NECKTIES

rockland falls book four

BESTSELLING AUTHOR
LACEY BLACK

Lacey Black

Love and Neckties

Rockland Falls book 4

Cover Design by Melissa Gill Designs
Cover Photographer Regina Wamba
Cover Models Nikki and Frankie

Editing by Kara Hildebrand

Proofreading by Joanne Thompson & Karen Hrdlicka

Format by Brenda Wright, Formatting Done Wright

Lacey Black

Index

Also by Lacey Black 5
Chapter One 7
Chapter Two 15
Chapter Three 26
Chapter Four 37
Chapter Five 49
Chapter Six 64
Chapter Seven 75
Chapter Eight 87
Chapter Nine 101
Chapter Ten... 107
Chapter Eleven... 114
Chapter Twelve 126
Chapter Thirteen... 135
Chapter Fourteen.. 163
Chapter Fifteen 171
Chapter Sixteen.. 183
Chapter Seventeen 191
Chapter Eighteen.. 202
Chapter Nineteen.. 212
Chapter Twenty.. 221
Chapter Twenty-One.. 233
Chapter Twenty-Two.. 237
Chapter Twenty-Three.. 245
Chapter Twenty-Four.. 254
Epilogue 265
Another Epilogue 272
Acknowledgments 278
About the Author 279

Lacey Black

Also by Lacey Black

Rivers Edge series
Trust Me, Rivers Edge book 1 (Maddox and Avery) – FREE at all retailers
> ~ *#1 Bestseller in Contemporary Romance*

Fight Me, Rivers Edge book 2 (Jake and Erin)
Expect Me, Rivers Edge book 3 (Travis and Josselyn)
Promise Me: A Novella, Rivers Edge book 3.5 (Jase and Holly)
Protect Me, Rivers Edge book 4 (Nate and Lia)
Boss Me, Rivers Edge book 5 (Will and Carmen)
Trust Us: A Rivers Edge Christmas Novella (Maddox and Avery)
> ~ *This novella was originally part of the Christmas Miracles Anthology*

With Me, A Rivers Edge Christmas Novella (Brooklyn and Becker)
BOX SET – contains all 5 novels, 2 novellas, and a BONUS short story

Bound Together series
Submerged, Bound Together book 1 (Blake and Carly)
> ~ *An International Bestseller*

Profited, Bound Together book 2 (Reid and Dani)
> ~*A Bestseller, reaching Top 100 on 2 e-retailers*

Entwined, Bound Together book 3 (Luke and Sidney)

Summer Sisters series
My Kinda Kisses, Summer Sisters book 1 (Jaime and Ryan)
> ~*A Bestseller, reaching Top 100 on 2 e-retailers*

My Kinda Night, Summer Sisters book 2 (Payton and Dean)
My Kinda Song, Summer Sisters book 3 (Abby and Levi)
My Kinda Mess, Summer Sisters book 4 (Lexi and Linkin)
My Kinda Player, Summer Sisters book 5 (AJ and Sawyer)
My Kinda Forever, Summer Sisters book 6 (Meghan and Nick)

My Kinda Wedding, A Summer Sisters Novella book 7
(Meghan and Nick)

Rockland Falls series
Love and Pancakes, Rockland Falls book 1
Love and Lingerie, Rockland Falls book 2
Love and Landscape, Rockland Falls book 3
Love and Neckties, Rockland Falls book 4

Standalone
Music Notes, a sexy contemporary romance standalone
A Place To Call Home, a Memorial Day novella
Exes and Ho Ho Ho's, a sexy contemporary romance
standalone novella
Pants on Fire, a sexy contemporary romance standalone

Co-Written with *NYT Bestselling* Author, Kaylee Ryan
It's Not Over, Fair Lakes book 1
Just Getting Started, Fair Lakes book 2

*Coming Soon from Lacey Black
Can't Get Enough, Fair Lakes book 3, with Kaylee Ryan
Double Dog Dare You, a new standalone (Royce from Pants on
Fire)
Grip, A Driven World Novel

Chapter One

Samuel

I adjust the small angel pendant on Mrs. Hammond's suit collar one final time, making sure everything is just right. Soft, classical music pipes through the speakers, while the video montage of her life plays on the screen in back. The flowers and plants are displayed perfectly, and the family is ready to say their final goodbyes with loved ones who came to share their condolences.

Her visitation will begin soon, just a typical Tuesday for me.

I make my way to the main office where Elma, our assistant, types an obituary for our website. She struggles with uploading to the site, yet can type like a court stenographer. Elma came from the typewriter era, and while she's the master at making sure the obits are worded correctly, she struggles with just about every other aspect of the process.

"Why does this line keep blinking at me? It moved up the page and now my words are typing in the wrong spot," the older woman complains, jabbing at the delete button with her frail finger.

"The cursor is supposed to move and blink, Elma. If it's not in the right spot, it's because you moved it," I tell her calmly. This is a daily occurrence and something I'm used to fixing.

"I just don't see the point of these machines. The Royal Epoch over there was working just fine," she grumbles, pointing to the antique device that hasn't been used in more than two decades, yet refuses to let me get rid of "in case they come back in style."

As I move to look at the screen over her shoulder, I'm assaulted with the scent of mothballs and Avon perfume. Timeless, I believe is what she calls it, though it really just reminds me of my grandma's bathroom when I was a kid.

I move the mouse, demonstrating once more how she can do so herself, but she's already getting up and moving on to filing. Elma's the only woman to ever have stepped foot in the office of Hanson Funeral Home. Her late husband, Ernest, started the business in 1964, with Elma running the office with an iron fist. In the eighties, their son, Robert, joined the family business, eventually taking over a few years ago when Ernest passed away. Now, Rob's son, Aaron, has finished school and joined his dad in their family legacy.

Unfortunately, Aaron doesn't actually care about working.

That leaves Rob and me, the one the young Hanson leans on to do, well, everything. I don't mind, though. I'm as dedicated to this business as the old man was before his heart attack, God rest his soul.

"The Hammond family should be here soon," Elma states, as I complete the upload of our newest obituary to the website.

"I'll meet them at the door," I reply, heading toward the wooden front entrance of our funeral home. I stop by the fireplace first, checking the knot on my navy blue tie in the mirror. It's already flawless, of course, but I always verify before meeting a family. Or before leaving the house. A perfectly executed double Windsor knot is on display, my favorite knot to tie.

I learned how to tie a necktie when I was seven, your basic four-in-hand knot. Over the years, I've learned four additional ways to display my tie, most of them named after British royals, and all based on the type of collar on the crisp dress shirt I'm wearing. I even took an online course on folding handkerchiefs. You never know when that will come in handy.

With my tie in perfect order, I head to the front door, holding it open just as the family arrives. I greet the grieving daughter and son-in-law, Debbie and Stuart, as well as their three children, handing them a small packet of tissues as they enter the funeral home. It's one thing I've learned over the years: be prepared. Always.

I escort them to the entrance of the parlor, where their loved one waits. They slowly make their way inside to say their goodbyes, while I wait just outside the door. After fifteen minutes, they come out to take a breather.

"I'll open the doors at four o'clock to the public," I tell them.

"Thank you, Samuel. You've been most helpful during this time," Debbie says, and I can tell already she's about to hug me. Grievers always hug, and why they feel the need to hug me is beyond my comprehension, especially when a handshake will suffice. Handshakes are professional. Yet here I am, being wrapped in her arms, a slight sniffle pulling my attention to the fact she probably just wiped her nose on my jacket sleeve.

"It's my pleasure to see your mother's final wishes were seen to," I insist, awkwardly patting her pack in an effort to return her affection.

"Oh, I almost forgot," Debbie says, taking a step back and wiping her nose on the crumbled up tissue in her hand. I try not to think about all of those germs. "I have someone stopping by after the visitation this evening."

"Oh?" I ask, running through tonight's schedule of events and coming up empty for an end of the night visitor.

"Yes, my Reiki healer is stopping by to see Mom."

"I'm sorry, Reiki?" I ask, racking my mind for what in the world that means. We've had our fair share of pastors, priests, and rabbis in the house, but I'm not sure what a Reiki healer is.

"Oh, it's this wonderfully relaxing Japanese technique that assists with many things, like your body's natural healing process, relieving emotional stress, and improving your body's overall well-being."

I stare at the woman as she easily pitches the concept of this Reiki bullshit as if she were reading it out of the brochure. "And this will help your mother how?" I find myself asking, unable to see the connection.

"Well, there's nothing better than sending Mom off to her final resting place when she's free of stress, right?"

Well, she's dead, so...

"Anyway, my Reiki healer has agreed to stop by after the visitation tonight to perform a treatment on Mom. It'll only take about a half hour or so," Debbie says matter-of-factly.

"Okay, I'm sure I can accommodate your...healer."

"Oh, thank you so much, Samuel. This means a lot to me," Debbie adds before, yep, you guessed it, pulling me into another tight hug. "Mom's spirit will fly free thanks to this woman."

"I bet she will," I mumble, standing perfectly still as the woman finishes her hug. Before she completely removes her hands from my body, however, she reaches up and adjusts the knot on my tie. My heart stops in my chest as this woman paws all over my perfectly executed double Windsor.

Completely horrified, I gently pull back, reaching up automatically and tweaking the soft silk tie. I can tell the tie is askew and not at all where it should be. The tightness in my throat is almost choking as I try not to make a big show of moving it back into place.

"You're such a handsome man, Samuel. I can't believe you haven't married yet," Debbie says, heading over to the mirror and adding a second coat of a light lipstick.

"Guests will start to arrive any moment. I'm going to greet those attending at the front door," I state professionally, completely glossing over her comment as if I didn't hear her.

Debbie just nods and heads into the main parlor, her family hot on her heels.

As soon as she's gone, I step up to the mirror and frantically correct my tie. I can practically see her finger smudges on the pristine material, even though they probably aren't visible to the naked eye. But I know they're there, taunting and mocking me with their imperfections.

I do the best I can to eliminate the tiny wrinkles from her fingers and head to the entrance. It's only a few minutes later that the early birds start to arrive to pay their respects. I can always count on them to arrive ten to fifteen minutes prior to the start of any visitation. There's no time but "their" time when it comes to schedules. Most of them will head out to dinner by four thirty, followed by *Jeopardy!* in their favorite recliner by six, and napping by six thirty. The elderly are as predictable as the sun rising in the morning and setting in the evening.

Though, as much as their early arrival used to bother me, I completely understand it on a personal level. If you're not ten to fifteen minutes early, then you're already late. It may drive my family crazy, my constant need to be on time, but that's better than the alternative. Tardiness makes you sloppy, and sloppy leads to mistakes. Mistakes create chaos, and the thought of chaos in my life brings a cold sweat to my skin.

"Good evening," I greet to everyone as I open the main entrance door, shaking hands with those gentlemen who offer theirs. Some of them even feel the need to fill a few uncomfortable seconds with small talk before they step into line with the rest of those in attendance. Usually, it's about the weather or something else as casual, but other times they try to ask me how the local high school football team is doing, or even how the fishing is this time of year. Things I have no interest in following.

As the evening draws to a close and the visitors trickle down to only immediate family left in attendance, I make my way to the daughter and explain tomorrow's schedule. "We'll be set up at the church by eight thirty. The family should arrive by nine, with the one-hour visitation set for nine thirty to ten thirty. Then, we'll have the pallbearers help move your loved one to the church chapel for the funeral service."

"Thank you so much, Samuel. I appreciate you taking care of Mom's final wishes," Debbie states, her eyes dry, yet tired and puffy.

"We appreciate you trusting us with these details."

Debbie steps forward and places a warm hand on my cheek. "You're such a good boy," she says with a sad smile. I don't scoff at her comment, even though I bristle a bit on the inside. I haven't exactly been a *boy* in nearly two decades. Although, if I'm being honest, I never was a typical boy.

I like things in order, even as a child. I enjoyed making sure lists were completed on a satisfactory level, even if they pertained to chores. My siblings never appreciated my obligation to following the rules, and even now, as adults, they find great pleasure in ruffling my feathers. I've also always felt a strong appreciation for proper dress. You've heard the phrase 'Dress to impress,' right? Well, I live by that rule. You never know who you'll run into at the grocery store or at the dentist. In a small town, your next business referral could come at any moment, by anyone. Always put your best foot forward, and that includes your appearance.

I'm the oldest of four. At thirty-six, I've been taking care of them since my teenage years. When our dad left following an affair, I readily stepped into his shoes as the man of the house. It was a role I filled easily, even if my siblings didn't find it necessary at the time. Mom ran a bed and breakfast out of our home and her days, and most of her evenings, were filled with caring for others. That left me to make sure they were showered, transported to and from ball practices or club activities. Not to mention helping take care of the homestead.

Harper is three years younger than me and owns a boutique in town. Kiss Me Goodnight carries unmentionables and other body care products, and despite the questionable product lines she sells, her business is doing well, and for that, I'm grateful. Harper lives with Latham Douglas, a gentleman she attended school with. They reunited following his extended stay in the service and have been living together for a few months now.

Jensen is third in line at thirty-one years old. He's a brilliant landscape architect, and despite the fact he always has dirt under his fingernails, I can appreciate the fact he works hard and has an eye for design. Jensen recently reunited with his former high school love and moved into her family's estate at the edge of town. Jensen is also the father of my only nephew, Max, who recently turned five.

Finally, there's Marissa, my youngest sister. Since she was a small child, Marissa knew what she wanted to do with her life. Now, at twenty-nine, she is fulfilling that dream by assisting our mother with her bed and breakfast. She manages much of the day-to-day aspect of the business and particularly enjoys handling the cooking feature of owning one of the few bed and breakfasts in our small North Carolina town, Rockland Falls.

"Are you ready, dear? Let's get home and rest," Stuart says, placing his hand on his wife's back and gently guiding her toward the exit.

"Yes, of course."

I meet the couple and their children at the exit, holding the door wide for them to pass through. "Oh, don't forget, my Reiki healer will be here any minute," Debbie adds, glancing at her watch. "She must be running a few minutes late."

My eye twitches at the thought, but I don't let my irritation show. "No worries, Debbie, I'll hang around a few more minutes until she arrives."

"Thank you, Samuel."

Then they're gone, leaving me alone in the funeral home with her deceased mother. I check my watch and notice this individual is approaching fifteen minutes late, assuming she was instructed to arrive at the end of the visitation. I activate the door buzzer, which allows us to hear a noise every time the front door opens. This helps when we're off somewhere within the building, we don't always have to lock the door.

Once I know I'll be made aware of her arrival, I head to the family room. This is an area down the hallway where family can gather to take a break. We offer a television, comfortable seating, and mini-kitchen area. Most families will bring in food or have it delivered to the visitation. Tonight's family cleaned up after themselves, so the only thing I need to do is take out the trash and wash down the table and counter. That job takes all of four minutes, and once it's complete I head back to the front, turning off the lights as I go.

When the clock strikes eight thirty, I figure this Reiki quack isn't coming. Maybe there was some sort of magical voodoo healing emergency? Flipping the lights off in the office, I step out, locking the door behind me, just as the front entrance opens. "It's raining harder than a cow pissing on a flat rock."

I know that voice.

And those crude words.

Exhaling, I stick my keys in my suit pants pocket and turn to the doorway. "Freedom."

Chapter Two

Freedom

"Sammy!" I exclaim, shaking the rain from my drowned hair. It hangs heavy and limply around my face and the water flies freely around me. Samuel sighs dramatically, which, of course, is just the response I'm going for.

"It's Samuel," he retorts rather heatedly, and I have to fight the smile.

Reaching up, I wring my brown hair out, watching small droplets of water fall on the floor. My long, Bohemian skirt clings to my legs and my top hangs awkwardly around my shoulders. "Seriously, this rain is nuts."

"It was forecasted," he replies, straightening his tie and avoiding eye contact. I've always felt like I made him nervous, which is why I go to such extended lengths to do just that. "I was just locking up," he adds, finally turning those blue-green eyes my way. He watches me for a few seconds, his Adam's apple bobbing in his throat as he swallows. "You know, they make these great inventions called umbrellas."

I wave my hand dismissively. "Ehh, a little water isn't going to hurt me." I take in the darkened foyer and ask, "Were you leaving?"

He sighs again. "Yes, Freedom, I was heading out for the evening. I have to return at seven."

"But didn't Debbie tell you I was coming?"

He crosses his arms and I try to ignore how his arms look with his suit stretched over his biceps. "She did, but I was under the impression you were arriving at the end of the visitation. That was more than thirty minutes ago."

"Where's the fire? Or did you have plans this evening?" I ask, waggling my eyebrows suggestively.

Samuel clears his throat and straightens. "I could have had plans."

"Of course you could have. I hear the coin club meets on Tuesday nights at the library." I give him the best, sweetest smile I possess, showing all of my teeth.

Again, he straightens his necktie, almost like a nervous twitch. There's something about his necktie that does weird things to my lady parts. I can almost picture Mr. Anal-Retentive wearing one of his fancy silk ties…and nothing else. "I'm not a part of the coin club, but I am starting to get hungry. Can we get the weird part of the evening over with, please?"

I strut past him, my wet skirt cooling my overheated legs. He doesn't make a sound as he follows me to the parlor, my bangle bracelets clanking together as we go. Samuel turns the light back on and my client for this evening comes into view. Technically, Debbie is the client—my client—but that's beside the point.

When she asked me at the end of our session on Sunday night to perform a Reiki treatment on her mother, I readily agreed. I didn't realize her mother had passed until the end of the conversation, and there was no going back—especially when she agreed to pay me twice my fee to accommodate the odd circumstance.

Have I ever performed on a dead woman? Umm, that's be a big fat no, but the dollar signs kept flashing through my mind, and honestly, I couldn't turn down the job. Being a Reiki practitioner doesn't exactly pay all the bills. That's why I work part time at my bestie's lingerie shop in town, as well as work as a part-time massage therapist. That's actually what I went to school for, but I'm always interested in trying new things, which is how I became a certified Reiki healer too.

Samuel doesn't say a word as I pull out my phone and find some meditation music, but I can feel his presence behind me. He stays back yet is close enough that goosebumps prickle my skin. Of course, it could be a result of being soaking wet too. Clearing my mind, I step up to the coffin, only slightly weirded out with what I'm about to do. I place my nondominant hand above her head and slowly start to scan down her body, keeping my hand four inches or so above her body.

"What are you doing?" Samuel's words startle me. They're soft and full of skepticism.

"I'm scanning her body to see if there is anywhere she needs additional healing," I whisper, realizing this part of the process probably isn't necessary, all things considered.

Samuel snorts a laugh. "Unless she's going to get up and walk out of here, I don't think any additional healing will help," he mumbles.

Usually, my client would be lying on my massage table, but there really isn't any other option here, so I take position at the head of the coffin, sliding over the pillar holding a massive flower arrangement as I go.

"Let me," he says, carefully shifting the flowers until they're out of my way and I can stand at her head.

I place my hand over her head, grimacing slightly at the thought of touching her. No, this is not my first deceased individual I've touched, but it is the first one I'll be touching for a prolonged amount of time. Ignoring the shiver that slides down my spine, I position my hand above the third eye in her forehead.

For the next thirty minutes, I proceed to conduct Reiki over Debbie's dead mother. Samuel remains quiet and out of the way while I work, though I can feel his presence in the room. When the session is complete, I feel confident Debbie's mother is spiritually ready for her afterlife. "All finished," I state, moving away from the coffin, turning off the meditation music playing from my cell phone.

Samuel stares at me as I approach. "That was…the biggest pile of bullshit I've ever witnessed."

I gape at him, trying to give my best shocked expression, when all I really want to do is laugh. Samuel is the last person on earth I'd expect to trust and believe in the healing powers of Reiki. He's more of a hold it in your hand or witness it with your own eyes to believe it man. "I can't believe you said that, Sammy. After witnessing her relaxation and ultimate spiritual healing in the flesh, you still doubt the power."

The tips of his ears turn red. "It's Samuel, and I'm pretty sure she's already as relaxed as she can get."

It's pretty much my goal in life to argue and make him as uncomfortable as humanly possible, which is why I follow up with, "I think you could benefit from a few Reiki treatments." I step closer, invading his personal space. His Adam's apple bobs again, letting me know I'm affecting him. "Oh, what I would do to get ahold of your…*chakra*." Yes, I intentionally make it sound dirty just to watch him blush.

He does.

"You keep your paws away from my…chakra."

I step back and turn around, grabbing my purse that I discarded on the floor. "One of these days, Sammy, I'm going to get ahold of your…chakra, and make you feel so good, you'll never want me to stop having my hands on your…chakra." Grinning inwardly to myself, I turn back around to face him. His eyes, however, are cast downward.

Where my ass was.

Knowing he was just busted ogling my behind, he quickly makes his way to the flower arrangement we had moved and rights it.

It actually takes him several minutes as he steps back and inspects the angles of the flowers multiple times to ensure it's displayed properly, which I find comical, considering tomorrow he's moving them all to the church for the funeral service. "You know, no one is going to see that bad boy, right? Live on the edge. Let it be out of place for the night."

He glances over his shoulder, giving me his best "zip it, Freedom" look before turning back around and adjusting the display once more. This time, he crouches down, looking at it from the floor angle. Why? No freaking clue.

My eyes automatically start to scan his physique. Samuel isn't as muscular as his younger brother, Jensen, who works outside all day, every day, but you can still tell he works out. His arms hold just enough definition to them without screaming gym rat, and his ass is firm, framed in a pair of expensive trousers. Once, I even caught sight of him shirtless. His nephew, Max, finally talked him into playing in the sprinkler at one of their summer gatherings. He strolled out of the house as uncomfortable as could be, wearing a pair of his brother's swim trunks hanging dangerously low on his narrow hips. I did things to myself later that night when I was alone a lady never speaks of in public.

Since I'm no lady, you should know I got myself off twice with images of a wet Samuel standing in the middle of the yard, pretending to have fun with his nephew in the sprinkler. Oh, I think he had fun, in the only way he knows how. Even though he stood paralyzed while Max ran repeatedly through the water, he enjoyed watching his nephew play.

As I finish my perusal of his body, that's when I notice something…off. This man wears suits for a living and is always so well put together. I'm even willing to place a bet on the fact his underwear probably matches his tie. No, wait. I take that back.

Samuel is definitely a tighty-whities guy. His dress shoes probably cost more than my entire outfit, and I know for a fact he gets monthly manicures because my bestie told me. That's why when my eyes reach his feet, I know something is much out of character for Mr. Samuel Grayson.

I bust out laughing, which causes him to look over his shoulder from his crouched position. "Oh my God, Sammy, I knew you loved my gift!" I exclaim, my eyes riveted to the completely inappropriate trouser socks I found online for Samuel's birthday this past summer.

Realization sets in, causing him to stand and spin around. "I don't know what you're talking about," he scoffs, embarrassment marring his handsome features.

Of course, I can't let this go, which is why I fling myself onto the floor at his feet, pull up his pant legs to get a good look at what he's wearing, not even caring my long, flowy skirt is bunched up around my thighs. "Let me see!" I hang on for dear life to his legs as he tries to shake me off like a dog trying to hump his leg.

"Get off me," he grumbles, trying to buck me from his body, but I'm part spider monkey and there's no way I'm letting go of his legs without seeing the goods he's trying to hide first.

Suddenly, though, he stops moving. I stop moving. I look up and realize our position would definitely border on scandalous if the right individual were to pop their head in this room. My face is there—right *there*—and he knows exactly how close I am to his pool stick because it starts to grow inches from my face.

"You're wearing my socks." The words come out raspy and needy as my eyes connect with his.

He swallows hard but maintains eye contact. "It was laundry day and I didn't have a chance to stop by the dry cleaners to pick up my clothes."

"You dry clean your socks?" I ask, glancing back down at the multiple sex positions socks he's wearing beneath his fancy suit. Yes, you heard me right. Sex position socks. I thought they were hilarious when I found them online, knowing he'd hate everything about them. So I bought them for his birthday.

"Doesn't everyone dry clean their socks?" he asks, incredulously.

I shrug. "I don't wear socks," glancing down at my well-worn brown sandals with my painted toes on full display. He does the same, his eyes lingering a few extra seconds on my hot pink toes. Looking from his face to his socks, I can't help but smile wide and say, "You love me."

Now he rolls his eyes dramatically. "I do *not* love you," he jeers as he reaches down and helps me stand, brushing off his pant legs as if I left some sort of hippie-inspired, tree-hugging dust behind.

"You're wearing my sex socks. That means you love me."

"Christ, Freedom, why must you be difficult about everything?" he asks almost absently, rubbing his right temple with his thumb.

"Just admit it and I'll leave you alone," I tell him, grabbing my purse I again dropped on the floor.

"I will do no such thing." He crosses his arms over his chest and stares at me. "Are you finally done with your weird voodoo shit so I can go home? It's been a long day."

Knowing that he'll hate it, and I'll love it, I reach up and lightly pat his cheek, much like a pacifying grandmother would a young grandchild. "Of course, little Sammy. It's after nine o'clock, way after beddy-bye."

Silently, we walk toward the front door. I step aside while he locks it, triple checking it latched, and together, we turn and head toward the back of the parking lot. "Why did you park back there? The lot was empty when you arrived," he asks.

"I wanted to prolong our time together as much as possible," I tell him sweetly as I walk beside him. I can smell his familiar cologne. I don't know what it is, but I'm sure it's expensive. Something else that reminds me of our differences. I'm more of a cheap body spray kinda girl; anything that's light, breezy, and reminds me of the outdoors.

Samuel walks me to my car. He's a stickler for the "rules." He was raised a gentleman by his mom, but more than that, he's just a good guy. Even if he's as anal as they come, and while his siblings tease him about his strange "qualities," I find them endearing. Most guys would just let the door hit you in the ass, but not Samuel. He always does the right thing, including walking me to my car, even when I could drive him to drink most days.

"Thanks, Sammy," I say sweetly, opening my car door.

He sighs loudly. "Don't you lock your car? That's not safe."

I glance around the interior of my ten-year-old Honda, packed with my portable massage table, a bag of my oils and lotions, and a few other necessities I picked up from Harper's shop earlier today. Plus, there's a few empty water bottles, some wheat cracker wrappers, and even a few takeout veggie burger bags on the passenger floorboard. "You think someone's going to steal my baby?" I ask, batting the roof of my car.

"Steal it? No, I'm afraid someone will get lost inside there," he grumbles, glancing at the piles of stuff in the back.

"I'll have you know that's all stuff for work," I tell him, placing my hands on my hips and glaring at him.

One eyebrow arches skyward. "If you get in an accident, your cause of death will be blunt force trauma from all the crap in your car hitting you."

I almost crack a smile as my foot hits one of the puddles in the lot from tonight's downpour. "That's descriptive."

"Clean out your car, Freedom. And when was the last time you had the oil changed?" he asks, almost absently.

"I changed it two weeks ago."

Now both eyebrows are raised. "*You* changed it?"

My mouth drops open. "Of course *I* changed it. Who else would do it?"

"A shop?"

I roll my eyes and slip into the driver's seat, my knee hitting an angel charm that dangles from my ignition switch. "I don't need to pay someone to change my oil, Sammy. I am more than capable," I answer, shoving my key into the ignition and turning it over.

Only the car doesn't start. It makes a sad, crying noise. I try a few more times, silently willing the car to fire to life, but the Gods of Car Care ignore my pleas.

Samuel sighs again. He does that a lot around me. I sort of turned it into a game years ago. You know, trying to see how many times I can get him to sigh in resignation or annoyance. I lost count years ago on how often he does it, but I believe that means I win the game regularly.

"Come on, Freedom. I'll give you a ride home."

"But what about my car?" I ask, slipping out of the seat and pulling the hood lever. "Let me just check under the hood."

A big fat raindrop falls on my forehead, followed quickly by a few more. "You can check it out tomorrow," he says, just as the skies let loose another downpour. "Lock your doors!" he hollers, taking off his suit jacket and holding it up over my head.

I reach inside the vehicle for my keys and bag, slam the door, push the lock button and make a mad dash for the passenger side of Samuel's car. He tries to hold up his jacket, but with the amount of rain falling from the angry sky, it's no use. We're both soaked in a matter of seconds. He doesn't seem to care that he's getting drenched as he holds the door open for me, trying to shield me from the rain with his jacket and body. Inside the car, I shake like a dog. There's no use trying to preserve his expensive leather seats at this point. I'm soaked. He's soaked. There's water everywhere.

The driver's door opens and he jumps inside, tossing his jacket onto the back seat. Samuel grumbles under his breath, something about dry cleaning and car details, but I don't really pay much attention. Instead, my eyes are locked on his shirt. Specifically, the way his crisp white dress shirt molds wetly to his torso. I can see his undershirt beneath it, but it does nothing to prevent the material from casting to his upper body.

My mouth waters and I glance away.

He fires his much newer car to life and cranks up the warm air. "Let's get you home," he says, his voice sounding…deeper.

I can only nod as images of his arms parade through my mind like the opening scene of a porno.

When he doesn't pull out of the parking spot, I finally glance his way. His eyes are locked on me, on my…chest. Glancing down, that's when I realize I'm soaked clean through, my blue tank top no longer flowy and light. Instead, it clings seductively to my body, giving him a clear view of my nipples. My very hard nipples.

I look up, watching his throat work hard to swallow. He turns away from me, throws the car in reverse, and drives out of the lot. I take in his defined arms, his wet hair, and the hint of his sex position socks peeking out of his trousers. Even soaked, he looks hot. He shouldn't look hot, but he does.

He always looks hot.

Dammit.

Yeah, I'm pretty sure I'll be diddling myself later tonight to images of Samuel Grayson.

Chapter Three

Samuel

Classical music softly plays in the sterile, cold room, as I prepare to embalm Mrs. Portman. Embalming is an art that requires a strong stomach, patience, empathy, and a special license. Mine hangs prominently on the wall by the door.

Did I always know I wanted to work with the dead? Not really. I always thought I'd be a dentist, but I quickly learned I much preferred deceased people to those living. I have a mortuary science degree and did my apprenticeship right here at this very funeral home under Ernest Hanson. His son, Rob, is also an embalmer, but I'm the one on-call most of the time. Aaron, Ernest's grandson and the third generation Hanson mortician, chose not to seek that specific license, probably because it required more schooling and training, and less partying.

My career isn't one most would consider on Career Day. It's messy, potentially hazardous, and requires you dealing with people on the worst days of their lives. But believe it or not, I find it wildly fulfilling too. I help those people as they deal with their grief, preserving and presenting their loved ones the best way I can. The final time they will see their loved ones is in my hands, and I take this obligation very seriously.

I take everything very seriously.

Just as I make my incision, the intercom buzzes on the wall. "Samuel?" Elma's gruff voice pipes through the room on this fine Friday morning.

"Yes?" I ask, holding my hand steady as I prepare to inject the preservation chemicals into the body via the embalming machine.

"Your sister is here. She says it's important," Elma replies.

I set my tools down, the process on hold for a few moments, and glance at the clock. It's very rare that one of my siblings actually stops by the funeral home. Usually, they text, knowing I could be very busy at any point in the day. Worried something is wrong, I state, "Please send her down. I'll meet her in the hallway."

I don't know which sister it is, but that doesn't matter. If one of them is here, it's important. I head over to the washing station and remove my gown, gloves, and mask. Once they're disposed of, I scrub my hands and head toward the door. A burst of warmth hits me as soon as I step into the private hallway in the basement of the funeral home. Families never come back this far, as this is where we prepare the bodies for burial or cremation.

My eyes land on Harper and the wide smile on her face. A smile can be deceiving, but hers seems to be one full of happiness, which causes me to pause in confusion. "What's wrong?" I ask, adjusting my cuff links as I tend to do when nervous.

"Nothing," she replies right away, still the smile plays on her face. "Do I need a reason to stop by and see my older brother?"

I think for a few seconds about her question. No, technically, she doesn't need a reason to stop by, however, we've never been much for random visits at the workplace. Especially her workplace. In fact, I've never casually dropped by. It's not that I'm against it; it's just her boutique makes me...uncomfortable. Panties and bras everywhere. I never know where to look.

"Uh, well, no, I guess not. Though, I was just getting ready to embalm Mrs. Portman."

Harper pulls a face. "Your job is so...weird."

Again, I adjust my cuff links. "The same could be said for yours."

She stops and considers my words before bursting into a fit of laughter. "Touché, brother. Anyway, there was a reason I stopped by this morning and interrupted your dead-person time."

Her blasé statement gets on my nerves at little. My siblings have never really understood why I went to mortuary school instead of dental school, but that's okay. It's not for them to understand or like. It was my choice, my career path. "Get on with it," I state, crossing my arms over my chest and waiting her out.

"Oh! Yeah, guess what?" she asks, her eyes sparkling like diamonds. "I'm getting married!" she squeals before throwing herself into my arms.

A smile crosses my face. A real one. I'm genuinely happy for Harper and Latham. They went to high school together and upon his return from the military, set out to make each other's lives miserable. Of course, it was a front for their true feelings, which is very evident in the way she flashes a large, gaudy diamond in my face. "Congratulations, Harper," I reply, awkwardly patting her back.

"Thanks," she replies, grinning down at the sparkler. "Anyway, I stopped by to ask you a question. You're off next weekend, right?" She nibbles on the corner of her lip, which is a telltale sign she's nervous about something.

I mentally pull up my schedule. I'm on-call most weekends, however I'm completely free next. Aaron takes one weekend a month, while I take the other three. I don't mind, really. This work is my life, and I prefer to be here than at home most days. I want to oversee everything, from the arrival of the body to the services and final resting place. "I'm free. Why? Do you need something?"

"Yes," she starts, taking a deep breath. "We're getting married next Saturday. In Las Vegas."

That gives me pause. Next weekend? In Vegas?

I adjust my necktie, suddenly struggling to pull air into my lungs. "I can't go." My words come out slightly strangled.

"Sure you can. The flight is less than five hours."

"Five horrible hours, suspended thirty thousand feet above the earth. If we fall, it's a fiery crash."

Harper gives me a sympathetic smile. "Look, Samuel, I know flying isn't really your thing," she starts and steps closer, a sympathetic grin on her face and a look that lets me know she's about to drop the bomb. "It's just that, well, I was hoping you might walk me down the aisle." She swallows and her blue eyes starts to shine with unshed tears.

Little sister goes for the kill.

I clear my throat. "You're not going to invite him?"

Harper shakes her head. "I know Jensen has talked to him a few times, but I'm not ready yet."

I completely understand that. I haven't been ready yet either.

"They serve alcohol on flights," she adds, as if the concept of getting drunk on an airplane at seven dollars a drink holds any weight with me. I'm sure the look I give her shows my displeasure. "Fine, maybe you could join the mile-high club?" she adds with a laugh. "That's a surefire way to relieve some stress."

"Do you know how small those bathrooms are, Harper? And not to mention the germs and whatnot that cover every single conceivable surface. What could possibly be enjoyable about contracting norovirus from an airplane toilet? It's bad enough I'll be breathing the same filtered air for five hours with everyone else," I huff, not really sure why I'm getting myself worked up over this.

Harper raises an eyebrow. "You seem to know an awful lot about airplane sex for a man who's never been on a plane. Is that like a porn fetish or something? *Stewardess Seduction*? *Bang Me at Thirty-Thousand Feet*? Oh! What about *The Randy Pilot's Cockpit*?"

I groan, knowing she'll not drop it now that the door has been opened. "Stop."

"Maybe *Debbie Does It Over Dallas*? Or *First Class Cum-Guzzlers*?"

That one makes my stomach clench. "Fine, I'll go," I reply, willing to tell her anything to avoid further discussion about porn with my sister.

"You will?"

"Yes, now please stop talking."

Harper giggles and throws her arms around me. I return her hug, even if I've never been much for displays of affection. That's how sicknesses are spread, you know? She quickly pulls away and smiles widely. "Thank you so much. This is going to be the best trip ever!"

"If you say so," I mumble, the panic of my commitment standing right there in front of me, ready to take over.

"It'll be fun," she starts, tapping me on the chest. "You'll see. It's going to be small and intimate and perfect. Latham and I are flying out Thursday, but you can join us anytime. Mom, Marissa, Rhenn, and Latham's parents are flying out early Friday, and I think Jensen and Kathryn are taking a later flight."

"Okay," I respond automatically, my mind reeling. On one hand, it would probably be better to fly with familiar faces for my first time. On the other, if I freak out, I'd rather they not see my fear in the flesh.

"I'll email you the hotel information. We're all staying at the same one. We booked a chapel on the strip for Saturday night at seven and dinner at the hotel restaurant at eight. Then, everyone has the rest of the evening to do whatever they please. I know what I'll be doing," she says, bumping her shoulder into my arm and wiggling her eyebrows.

"Jeez, Harper," I groan, trying to push that mental image as far from my mind as humanly possible. Hell, another universe wouldn't be far enough.

My sister giggles a happy little sound and hugs me again. Three hugs in one day; that's definitely not the norm. "Anyway, I'll let you get back to your dead person. I'll email you the hotel info and the flight confirmations for everyone else. Try to get on a flight with one of them. It'll help," she says, giving me a sympathetic look.

"Fine," I state, straightening my necktie.

"Oh, I think everyone is staying until Monday, so it might not be a bad idea for you too. Take a day off work. Live a little."

Ha. Live a little? I almost laugh out loud. I live just fine, thank you very much. My idea of living isn't traveling two thousand miles to the fucking desert, surrounded by too many people, all bumping into each other and spilling their drinks on you. And let's not forget the selfies. Why this is a thing, I'll never know. I don't need a hundred photos of myself standing in different places, making stupid faces that resemble animals at my phone.

"Anyway, I'll let you get back to work. Make sure you get your stuff booked tonight," she says, hugging me a fourth time before disappearing down the long hallway.

Running my hands over the back of my neck, I let the immensity of our conversation settle over me. Yes, I'm happy my sister is getting married. Yes, I'm thrilled I'm gaining Latham as a brother-in-law. Yes, I'm ecstatic to walk her down the aisle. I'm not so thrilled that particular aisle is in Nevada.

Not-so-pleasant images parade through my mind as I think about getting on an airplane. Statistically, the chances of being involved in an airplane-related crash are one in five point four million. I'm more likely to die crossing the street than in an airplane.

But there's always that one time…

* * *

The airport is busy on this Friday morning. There are people everywhere, from countries all over the world. I try to blend in, but it's hard when most are in tropical shirts or what looks like pajama pants. Do people really leave their houses like this? Like everywhere they go, they just rolled out of bed? I straighten my necktie and try not to get caught gawking, but one particular woman in slippers and flannel pants catches me looking.

I guess they take casual flying to the extreme here.

I open back up the newspaper and scan today's headlines, a cup of black coffee between my legs. The man to my left has his carry-on bag in the empty seat between us, which grates on my nerves. There are people standing, yet this jerk takes up an available seat with a suitcase. Do people really act like this? I can already feel a headache coming on, and I'm starting to think the alcohol my sister was boasting about sounds better and better by the second.

Before I have an opportunity to say anything to the man, the hairs on the back of my neck stand up and my body becomes hyperaware of…something. No, not something. Someone.

"Excuse me, excuse me," the familiar voice sings politely.

I focus on my newspaper, as if it might have the answers to world peace and try not to draw any attention to myself. It's not working, though. I can practically feel her drawing near, smell her familiar earthy fragrance.

"Yo, move your bag, friend, or I'll move it for you."

I glance up to see Freedom standing directly in front of the seat right next to me, staring at the guy with his carry-on in the seat. Her hands are planted firmly on her hips and she taps her foot impatiently. The man glances up, clearly getting ready to ignore her request, but Freedom pins him with a look that could melt the glaciers in Antarctica. Sighing loudly, he grabs his carry-on and places it beneath his seat.

"Well, isn't this an unpleasant surprise," I mumble, keeping my eyes locked on the paper as she sits right beside me. If I don't, then I might notice the way her skirt shifts around her trim legs. Freedom always wears these gaudy, awful skirts that look like they were cut from Grandma's couch material.

"Don't pretend to be annoyed with my sudden appearance, Sammy. I know you're secretly excited to see me," she sings, setting her bag on the floor between her legs. Instantly, I'm assaulted by her perfume. You know, the one that smells like fresh air and spring rain? My dick actually twitches in my pants.

Finally, I set my paper aside and look her way. She's pulling a small container from her purse, which is big enough to fit small children, and pops open the lid, holding it up for me. It looks like some sort of bread, but there's definitely some extra ingredients like nuts, maybe? "What's that?"

"A snack," she says, waving it in front of my face. "Try it."

Part of me wants to tell her no thank you, mostly because I have no clue what the hell those green things are, but then I recall this is Freedom we're talking about, and she'll just push harder until she gets what she wants. And apparently, what she wants is me eating her weird nut bread. "What's in it?"

"Things that are healthy, Sammy. Try. It."

Exhaling loudly, I reach over and pull off a small piece of bread, carefully examining it first. "Why is it green?"

"I'm not telling you what's in it until you try it," she adds matter-of-factly, as she breaks off her own piece and shoves it in her mouth. There's something oddly sexy about the way she chews, which is a little concerning. No one is sexy when they eat. The last woman I dated used to continually dab at the corner of her mouth with a napkin because she was concerned about residual food, and there was definitely nothing sexy about that. But the way Freedom licks the breadcrumbs off her fingers?

Yeah, that's alarmingly sexy.

Needing somewhere else to focus my attention, I bring my eyes down to the bread in my hand. The fact that it's green and has little chunks has my heart palpitating in my chest. I can also feel her eyes on me and know she won't be able to refrain from commenting much longer, so I slowly bring the questionable food to my mouth and chew.

When it hits my tongue, it's surprisingly sweet, with just a hint of something fruity. "What's in it?"

"Do you like it?"

Swallowing, I turn my attention her way. "Yes, Freedom, it's tasty. What's in it?"

"It's pistachio cranberry bread with Greek yogurt and roasted salted pistachios. Oh, and coconut."

I blink once. Twice. Surely I heard her wrong. My throat starts to tighten. "Did you say…coconut?"

Freedom turns her big, innocent eyes my way. "Yes, why?"

"Dammit, Freedom, I'm sensitive to coconut," I grit through clenched teeth as I grab my carry-on bag from beneath my seat and start to riffle through it.

"What do you mean sensitive to it?"

Ignoring her question, I look through my bag for the small ziplock I bring, containing some common over the counter medicines. Tylenol, Motrin, cough drops, Neosporin, and Tums. I pop an antacid out of the container and throw it in my mouth, chewing rapidly. I glance down in my bag once more, but don't find what I'm really looking for.

"What's happening?" she asks, taking my hand in hers, halting my frantic movements. Her skin is warm, her eyes full of concern as she looks over at me.

"I've always been sensitive to coconut."

"I didn't know. What does that mean?"

My stomach rumbles and I swallow the extra saliva gathering in my mouth. This isn't good. "It means I need to go and get something for my stomach," I state just as my belly turns angry. There's no way I'll have time to get to the store before I hit the bathroom, and if there's one thing I know, I'll need to find the bathroom fast. Everything in my body is about to come out—very quickly—and I definitely don't want to be here when it happens.

I stand up, wishing I was at home and as far away from Freedom and her coconut as possible. Unfortunately, the only place I'm going is the public bathroom, in which I will expunge all of my bodily fluids from my ass, while in a multi-stall public bathroom.

Fun.

"I'll help!" she hollers, surely drawing the attention of everyone around us, as she grabs our bags and pulls me through the gathering crowd at our gate. Even in my pre-disaster ass state, I still wish she'd keep her voice down and her hands to herself. Her touch just…affects me.

"I'm fine, Freedom," I mumble, yet still allowing her to pull me through the mob.

She stops in front of the bathroom. "You go take care of your problem, and I'll run down and get some Pepto or something," she states loudly before disappearing into the crowd, my bag still in her hand.

I'm about to holler after her when my stomach not-so-subtly reminds me that the bathroom usage is imminent. I make my way inside, finding an available stall in the back of the large room avoiding eye contact as I go. There's no way to hide what's about to happen, and I can already feel the embarrassment burn my face. My stomach turns once more, an angry howl echoing off the concrete walls, as I lock myself in my stall.

"Attention passengers, American Airlines flight 4382, nonstop service to Las Vegas, will being boarding in five minutes. Please make your way to gate twenty-three for boarding."

I drop my drawers and pray for a swift death.

Chapter Four

Freedom

I grab everything I can from the small pharmacy selection available.
Everything.

How was I supposed to know he had a sensitivity to coconut?
I mean, who actually gets the squirts from coconut? I pull out my
phone, carefully juggling all of the over-the-counter products in my
arms, and Google search coconut allergies. It's actually quite rare,
however a person can be sensitive to just about anything. Figures
Samuel would be sensitive to one of my favorite add-on ingredients.

The young girl at the counter seems completely unfazed by
my wide selection of products on the counter and slowly starts to scan.
This is also the time when I hear our flight announce the pre-board
process is about to begin over the intercom. I grab two bottles of water
from the cooler beside the counter, ignore the astronomical dollar
amount on the small cash register screen, and swipe my card. The girl
throws my products in a bag and I take off, almost leaving our luggage
behind.

I juggle my way quickly to the bathroom where I left Samuel
and wait. They announce the boarding of our flight, beginning with
first-class passengers. No way in Hell's half acre could I ever afford
a first-class ticket. No, I'm stuck in coach. In the back. The way back.

Watching our gate, they start to call the next series of
passengers to board. I'm getting a little nervous we'll miss our flight
when Samuel finally appears. He's gray and sweating a bit, but he's
alive. I'd feel really bad if I killed my best friend's hot older brother
the day before her wedding. "You okay, champ?"

Samuel doesn't say anything but reaches into the bag for one of the bottles of water. He chugs it swiftly, almost draining the entire bottle in one long gulp. Just as he goes to reply, a little boy comes running out of the bathroom, his dad hot on his heels. "Mommy! The baffroom smells willy bad!"

I watch as Samuel's face turns beet red. He reaches for his carry-on bag, which is wrapped up in my arms, and starts to head away from our gate. "Hey, where are you going? Our flight is boarding."

"I'm going home. I can't fly like this."

"You can't go home, Sammy."

"My name is Samuel," he grounds out through clenched teeth. I fight the smile, because, well at least he's well enough to give me shit for calling him by his nickname.

"Sorry, *Samuel*," I say, drawing out the word like it has fourteen syllables. "You can't go home. Your sister needs you."

That makes him pause and slowly turn my way. "My stomach is a mess, Freedom. I'm not fit to fly."

Reaching for the white bag, I start to pull out some of the over the counter products I purchased for him. "I have stuff. Lots of stuff. Surely something in here will help your stomach calm down. Oh, here! This one!" I yell, pulling the package of DiaResQ and waving it in his face. "This one says it addresses the issue of diarrhea, not just the symptoms." I ignore the fact it just cost me almost twelve dollars for this one-dose package.

Someone snickers as they walk past.

"Final boarding call for American Airlines flight 4382, nonstop service to Las Vegas. Please make your way to gate twenty-three at this time for takeoff."

"Shitballs, Sammy, let's go," I holler, grabbing his hand and all of our stuff and dragging him behind me toward our gate.

Fortunately, it's just down the corridor, so we're there within a minute.

At the gate, I hand him the box of medicine and the last bottle of water. Then, I dig in my purse for my boarding pass and his travel bag for his. He grumbles as I move all of his stuff around, probably because he knows I'm wrinkling the extra set of underwear he no doubt carries in his bag, in case his luggage gets lost.

"Found it!" I holler as I pull his paper from the side of his bag. "Let's get on this plane and get your tummy settled. I found crackers," I state, pulling out a sleeve of wheat saltines from my bag.

The woman scans our passes, trying to hide her smile, while Samuel mumbles something about jumping from the plane without a parachute. "Enjoy your flight," she adds before grabbing the door, clearly ready to secure the walkway once we step inside.

"Thanks, love!" I chirp, heading down the chute toward the awaiting jet. I know he's behind me. I can sense his presence. That and smell his cologne. It's like an aphrodisiac. I actually went on a date with a guy months back because he wore the same stuff. He was nothing like Samuel, though.

Samuel isn't married.

The plane is already packed to the gills when we make our way to the small aisle. "Jeez," he mutters behind me, his body very close to my backside that I can feel his heat. I have our bags in front as I push my way through the aisle. Everyone is already seated, their carry-ons stowed in the overhead bins, and noses stuck in their electronic devices.

Finally, I spy my seat in the very back of the plane. It's not a coincidence the final remaining seats are right next to each other. "We're here, Sammy," I state, trying to shove both of our bags in the very tiny space left in the overhead bin. It doesn't work.

"I'll just put my bag under my seat," he says, reaching around me and taking the bag from my hand.

"Get buckled in. The crew is preparing for takeoff," the flight attendant says politely, closing the bin without my bag inside. She hands it back to me to put under my seat.

I glance at the gentleman sitting in the aisle seat, waiting for him to get up. He's a tad on the larger side, and there's no way I can slip past him without crawling all over him like a jungle cat. I'm totally prepared to do it, but I can't envision Samuel following suit. The man finally sighs and unbuckles his seat belt.

"Thank you, kind sir." Then I glance over my shoulder and ask, "Window or middle?"

Samuel has gone pale again. "What?"

"Window or middle? You have to choose before that flight attendant comes back and makes us sit in the aisle." His jaw unhinges and panic starts to set in. "I'm kidding, I'm kidding."

"I can't sit by the window," he whispers, pulling at his necktie. It's a deep red with satiny stripes of the same color and does weird things to my lady parts.

"Middle it is," I state, sliding into the row and taking the window seat. I shove my bag under the seat in front of me and clasp my buckle.

Samuel moves in, plopping down in the seat beside me. He's clenching his carry-on to his chest like a life preserver, his body taut with tension. When the man in the aisle seat joins us, I can see the discomfort instantly on Samuel's face. The man is spilling into his seat, taking the armrest with his big, meaty forearm. My travel companion looks about as comfortable as a prostitute in church.

When the flight attendants start their pre-flight instructions, I try to pry the bag from Samuel's hands. The death grip he's got is fierce, but I have something extra special in my arsenal. Gently, I place my palm on his thigh, fingers spread wide, and slowly run it up his leg. I can feel his entire body tense, the corded muscles on his thigh tighten, and his wide eyes turn my way. I move my hand until I'm a millimeter away from touching something I know I shouldn't, yet can't seem to not want. My gaze remains gentle, even as the hormonal storm starts to twirl in my gut. With my other hand, I tug on the bag. It pops free from his arms easily, and I can't help but smile victoriously.

"Thank you," I coo, tossing it on the floor at his feet and reaching for his seat belt. Giving it a tug to lengthen the strap, I slip the two pieces together and clasp the safety device in place. Then, to be extra ornery—or because I just can't seem to help myself—I reach down and grab the extra belt, pulling it nice and tight. When I do, my hand brushes against…oh, you know exactly what it brushes against, and I'm not at all ashamed that it happened.

I grab the bag from the market in the airport and toss it on his lap. There's still a little water left in the second bottle, so I hand it to him. He definitely will need his fluids after what happened in that bathroom, and it probably wouldn't hurt him to see what else he can take for the flight. He glances in the bag, pulling out all sorts of small packages. Things for headache, motion sickness (which he pops in his mouth), antacids, even cough drops.

It's when he pulls the last box from the bag that has me pause…

And think about sex.

"Condoms? Really?" he asks, annoyed as all get out.

"What? You never know when they'll come in handy," I reason.

Samuel tosses them back in the bag, seeming to hide them beneath the plethora of other medical goodies I have in there. "I highly doubt I'll be needing them, Freedom."

"Well, you know what they say, sex every day keeps the doctor away."

He stops and stares at me, those yummy eyes shining under the horrible airplane lighting. "Seriously? *Who* says that?"

I shrug, reaching into the bag for the small box of condoms. "Dunno. A doctor?"

Samuel snorts, making a grab for them when he realizes what I have. "Put those away."

"What, these?" I ask, holding them up and waving them around. "Oh, look! These are lubricated and ribbed!"

"Jesus, Freedom, would you keep it down?" he harshly whispers, making a quick grab for the box of protection.

Ignoring him completely, I continue, "It's a three-pack. That's three days' worth of doctor-recommended sex on a five-hour flight."

"Put them away, Freedom. I mean it."

I stop and look him straight in the eyes before I say (quite loudly, I might add), "No, I will not have sex with you in the bathroom. There are children on this flight, Samuel Grayson."

He freezes, his eyes wide with horror. His mouth opens, but no words come out. It's one of my many talents to be able to render Samuel speechless, and something I take great joy in accomplishing. "You're horrible," he whispers, throwing the bag of medicine back onto my lap.

"You love me," I coo, tossing the condoms back where they came from.

The plane starts to move, pulling away from the gate and taxiing toward our runway, and I sit back to enjoy. I love this part of flying, though admittedly, I don't fly often. In fact, I've only flown on two other occasions, but both times, I loved the takeoff. The speed, the incline, the altitude. The fact we're relying solely on a machine to keep us suspended in the sky, moving us from point A to point B. The thrill of the adventure that awaits.

"Christ," Samuel mumbles beside me.

While I'm completely relaxed and gazing eagerly out the small window, my neighbor is pale as a ghost and gripping onto the single armrest like it's the only thing keeping him from certain death. His eyes are pinched shut so tightly it must hurt, and we've barely begun the journey. I realize real quick this isn't just about the whole coconut thing from earlier. Samuel's afraid of flying.

"Sit back and enjoy your flight," the flight attendant says over the speaker, as they all make their way to their seats and strap in.

With Samuel on the verge of a panic attack, this flight is going to be the longest of my life. He needs to relax or he's going to make himself miserable, or worse, divert the plane for an emergency landing.

We slow as the reach the runway. I slip my hand against his, the whites of his knuckles clear as he grips the plastic. I'm fearful he'll actually shatter the armrest if he doesn't let up, but fortunately, that doesn't happen. Instead, he lets go and takes my hand in his. His palm is warm, a little sweaty, and his grip fierce, but he doesn't strangle my hand with his.

Just as we start to move, his eyes open, a combination of fear and panic laced in those blue-green orbs, so I do the only thing I can think of to redirect his focus. I kiss him.

At first, he stills, completely shocked by the fact we're lip-locked as we scream down the runway. But then, something else happens. He relaxes. And kisses me back, taking complete control. His lips are urgent, his tongue insistent as it sides against my lips, begging for entrance. A gasp slips from my lips, giving him complete access to my mouth. His tongue dives in, tasting and teasing me in the best way possible. My hand moves to his chest, gripping the smooth, silky tie, as he takes my mouth for the ride of its life.

A throat clears behind Samuel, breaking the fan-tabulous sex-fueled fantasy I find myself starring in. My lip-tango partner rips his lips from my own, his breathing labored as he tries to suck sweet oxygen into his lungs. "What the hell?" he whispers, his eyes glassy and unfocused as he glances around to catch his bearings.

"Damn, Sammy, if I'd have known you kiss like that, I'd have taken you flying way before now," I gasp, my voice not quite sounding like my own.

He turns and sits like a statue in his seat, his discarded bag and the takeoff all forgotten. Instead, he looks completely shocked, a little beside himself, and definitely a lot kissable, his lips all swollen and wet. Just then, the flight attendants start their drink service, stopping at our row. I watch as we soar above the clouds, mere hours away from landing in Las Vegas. All the while, my mind races with the knowledge I kissed Samuel.

And like it.

A lot.

"Drinks?" the smiling attendant asks.

"Alcohol," he answers. "Give me all the alcohol."

***

"You're here!" my best friend hollers as Samuel and I enter the hotel lobby. Harper is all smiles as she throws her arms around my neck and squeezes me tightly. Latham is behind her, his hand extended toward the man who will become his brother-in-law tomorrow evening.

"We're here," I tell her, returning the smile on her face.

"And you survived?" she asks her older brother, giving him a quick hug.

"Barely," he mumbles, kissing her on the cheek.

"After a bad bout with the squirts and a few mid-flight shots of cheap vodka, we got ol' Sammy here, safe and sound," I add, loving how the tips of his ears turn fire engine red and his cheeks pink with mortification.

Harper and Latham seem to both choke. "Did you say…squirts?" she asks, her wide eyes full of humor and so many questions.

"Let's pretend this entire conversation didn't happen," Samuel says, walking toward the desk to check in.

Harper places her arm over my shoulder as she guides me to follow behind her brother. "What the hell happened?" she whispers.

"Apparently, he has an issue with coconut."

Harper's eyes widen. "Shit, yes, he does. It makes him…ill."

"Ill as in giving him the screaming shits about five minutes after it hits his gut."

"No thanks to Freedom," Samuel mumbles, handing his credit card over to the front desk.

"I didn't know!" I reassure him. There's no way I'd intentionally poison his belly with sweet coconut. The next line opens up and I move to the counter. I drop a bag on the floor as I try to juggle my big purse to retrieve my wallet.

"I'll help," Latham says, crouching down at my feet to pick up the dropped items.

I glance down just as he holds up the small box of condoms. "Planning on getting lucky in Vegas, Free?" he asks with a big grin on his face.

"Not me. Those are Sammy's," I announce in the middle of the hotel lobby.

Both Harper and Latham turn to look at the man beside me. He stutters and stumbles, and finally spits out, "Those aren't mine!"

Before anyone can say anything further, Mary Ann comes into the lobby, her phone pressed to her ear. "There you are! I have the ticket agent on the phone. Who's in for the David Copperfield show tonight? They have open tickets."

"Definitely!" Harper exclaims without even consulting with Latham. But the smile on his face lets me know he doesn't care. He'd go anywhere, as long as it's with her.

"Me too," I state, slipping my wallet back into my bag.

"I'm out. Magic is nothing more than a fake mind illusion anyway," Samuel grumbles.

"What? No!" Harper exclaims, drawing more attention to our small group.

"Samuel, it'll be fun. I insist you go with the rest of the family," Mary Ann says, laying the guilt on thick. I love that woman. He grumbles a little, but doesn't argue with his mom.

Mary Ann finishes ordering the tickets to the show, and we all agree to meet in the lobby in an hour. She heads up to tell the rest of the group the plan, while we slowly make our way to the elevators with our luggage. "What floors are you guys on?" Harper asks as we step onto the elevator.

"Fourteen," Samuel and I both say at the exact same time. I flash him a wide grin, while the look he gives me is more of annoyance.

"We're on thirty-five. Do you need help with anything?" Harper says as the doors open on our floor.

"No, I can manage," I tell her, pulling my wheeled suitcase behind me off the elevator.

"We'll see you guys in an hour," Latham says. I turn to see him shove the small box of rubbers into Samuel's suit jacket while his hands are occupied. He shrugs at his future brother-in-law and says, "Just wanted to make sure you're prepared." Then the door closes, cutting off Latham's laughter and leaving us in the hallway alone.

I turn and start to head down the hall, glancing occasionally at the numbers on the doors. It would figure I'd be as far away from the elevator as possible. When I reach the end of the corridor, I turn to the left, only to realize Samuel is still behind me. "Following me?" I tease, glancing up at the numbers once more and realizing I'm finally getting close.

"Just looking for my room."

I finally stop when I hit 1447. Glancing over my shoulder, I see he does the same. He looks at the number on his door, then back down at the card in his hand, and finally over to me. "Seriously?" he whispers, as he swipes his card over the sensor to the room right beside mine. The light flashes red, much like the tips of his ears.

He does it four more times before I finally take pity on his poor, uptight soul. Dropping my bags on the floor, I walk over and grab his card. He huffs and puffs a little, but doesn't say a word as I slowly move the keycard over the sensor, the light immediately flashing green. "There ya go, Sammy. All set."

I hand him back his card, his finger brushing against mine slightly. My entire body erupts with awareness. His scent, his touch, the little noises of annoyance he makes without realizing it. I'm suddenly hyperaware of the fact we're standing very close, his finger grazing against mine. It's not meant to be sexual, but that doesn't stop my brain from conjuring up every dirty fantasy I've ever had, starring the man right in front of me.

Samuel clears his throat. "Thank you."

I back away, even though I'd much rather throw my arms around his shoulders and shimmy up his body like a squirrel. "You're welcome. Apparently, I'm right next door if you should need anything."

"I'm sure I'll be fine," he states, gathering up his belongs and stepping into the room. He stops, though, before he's completely over the threshold. "I, uh, am right next door too. Obviously. So if you need help, or anything, uh, let me know," he stammers.

"Thanks, but I'm sure I'll be fine."

He nods, swallows hard, and steps farther into the room. I turn my back to him and head next door. I use my own keycard, gathering up all my crap off the floor as I balance the weight of the door. I'm bent over when I hear a hiss behind me. Glancing over my shoulder, I find Samuel still there, staring at me.

Or specifically, my ass.

Warmth spreads through my chest as our eyes connect. His widen just a sliver as he straightens his necktie. "I was just making sure you got into your room safely." Then, he turns and disappears, the loud echo of his door shutting filling the hallway.

Just making sure I got into my room safe?

By staring at my ass?

Sure, Sammy.

That's what they all say.

Chapter Five

Samuel

The auditorium is packed by the time we finally get through the ticket line and security. Show, then dinner. The guys all head to the next line, a concession stand that serves over-priced beer, while the girls make a bathroom stop and plan to meet us at our seats. Even though I'm the only single guy here, somehow, it's assumed I'm with Freedom for the evening. She basically just walked up to me, told me to get her a beer, patted me on the chest, and walked away.

Typical Freedom.

I have two draft beers and a bag of popcorn as I follow behind the guys to our seats. I'm surprised when I find us heading down toward the floor, and even more shocked when I find the ladies waiting for us in the third row. "Damn, these are nice seats," my brother, Jensen, says as he hands his fiancée, Kathryn, a beer. Marissa and Rhenn also follow behind me.

"Aren't they? Mom scored big time," Harper replies, wearing the same smile she's had since her Las Vegas destination wedding festivities began.

I slip down the aisle, finding Mom and Latham's parents, Kitty and Bud. They're chatting animatedly about the show, discussing the bio in the book they purchased on David Copperfield. Reserved, I take the empty seat between my mom and Freedom, who quickly relieves me of one of my drinks. "Oh, you got popcorn too. Good thinkin', Sammy!"

She reaches for the popcorn, but I hold it up out of her reach. She's quite a bit shorter than my six-foot frame, so it's easy to keep the salty treat out of her grasp. What I wasn't expecting was for her to literally climb onto my lap to get it. Her long skirt pools at her thighs and I catch a glimpse of her bare ankles. Without truly knowing why, I find myself hard. And staring at those fucking ankles like a crazy man who hasn't seen a woman in decades.

"Freedom?" I whisper, grateful everyone around us seems to be lost in their own conversations.

"Yes?" Her warm breath hits me square in the neck and sends a shiver through my body. My overly heated, too responsive body.

"Why are you on my lap?"

"Why are you keeping the popcorn from me?"

Realizing I'm still holding it up and out of her reach, I lower the tub, setting it between us. Freedom dives right in and doesn't seem to care at all that she's still sitting on my lap, practically straddling my erection and munching on popcorn like it's no big deal. "Oh, you added extra butter salt, didn't you?" she asks between bites. Usually, I'd be a little grossed out and a whole lot offended if a woman devoured her food, licking her fingers, and moaning in orgasmic food delight, but not this time. This time, I'm aroused. So fucking aroused, and the worst part is my mom is sitting right beside me.

I clear my throat, that fact like a cold bucket of water thrown on my head, and move Freedom off my lap. She doesn't really say anything, or seem to notice for that matter, and continues licking the butter salt off her fingers and sipping her beer. No, not sipping. Ladies sip. Freedom devours. She consumes, and again, I don't understand why that image kicks my libido into overdrive.

"So, you don't like magic," she says between bites. "Why not? Scared as a young, impressionable child?"

I take my own drink of beer, grimacing a little at the brand I'm not too fond of. "No, nothing like that. Magic is just an illusion. It's not real."

"But it's real fun to watch, even if it's as fake as Darci Montgomery's tits."

Her words register a split second before the beer in my mouth comes back out. Everyone turns to look at me as I try to wipe the wetness from my chin. Thank Christ no one was sitting in the seats in front of us yet, or they'd be wearing piss beer all over the backs of their heads. "Jesus, Freedom."

She rolls her eyes. "It's true. She *claimed* she was away to some fancy spa for a long girls' weekend, but we all know where she was. No one goes to the spa a B-cup and returns a D with pointy nipples. If that doesn't scream surgically enhanced, I don't know what does."

"If you say so," I mumble, refusing to think about Darci's breasts. Instead, my mind slithers on over to another pair. Ones that are small, yet perky and would fit perfectly in my palm.

No, Samuel. We are not thinking about Freedom's breasts.

Oh, yes, we are.

And they're fucking fabulous.

I inwardly groan just as the stage goes dark. Everyone files into their seats and the show begins, the magician taking the stage. Freedom whistles—you know, one of those eardrum piercing loud noises that makes dogs howl—and claps her hands, spilling her beer. On my pantleg. There's no time for me to grumble or even brush off the excessive liquid as Mr. Copperfield starts to perform.

Admittedly, his show is fascinating, even if it is all a complete pile of crap. The crowd is enthralled, especially Freedom. The bright lights of the stage seem to reflect in her eyes, lighting up her entire pretty face as much as her smile does. I find myself studying her profile, from her narrow chin to her high cheekbones. She's wearing minimal makeup, as always, and has her hair pulled up in a high ponytail. She's wearing at least four necklaces and twice as many bracelets, and on anyone else, it would probably look at little weird. But on Freedom, it looks…normal. Pretty. Sexy, even.

"Las Vegas is the birthplace of sin and love. Might I have one lovely couple come on stage and assist me with my next trick?" David says to the crowd, and just about every hand in the joint flies in the air. "Ahh, yes, you two. Come on up," he adds, pointing down our row. I realize it's my sister and future brother-in-law who are being escorted onto the stage for the next part of David's show.

Freedom lets another whistle fly as our family cheers for Harper and Latham. He has her hand as he helps her navigate the stairs and step onto the stage. "Good evening. You are?"

"I'm Harper and this is my fiancé, Latham," my sister practically beams at the famous magician.

"Fiancé, huh? You sure you want to marry this guy?" David asks, clearly teasing, but getting a huge rise from the audience.

"I do," she giggles. Latham, on the other hand, pulls my sister into his side and seems to size up the man in front of him.

"When's the big day?" Mr. Copperfield asks, as his assistant brings out the tools for his next bit.

"Tomorrow evening," Latham announces proudly.

"Tomorrow, huh? Still plenty of time to change your mind," David says, nudging my sister and giving her a wink. "You know, if say, Latham here…*disappeared!*"

The crowd goes wild at the concept of watching Latham disappear, while the look on his face isn't so lighthearted. Latham looks a little concerned, in fact, and I admit, it matches my own feelings.

"Latham," David starts, throwing his arm over Latham's shoulder and guiding him toward the big box in the middle of the stage. "You're going to go for a little…ride. But don't worry, I'll bring you back!"

The crowd explodes with excitement as Latham steps up to the large, white box in the middle of the stage. Before Latham even knows what's happening, he's being blindfolded by the assistant, and shoved inside the box, with lid ready to close. "Give your fiancée a kiss goodbye," David announces with a laugh.

Then, the lid shuts and Harper is left on the stage with a big white box and a magician who's about to make her fiancé vanish. "Harper, sweetheart, you're going to do the honors. Are you ready? We're going to count to three and with each number, I want you to knock on the box lid. Can you do that?"

She nods, her eyes wide with excitement and even a little fear as she gets ready to make the man she loves disappear. "Are you ready?" he asks.

"One," everyone counts, while Harper knocks on the lid.

"Two."

"Three!"

When she knocks the third time, David rips open the lid to reveal the empty box in the middle of the stage. The crowd goes wild as they spin the box, showing no holes, no trick doors. My stomach knots as I think about Latham disappearing from the stage. Everyone else seems to be happy he's gone, clapping along and cheering for the magician. I'll admit, it's a cool trick, but at the same time, there's a logical explanation as to where he went.

No one just disappears.

"Thank you so much, Harper. You can take your seat and we'll move on with the show," David says, turning and walking away.

"Uh, but what about Latham?" she asks, a nervousness filling her laugh.

"Oh, you mean the big guy you thought you'd be marrying tomorrow?"

"Yeah. Him."

"He's in the box," David says with a shrug.

"What box?"

David Copperfield points to the big white box that's still in the middle of the stage. "That box."

Harper runs over to it, pulls on the lid and reveals a smiling Latham. She throws her arms around his neck and kisses him hard, in front of God and an auditorium full of half-drunks. David claps, helps Latham back out of the box, and points to the stairs at the end of the stage. "Thank you so much, Latham and Harper. Have a wonderful wedding tomorrow," he says before moving on with the rest of his show.

"That was amazing. I can't believe he made Latham disappear," Freedom boasts.

"He *didn't* make him disappear. It was an *illusion*," I insist, finally taking a few pieces of popcorn.

"Well, he definitely was *not* in the box the first time he opened it," she maintains, reaching down and grabbing a handful of my snack. Our hands touch, that familiar electricity coursing through my blood at Mach speed. It's recognizable, and a total nuisance at the same time. I've dealt with it for longer than I'd like to admit.

The show proceeds, Freedom talking off and on throughout. I make a conscious effort not to let our hands touch in the popcorn because it feels like a tsunami in my stomach every time they do. When something big happens on stage, she leans forward, her eyes wide with excitement, as she watches the reveal. Then, she hits me on the arm and explains what just happened, as if I didn't see it with my own eyes. Truthfully, I missed a few of them because I was so wrapped up in watching her excitement play out.

When the show is finally over, all I can think about is getting back to my hotel room, ordering some room service, and maybe a cold shower. It has to be cold because if it were any other temperature, I'd be tempted to picture a certain brunette on her knees, lips wrapped around my cock, and bangle bracelets jangling in rhythm with my hip thrusts.

And that isn't going to happen…

There's no room for those images, I think as I discreetly adjust my rapidly growing erection behind my trousers' zipper.

"Come on, Sammy, we're headed to get something to eat." Freedom says, leaving me in a precarious state.

"I'm not hungry," I reply, just as my stomach decides to betray me, letting out a loud growl.

"Right," Harper sings. "We're going to a club down the street. The concierge recommended it. It's got specialty burgers and steaks."

"Come on, brother. Let's go have a big, juicy steak," Jensen says, slapping me on the back and pushing me up the aisle.

"I'm not eating steak," Freedom adds. As if we don't already know she doesn't eat meat. She reminds us every time we have a cookout.

I lag behind our group as we fight our way out of the auditorium. Maybe they'll proceed to their dinner destination without me. Not that I don't want to join my family for a meal, but I'm still feeling a little off from the flight and I'm not sure I'd be good company. Plus, the constant earthy scent emanating from Freedom's skin is fucking with me, like always.

"Let's go," Latham says when we finally smell the freedom of the night air.

Freedom. See? I can't even step outside without somehow associating everything with her.

"We're going back to the hotel for dinner. We'll see you all tomorrow," Mom announces, pulling away from our group, along with Latham's parents.

"Are you sure?" Harper asks.

"Absolutely, You kids go have fun. We'll meet you tomorrow for brunch in the hotel restaurant," Kitty adds, walking over to give her son a hug.

"I'll go with them," I announce, ready to make a run for it. Just the thought of going to a club has me about ready to break out into hives.

"No way! You're definitely coming with us," Harper insists, latching onto my forearm with her little sister claws.

"But Mom…"

"I'll be fine. I'm having dinner with the Douglases and then will be turning in to my room. No need to worry about me. Please, go with your siblings and enjoy yourself." Mom gives me a smile, but retracts away from the group, letting me know there's no room left for discussion.

Sighing, I turn toward my siblings. They're all smiling widely. "We're going to have fun, Samuel," Marissa insists, Rhenn wrapping his arm around her shoulder and guiding her toward the club.

Fun.

Right.

I fall into step with the rest and walk the two blocks to the club. The lower floor is a restaurant and bar, while the top two floors are for dancing. Latham gives our name to the hostess, thanks to our hotel concierge for making the reservation, and we are led to a big round booth in back. Music from the floors above filters down, but not in the can't-talk way. Instead, it seems to add to the dark ambiance and comfortable experience.

"This place is great," Harper beams, taking her menu from the hostess.

"I can't wait to get upstairs," Latham croons over the music. Her eyes light up with excitement and I have to look away. They're clearly sharing a private moment, and I don't want to be subjected to it.

Our waiter arrives, delivering glasses of water and a smile he offers right to Freedom. My gut tightens when she returns the gesture, and I have no clue why. Freedom isn't mine, and if this guy wants to flirt with her, so be it. Yet, at the same time, that thought makes me want to rip off his arm and beat him to death with it.

It's confusing as hell.

Latham orders a round of Patrón for our group while we browse the menu. The ladies are all excited, ready to let go and have fun in Vegas, while all I can think about is how we're going to all get safely home and how often they clean the club bathrooms. No way am I taking a shot of anything, let alone Patrón.

"No thanks." I wave my hand as the shot glasses are passed out.

"You have to," Jensen states, pushing my hand away and setting the little glass in front of me.

"I do not. I'm not five."

"We're celebrating!" Harper bellows.

"We haven't eaten yet. It'll go straight to our heads," I argue, refusing to even glance at the tiny glass of temptation.

"Exactly," Latham replies, raising his hand.

"Please," Harper whines. Yes, whines. That over-the-top fake voice that some use to get their way. She used it all the time when we were little, so no surprise she'd pull it out now for this special occasion.

I push the glass to Rhenn, who's sitting next to me. "You do my shot."

"Hell no, my friend. You're in this with us," he deflects, pushing it back my way.

Suddenly, I feel her hand creep across my thigh. I jump so hard I hit my knee on the bottom of the table, making everyone around me jump. "Shoot, sorry," I mumble, refusing to glance to the vixen beside me. The one who's digging her nails into my thigh hard...and harder...and, "Ouch!"

She just smiles sweetly at me, fluttering her long lashes like it's her job. "Sammy, please take the shot."

My heart jumps around in my chest as I stare at the only woman to make me want to put liquid death into my body. Yes, death. One time, a long, long time ago, I almost died from alcohol consumption, but if you ever tell anyone, I'll deny it until my last breath.

Realizing it's a futile point, I sigh my resignation and reach for the glass. "Fine. One shot."

"Yay!" Marissa and Harper both cheer as they raise their glasses with the rest of us.

"To Harper and Latham and a long, happy marriage," Jensen toasts.

"Cheers!" we salute, bringing our glasses to our lips.

Cool liquid hits my lips and throat as I toss the alcohol back. The first thing I notice is the smell. It's smooth, just like the taste, yet I know they're both deceiving. The contents of my glass are about to hit me like a sucker punch to the gut, especially on a mostly empty stomach. I set my glass down on the tabletop as warmth spreads through my blood. It could be from the liquor. It could be from the hand. Yes, Freedom's hand that still rests on my thigh. No, she's not digging her nails into my flesh, but she hasn't moved it yet either.

For some reason, I don't say a word.

I let her hand rest mere inches from where my cock twitches with eagerness.

Chasing the liquor with big gulps of water, I finally ask the group, "What is everyone having?"

We order food and visit, discussing details of tomorrow night's wedding, as well as the dinner afterward. Again. Like we haven't discussed it to death in specific detail since the news spread that they were getting married in Vegas. I try to focus on the words around me, but I can't. Her hand. It's still there. On my leg. And it's doing crazy things to my mind. Things I shouldn't be thinking about, especially as we discuss my sister's impending nuptials to the man sitting next to her with stars in his eyes. The thing going on in my pants shouldn't even be a blip on the radar at this point.

Jensen orders a round of drinks and groans when I order another water. He mumbles something to the waiter that has the hairs on the back of my neck standing up. I already know he's up to something.

"I can't wait to dance," Marissa says, smiling at the couples heading up the stairs toward the music.

"Me either!" Harper agrees, her eyes sparkling under the lights.

"I can't wait to watch you dance either," Rhenn mumbles, placing a kiss on her exposed shoulder. My little sister blushes fiercely but smiles in response. She leans in and whispers in his ear, and I have to look away when his face transforms into something that definitely speaks of dirty talk.

Averting my eyes, I find Jensen kissing on Kathryn's neck and Latham running his finger down Harper's cheek like he can't stop touching her. My gut clenches with something that feels like…jealousy. I'm extremely happy for my siblings that they found love. So why am I suddenly wishing it were me sitting there, gazing at the woman I love like I can't wait to be alone with her?

I've never felt that kind of longing. Even when dating over the last decade. They were nice—great, even—but they didn't bring out this primal urge to rip off all their clothes in a public place. Something I'd never do, mind you, but still. You get the point. My siblings are there. They're happy and engaging in healthy relationships, while I'm sitting here *alone*.

No, not alone, I'm reminded as Freedom flexes her hand on my thigh.

Subtly, I glance her way and study her profile. She's smiling softly at my sister, her best friend. Her hair is up, a high ponytail with a little butterfly clip on the side. My fingers twitch to slide through those long locks. Something tells me they're soft and smell amazing, and suddenly, I'm leaning just a little closer to see if I can catch a whiff.

There.

There is it.

That familiar earthy scent I only associate with Freedom.

Our waiter returns with drinks and appetizers. My stomach growls, the warmth of the alcohol still very much present, as a glass of something dark is set in front of me. I glance over at my brother, who just winks and lifts his own glass. It's definitely not beer, and something tells me whatever's in this glass is going to kick my ass. That's the prime reason I won't be drinking it. I'll politely decline, settling for my water for the rest of the evening, but then that damn hand moves. The touch, the heat, the familiarity is gone as she turns and talks to Harper. An odd sense of longing sweeps through my blood, a sadness I can't describe, and that's when I reach for the glass.

That weird feeling I've been trying to ignore but keeps returning all the same.

That weird pull I feel in my chest whenever she's around.

That horrible twist in my gut when some guy passing by our table stops and engages her in a conversation.

She laughs.

I hate it.

It's real and natural and…

Fuck.

That's why I bring the glass to my lips and drink half the contents. It's sweet and goes down easily, and I'm surprisingly shocked. I've never been a liquor guy, not after that one time, indulging too much in college. Now, here I am, begging for that long-forgotten numbness to sweep through my blood, as I finish off the rest of the glass without any food in my belly.

Freedom laughs again, and whatever he says, she agrees. He walks away, a little too much pep in his step, glancing back over his shoulder once before rejoining his small group of friends. I hate him. I don't know why, but I do. The fact he evoked laughter from Freedom so easily, so eagerly, leaves me feeling like a caged animal, ready to pummel my way to freedom.

Freedom.

My complete undoing.

I want to stay away, but I can't.

She calls to me like a siren, drawing me in, most likely to my untimely death.

No, Samuel may not die, but the carefully constructed façade I erected around him will. It's slowly crumbling, and there's nothing I can do to stop it. Nothing I can do to go back. Nothing I can do but go to her.

She calls.

I answer.

***

The pounding.

So much pounding.

My head feels like it's going to vibrate right off my neck, and knowing the way I feel, it'd be a welcome relief. I squint my eyes and glance at the clock, which reads ten thirty. The room is bathed in darkness, thanks to black-out curtains, and I've never been more grateful for decent window coverings before in my life. I also can't believe I drank as much alcohol as I did. That's completely out of character for me, especially when surrounded by my family.

The pounding starts once more, and I realize it's the door. I stumble from bed, my legs tangled in the sheets and almost causing me to fall. It takes me a good five seconds to stand there, waiting for the waves of nausea to take over my body, but fortunately, it doesn't happen. At least not yet.

Cool air-conditioning hits my body—I mean my *whole* body. Why in the hell did I go to bed naked last night? How did I even get to my room? Where the hell are my clothes? All good questions and yet, I have no answers. None. My mind is a big blank sheet of paper where last night was concerned. I remember the show and club we ended up at. My brother talked me into a shot—or was it two? Hell, if the way I'm feeling is any indication, I'd say it was way more than two.

I find a towel thrown on the floor over by the bathroom, so I wrap it around my waist and head toward the door. The pounding starts a third time, and I almost say screw it and go back to bed. But whoever is there is insistent as hell and probably won't leave until I answer. Throwing the lock, I pull the heavy door open, the light from the hallway blinding me.

I hear a gasp and crack open my eyes, only to find my sister, Harper, standing in front of me. Her mouth is hanging open so far, it practically drags on the ground. "Hello," I grumble running my hand over my forehead as my eyes finally adjust to the onslaught of light.

She takes in my appearance at the door, probably just as shocked to see me in a towel as I am to be answering the door wearing one. "What are you doing?" she whispers, her eyes bouncing from my bare chest to my eyes.

"Sleeping. It's what people do in a hotel room," I tell her, already wishing I were back in bed, back in the darkness.

"Why are you here?"

That gives me pause. I know I drank a lot last night, but why the hell is my sister surprised to find me in my room? "Why are *you* here?"

She seems to glance around, checking the number on the door and looking back my way. There's no hiding her confusion. "Did you sleep here last night?"

"Yes," I grumble. Why the hell is she asking stupid questions.

"Naked?"

I pull my towel tighter around my waist. "Apparently."

"Samuel," she starts, then stops.

"What, Harper? Why are you at my room?" I ask, hating that I'm being a tad rude to my sister on her wedding day, yet really just wishing for another hour or two of uninterrupted sleep before all of this wedding whoopla begins.

I expect her to be a little snippy by my impoliteness, but what I wasn't expecting was her response. A response that changes the entire course of my life. A response that rocks me clear down to the core.

"This isn't your room. It's Free's."

Chapter Six

Freedom

Voices.

They're close, yet seem so far away. Through the fog and clouds, a ray of sunshine peeks through, beckoning me awake, yet making me want to hide and pull away at the same time. I bury myself under the thick comforter, trying to grab on to any piece of recollection I can find.

Las Vegas.

Dinner.

Drinks.

Dancing.

More drinks.

More dancing.

There was a guy. I remember his light hair and bright eyes. He couldn't really dance, but I'd had enough drinks I didn't care. The beat in the club was deep and heavy, much like the beat in my head right now. We swayed to the music, laughter from my friends settling around me as they did the same.

Eyes. I felt them on me the entire time, drinking in my moves like a fine scotch that's aged to perfection. Savoring. Tasting.

Hands. Not the ones from before, but a different set. Familiar hands that not only touched my skin, but my soul. I can still feel them sliding against my arms, his long legs moving in time to the music as he pressed his body to mine.

And that body. A flush spreads over me as pieces of the night before start to slide together like a jigsaw puzzle. That torso, surprisingly rippled with hard muscle, and those arms, strong and steady as he held me close. He could move, I recall, as we danced to the thick pulse at the club.

It wasn't the only thing…thick. I definitely remember *that* as he pressed against me, hard and ready.

More booze.

I should have stopped, but I didn't—I *couldn't*.

Like courage, I needed it to advance my night to the next phase. There was only one thing I wanted, and I wanted it with this man. This stranger. Who danced like a god and enticed me, drawing me in with his magnetism and ease.

And yes, it was familiar. His scent, his touch, his everything.

I remember leaving the club, my hand tucked securely in his. We walked, laughed, and…kissed. God, so much kissing. He pressed me against every wall, every doorway, every hard surface as we made our way to our destination. We stopped along the way, another club with a harder beat. Rap music filled the air, but I didn't seem to care. Neither did the mystery man.

We danced, our bodies so close I didn't know where I ended and he began. His lips were soft, yet firm, as they skimmed my hot skin, leaving me completely breathless. We drank from shot glasses a warm amber liquid that was smooth, yet potent. Then, we danced some more, our bodies mimicking sex. Hot, sweaty, stinky sex.

I don't recall what happened next, really. I needed air desperately, my body craving it as much as it was the man. We stumbled outside, giggling and kissing the entire way. I recall…the lights. So many lights, which I guess, is pretty common when you're on the strip in Vegas.

And then there was music.

It was different.

It was low and intimate.

It was…recognizable.

My brain struggles to piece it together, slivers of the beat refusing to connect or make any sense. I stay buried beneath my blankets, struggling to remember the end of the night. Or early morning? Hell, it could have been any time. Obviously, I met someone and enjoyed the hell out of my evening. I'm currently hiding in the darkness, completely naked, and listening for those voices.

An odd sense of awareness seeps through my pores as the voices grow loud—or at least, one particular voice.

Harper.

Suddenly, it all comes back with the intensity and shock of a twelve-car pileup.

The walk in the night.

Kissing.

The jewelry store.

Elvis.

A hummingbird.

I sit up, my hair hanging in my face like a protective shield from the onslaught of sunlight. My hand shakes as I slowly bring it to my face, the ruby and diamond ring shining like a spotlight in the night. A gasp is heard, but I'm not really sure it's from me. No, definitely not from me. I couldn't form coherent sounds if my life depended on it. I'm too busy trying to figure out how the hell I managed to get married in the last ten hours and barely remember it.

"Free?"

I slowly raise my head to face my best friend. Sure, Harper looks like she's seen a ghost, her eyes wide with shock and disbelief, but it's not really her I'm focusing on right now. No, my eyes are riveted to the man standing beside her. He's wearing a towel and nothing else. His hair is in complete disarray, a look I'm definitely not used to seeing, yet turned on by that image all the same. It's also the first time I've noticed the length of his hair. It's definitely a little longer than usual, like he missed a cut or something. His jaw hangs as low as his sister's as he stares back at me with big distressed eyes.

Samuel.

I fucking married Samuel Grayson last night.

Or this morning.

Whatever. Semantics.

His eyes drop as he stares at…my chest. I pull up the blanket, the starch white comforter that's slightly tangled around my legs. "Holy shitballs," I mumble, falling back onto the pillow, my brain jarring and my vision blurring.

"Holy shitballs is right!" Harper hollers, completely inside my hotel room now.

"Can you quiet the noise a little, please?" I ask, my brain trying to crawl from my skull.

"Did you two… Are you… Oh my God, Samuel, what is that on your finger?" she bellows, trying to keep her voice down but failing miserably, as she points at his hand.

I glance up and watch as he tries to hide his left hand behind his back, but I already know what she's referring to. I put that ring there. I have no clue how we were able to stand up straight, let alone long enough to speak words and follow tasks. Yet, we did it. Beautifully.

Suddenly, my best friend starts laughing. She throws her head back and lets loose a full-body laugh that has her eyes leaking water. "What's so funny?" Samuel mumbles, trying to process her sudden shift in personality.

"I can't believe you two got married! I mean, I honestly knew this day was coming, but I never thought it'd be this soon. I thought for sure we had a few more years before you two realized you were secretly in love and pining for each other."

Samuel scoffs and stutters. "I'm not…we're not in…love. Far from it."

Harper snorts. "Right," she replies, pushing the long strands of red hair that fell from her face during her giggle-fest. "Anyway, I should let the newlyweds get back to it. I'll make an excuse for the brunch, but Free, you should probably make sure you're down at the spa at three, and Samuel, you're meeting in Mom's suite at five."

My lips don't seem to want to work. I can't believe how blasé she is about this entire thing, like it's totally natural for her brother and her best friend to marry in Las Vegas mere hours before her own wedding.

She waves her hand. "It's fine."

"What?"

"You said that out loud, silly. It's totally fine. If it were anyone else, I might be a little perturbed, but not you and Samuel." She shrugs. "You two were meant to be together, and I'm happy for you. Though, I guess I'm a little ticked I didn't get to stand up beside you."

Realization sets in.

I got married. Without my best friend. Without the only person who's stood by my side through life's many ups and downs. And boy have there been a lot of downs. My childhood which was a tad bit unusual than most, moving to Rockland Falls to live with my grandma, growing up and always feeling, well, different. Boys were always curious, which is why they dated me, but they always ended with disappointment.

"We're not married, Harper." Great, Samuel finally finds his voice.

"Actually, we are," I mumble, wishing I could just crawl back under the covers and wake up in someone else's life.

"I'm going to go downstairs. If you guys decide to join us, brunch is in the restaurant," Harper adds with a smile as she heads toward the door.

"Well, we'll just get it annulled," he states to me, as if he isn't standing in front of me wearing nothing but a towel and a scowl on his face.

Harper snorts as she reaches the door. "Uhh, I don't think you can do that."

"Why not?" he asks, incredulously.

I follow her eyes as they settle on the nightstand beside the bed. "Well, it looks like this marriage was already consummated. Twice." Her laughter spills into the hotel hallway as she leaves our room.

The silence is heavy as realization sets in. Oh yeah, there was definite sex here last night. Twice. It comes back to me piece by piece, in vivid Technicolor. The wall, the shower, the vanity, the couch, the bed. We may have only used two condoms, but we pretty much christened every surface in the room until we were both exhausted.

There's an ache between my legs as I recall how we spent our morning as husband and wife. My eyes glance up and connect with the bulge, the one barely concealed behind thick terrycloth, and my body starts to hum with anticipation and need.

"What are you looking at?" he asks, glancing down to his growing erection. Yes, it's growing. And growing and growing. Yes, definitely a grower. Apparently, Samuel has been hiding a Louisville Slugger behind his formal suit pants on a daily basis that even I couldn't have been prepared for.

"Nothing," I reply, trying to avert my eyes, but I can't seem to look away. My nipples start to tingle.

His sigh fills the hotel room. "Listen, Freedom, I don't know what happened last night. I never drink hard liquor, let alone that much. Everything is very...well, it's missing. I don't remember anything after a certain point."

"What do you remember?"

Samuel comes over to the bed and has a seat on the edge. His back is...ripped. Holy shitballs, his back is fucking cut like a diamond, but that's not all. There are red welts in long streaks. I lean forward, my face burning with mortification as I realize they're scratch marks. A lot of fucking scratch marks, actually.

He lowers his head, only making those damn marks on his back stand out that much more. "I remember drinking before our dinner was served. Your hand—" he starts, but cuts himself off.

"My hand what?" I press, recalling exactly where my hand was. I was surprised he didn't push it away. Instead, he let it sit on his upper thigh, dangerously close to his groin. I had done it to settle him down. He seemed to get a little worked up when the shots arrived, refusing to take one in celebration. So I set my hand there, which seemed to work. He calmed down and took the shot, and for some unknown reason, I left it there until our dinner arrived. Okay, fine. I know the reason.

I liked touching him.

He clears his throat. "Nothing. Never mind. The point is, I drank a lot, and I never let that happen. This is why."

"Because you wind up married in Las Vegas?" I quip, a smile on my face. I mean, in the grand scheme of things, there are a lot worse things in life than being married to the man you're secretly in love with, right?

Yes, you heard me right.

It's a carefully guarded secret I've carried with me a while, surrounded by locks and chains, guard dogs, and an electric fence. How my bestie figured it out, I have no clue because I'm pretty sure my acting skills have been on point.

"No, because I wind up doing something stupid," he states, the edge of his words striking my heart like a sword.

"Ouch."

He turns around to face me, lifting his leg up on the tussled bed. Of course, when he does, things...dangle out from where the towel is gathered. My eyes are drawn to it like a moth to a flame, and I'm not even embarrassed.

If he feels the breeze, he doesn't adjust, just keeps talking, trying to let me down easy. "Listen, Freedom, I don't know what happened last night, but the bottom line is we can't be married."

"And why is that?"

"Because."

"Because why?"

"I... I can't be married, Freedom."

"Why? Do you have another wife somewhere?"

He scoffs at my comment. "Of course not."

"Well, I'm not getting divorced," I tell him, turning until we're face-to-face.

"What?" he huffs.

"I told myself I'd only get married once, Sammy, so like it or not, you're stuck with me." I shrug, feeling the cool air kiss my chest.

His eyes drop and dilate, as he drinks his fill of my bare girls. If he's going to freeball it, I'm going to let it all hang out too. It's not like we haven't seen those parts that dangle anyway. It was mere hours ago he had his mouth all over my dangles.

I snap in front of his face. "Eyes up here, Sammy."

"What? Oh. Sorry, you're exposing yourself," he defends weakly.

"So are you, and clearly little Sam is ready to play," I state, thumping his erection with my pointer finger. I almost giggle when it jumps, springing back like a bobber. "Though, *little* might not be the right adjective."

"Stop that." He adjusts his towel so his goods are covered, but I don't do the same. Instead, I let them all hang out. "Anyway, we have to get divorced. We can't stay married."

"We can and we will."

He exhales deeply and closes his eyes, rubbing the headache I'm sure he has with his right hand. "Listen, Freedom, this isn't going to happen. I don't even remember the wedding, and that's not the way to start a marriage. I think we need to get this taken care of right away."

"Taken care of? I'm not a wart on the bottom of your foot. I'm you wife. Clearly you have a lot to learn about sweet talk, Sammy. Is that why your previous girlfriends only lasted a few months?"

He growls, the sound low and possessive. A memory flashes through my mind. Wet skin. Kissing. My hand wrapped around his…you know. His low growl. Shower sex. It was pretty much the best sex I've ever had, I'm certain, and I can only remember pieces.

"I'm not trying to sweet talk you, Freedom. I'm trying to be rational. We can't stay married," he exhales, his shoulders sagging a little.

"We can and we will. Come on, Sammy. Let's get cleaned up and head downstairs for brunch. I'm starving," I state, climbing off the bed and letting my full nakedness hang out. "I'm not sure if it's from the booze or the bedroom Olympics." I reach the doorway to the bathroom and glance over my shoulder. When I do, I find his eyes glued to my ass. "Of course, most of our Olympics didn't happen in the bedroom."

His eyes flare with something that looks a lot like desire right before they drop to take in my clothesless state. I hum a little tune, something deep and pulsing from the night before, as I shut the door, leaving it cracked just an inch or two for ventilation. I turn the water on as hot as I can stand it, ready to wash away the aches and pains associated with this hangover. Of course, as soon as I step under the stray, I moan in both pleasure and pain. The water practically scalds, but the jet spray on my neck is heavenly.

"Are you okay?" Samuel asks hesitantly from the doorway. He's standing in the cracked door, staring at me through the glass shower enclosure. I can tell he's trying to keep his eyes glued to my face, but he's failing. I, being the super human I am, decide to toy with him just a little bit. Stepping forward, I press my girlies against the slowly steaming glass.

"What?" I ask, pretending I can't hear him.

"Jesus, Freedom," he groans, averting his eyes.

"You're the one who's lurking by the door like a voyeur," I reply, running my hands over my wet hips.

"I heard you moan. I thought you were hurt," he insists.

"I do have this ache…" I start, leaving my innuendo wide open like a door.

Samuel doesn't kick it open though, ready to alleviate the sudden ache in my girly bits. Instead, he steps back and reaches for the knob. "I'll let you shower," he says, closing the door securely behind him.

He wants me. It's written in his eyes and all over his face. Samuel is just having a hard time coming to terms with everything he's feeling and what has transpired over the last twenty-four hours. I mean, traveling out of state by plane is kind of a big dealio for him. Throw in alcohol and waking up married, yeah, he's sure to feel a little out of sorts in his uptight little world of his.

That's why I'm going to help him.

I'm going to make him see our marriage isn't one of inconvenience or a mistake.

Oh, no.
Our marriage is for life.

Chapter Seven

Samuel

I have to get out of this hotel room before it swallows me whole or I do something I'll regret, like take a very naked Freedom against the tile wall in the shower.

Again, apparently.

I throw on my discarded pants, shove my arms into the wrinkled button-down, and head toward the door. Before I make my exit, I stop, considering all that's transpired in the last half hour. I don't know if we're legally married or not, or what the hell happened or didn't, but something has my feet halting at the door. Instead of making my retreat, I turn and face the bathroom door. I run a shaky hand through my hair, wishing I had time to get it cut before making this trip to Hell, population one.

No, check that.

Apparently, there's two at this party.

Images flood my mind. Freedom's bare chest as the sheet fell to her waist. Freedom's pert breasts pressed against the shower glass. Freedom's rose-colored nipples wet and hard. Freedom's grin that was like a siren's song calling me home.

Freedom, Freedom, Freedom.

I exhale to keep the walls from closing in on me. "I'm going to head to my room and change," I holler as I finish my quick retreat. "I'll meet you downstairs."

Then the door closes, bathing me in silence.

I'm alone in the hallway without any shoes or socks and looking like I was possibly mugged. I haven't even found my tie. I walk the handful of feet to my own room and search my pockets for my keycard. My hand comes in contact with a lot of things, but no keycard. Sighing, I dig for my wallet in my back pocket. Fortunately, it's there, along with all of the contents, including a few more pieces of paper I'll need to look over. Right now, all I really want is about a dozen Tylenol and a hot shower.

The room is cool when I step inside, lacking the life and joy that seemed to be vibrating off the walls in Freedom's room. That's why I need to stay away. Not because of the life and joy, per se, but because it's very out of the box. She's all sparkle and sunshine, while I'm more cut and dried with primary colors.

Taking a seat on the bed, I run my hands through my hair once more. Damn it, I should have taken the time to get that haircut. Something shiny catches my eye and I find myself staring down at the simple platinum band on my left hand. It's as foreign to my finger as an ex-spouse at a funeral. Although, that's not really that uncommon anymore. It seems more and more exes show up at memorials with their big wooden spoon to stir the proverbial pot.

"What the hell did I do?" I ask aloud.

No answer is given.

Standing up, I start digging in my pockets to empty them. The first thing I notice is the small velvet box. It's light in comparison to the heaviness I feel when I open the lid. It's empty, of course, considering the items once inside are now wrapped around our fingers. Tossing it on the bed, I grab a sheet of paper folded into a small square. When I unfold it, I gasp at the bottom number printed in black ink. Three thousand dollars. I bought a damn engagement and wedding ring set, as well as my own ring, and spent just under three thousand dollars.

I start to get a little sweaty in the pits.

My signature stares up at me from the bottom of the receipt, my credit card used for the purchase. Glancing back down at the ring on my finger, I don't exactly see seven hundred dollars in material there, but it's not like pricing wedding bands is something I do in my spare time. Not that I have any of that either.

I toss the receipt on the bed beside the ring box and thumb through the rest of the items. A ticket stub from the magic show and a handful of drink receipts from, apparently, several stops we made after we left the club. The time stamp on them drifts into the wee hours of the morning, until I finally get to the last one.

Happiness Wedding Chapel.

A receipt for the Ultimate Vegas Package.

Five hundred ninety-five dollars included our ceremony, staff photographer, and Elvis and Marilyn witnesses.

Signed. Dated. Stamped.

We're married.

Fuck.

***

Feeling a little more human after a shower and a few aspirin found in my bag, I make my way down to the restaurant for brunch. My stomach growls as the elevator starts to drop, and all I can do is pray the food will stay down. I'm starving.

When I step into the lobby, I run into Rhenn. He's coming from the hallway and heading for the restaurant. "Hey, Samuel," he says.

"Rhenn," I reply, nodding in greeting. I keep my head down and shove my hands into my suit pockets. I'm not sure why I'm still wearing this ring, to be honest. I should have taken it off and left it in the safe in the room. Now, here I am, getting ready to have lunch with a big neon flag on my finger, so I slip it off and slide it into my pocket when he's not looking.

"You ready for today?" he asks, as we enter the restaurant and find our table. Freedom isn't there yet, but everyone else is. They're all sitting around and laughing, telling stories about last night.

Boy, do I have a story...

"Yes," I reply politely, even though I'm not really sure what I'm ready for. The pre-wedding festivities? The wedding? The reception? Seeing Freedom, who has apparently joined me in wedded bliss? Hell, I have no idea what I'm ready for, but I can't exactly say that now. It's not about me. It's about Harper and Latham.

"Where'd you disappear to last night?" Marissa asks as we join the table. Rhenn sits down beside her, while I take the empty chair across from her. Far away from my nosy sister Harper and her knowing smirks.

"I..." I clear my throat and take a sip of water. "I wasn't feeling well."

I also ignore the snort from the far end of the table. Marissa glances down at Harper but doesn't ask why she responded that way.

Before anyone can ask me further questions, Freedom blows into the restaurant like a whimsical goddess. She's wearing a long purple flowy skirt and black tank top. Her feet are adorned with strappy black sandals and her neck with layers of necklaces that dangle between her pert breasts. My mind instantly flashes back to waking up this morning, to the sheet that fell to her waist and giving me a nice little peepshow of said breasts. The small, hard nipples that were begging to be licked...

I clear my throat.

Not the image I need in my head as I sit with my family for brunch.

"Good morning," she singsongs as she approaches, all smiles and chipper disposition, like Snow White and her little woodland creatures.

I choose to ignore her, letting everyone else offer morning greetings. She takes a seat directly beside me, because, well, why wouldn't she? It *is* the only seat left available, but also because she's gunning to draw out this torture as much as possible. If there's one thing I truly know about Freedom Rayne, it's she'll do anything to get under my skin. Including refuse a divorce.

"Hello, lover," she whispers as she sits down and drops her napkin on her lap.

I inwardly groan, but my dick actually starts to harden with her greeting.

"Christ, Freedom, stop it," I mumble, taking another long sip of my water.

"You know, Sammy, I totally get not telling everyone right now. It's Harper and Latham's day, right?"

"My name is Samuel, and we're getting it fixed as soon as we get home," I argue, hating I'm so riled up in front of my family.

Freedom just smiles at me over her water glass. It's a smile I know too well, one that says she doesn't believe me. One that screams *We'll see about that.*

I shift uncomfortably in my seat, my stomach rolling and my head pounding. I'm pretty sure I should just head back upstairs and take a long nap. Maybe if I sleep long enough, I'll awaken from this nightmare to find I didn't actually get married in Las Vegas, that I didn't actually marry my sister's best friend.

Before I can get up and make excuses to leave breakfast, a commotion is heard at the door. We all turn at once, only to find my kooky aunt and uncle standing there, big grins on their faces.

"Orval? Emma?" Mom asks as she stands up.

"You didn't think we were going to let our niece get married without us, did you?" Emma says, as she makes a beeline toward our table, moving faster than most people half her age. Orval is my mom's half-brother from grandpa's first marriage. We didn't even know they existed until earlier this year, nor did I know Grandpa was married before Grandma Phoebe. "Look at this beautiful bride! Harper, you're glowing! You're not already knocked up, are you? You know, you can quickly become addicted to *the sex*. It's too hard to resist, especially when you have man candy like that one," she adds, nodding toward Latham as if he weren't sitting right there.

Harper just giggles and gives Emma a hug. "This day is complete now that you're here," she says before turning to Uncle Orval and giving him a hug too.

Jensen jumps up and grabs two empty chairs from neighboring tables and brings them to our table. Of course, the most convenient place to add seating is at the end of the table. Right by me. I go ahead and give my younger brother a stern look, just for good measure, and his returning grin lets me know this new table arrangement was all part of his master plan.

Emma walks around and greets everyone, offering hugs and warm smiles. She makes her way over to where Freedom and I sit, her aged eyes dancing with mischief. I can already tell I won't like this.

"Samuel, so good to see you again. And with the lovely Freedom, who looks like she enjoyed a few rides on the baloney pony last night too." Emma smacks her lips together and pulls Freedom into a hug. For a tiny, frail-looking woman, she's crazy fast and strong.

Freedom just snorts. "A lady never kisses and tells."

Emma returns with her own smirk. "That's why you come sit next to Aunt Emma. I'm no lady," she teases, and suddenly, the thought of Freedom sitting next to my crazy aunt has me all sorts of twisted up. Freedom doesn't need any of Emma's influence, that's for sure. She's perfectly capable of torturing me on her own.

"And how about you, Samuel? Keeping that joystick active? Even if you have to use your hand, regularly firing your love gun will do wonders for your complexion, let alone your stress level." She turns those big, innocent eyes my way, as if she wasn't just asking me about my… gun.

"No comment," I tell her, taking my menu and studying the brunch selection.

"Just ignore her, Samuel," Uncle Orval says as he takes a seat beside his wife. "That's not something you discuss at the table."

Emma snorts her indignation. "What are you talking about? We talk about it every night."

"No, we fire the gun every night. We don't always talk about it before it goes off."

My stomach is lurching. I'm stuck in a *Twilight Zone* hell with my crazy aunt and uncle and a woman who I married, yet don't recall any of it. "Please stop talking about your gun. It's a family establishment."

Freedom leans toward me, her long hair dangling on my lap as she whispers, "You know, I always heard a guy could go blind if he messed with that too much."

I groan.

"Oh, dearie, there's no such thing as *too much*. It's important to have a healthy sexual appetite. When you marry, you'll understand what I mean. If you find yourself with a man who doesn't make you want to drop your panties and grab your ankles on a regular basis, then you're with the wrong fella," Emma says, giving Freedom a decisive nod.

I concentrate on my menu and pretend I don't feel Freedom's gaze on me. I'm saved from any further discussion about ankles and grabbing them when our server arrives at our table and starts refilling coffee cups. A leg to my side slides against mine, whether by accident or on purpose, I'm not sure. I just ignore the way Freedom's limb is pressed against mine and the way her fruity shampoo is permeating my senses and making it difficult to think of anything but her.

"And you, sir?" our server asks as she steps behind Freedom to take my order.

"I'll take a cheese, mushroom, and green pepper omelet with a side of bacon."

A gasp echoes over the conversations around us. "Bacon?"

When I turn her way, I find Freedom's eyes wide in disbelieve. "I'm sorry, what?"

"Bacon? You can't eat bacon," she states, folding up her menu and handing it to the server. "He'll have the tofu cakes too."

My stomach does a pirouette straight south into Yuckville. "No, I will not eat that weird crap. I'll have the bacon," I tell our server, who just looks at us with a confused look on her face.

With one final glance our way, she quickly turns to Emma and Orval for their orders. I turn to the woman on my left, lower my voice, and ask, "What's wrong with bacon?"

"There's nothing *wrong* with it, per se, but I'm just really devastated about how they treat those pigs at the farm in Missouri. Did you hear about it?"

My television, when it's on, is usually on some news program, so yes, yes I've heard about the large hog operation where the owners were supplementing their food with some less than quality products. A few of the pigs even died from the bad diet and the owners left their corpses in the pens for the others to feast on. A worker finally called the authorities, which ended up hitting national news when it was discovered the owner of the farm is a senator's son.

"I heard," I finally confirm, chugging my too-hot coffee.

"Well, then you must agree with me, right? That's a horrible way to treat an animal," she states, her eyes a little glossy from unshed tears. One thing I've learned about Freedom in the last twenty plus years, she's incredibly soft-hearted, especially with animals, but while she doesn't eat meat, she's never pushed her beliefs off on anyone around her. She's never criticized Harper or our family for that matter when we eat cheeseburgers or steak. Freedom just politely declines and picks something else.

"Horrible," I agree, keeping my eyes ahead of me. Marissa and Rhenn chat with Kathryn and Jensen, completely oblivious to the fact I'm caught in my own personal hell, with Freedom on one side and our aunt and uncle on the other.

Once everyone has placed their orders, Latham's dad stands up and asks for our attention. "If I could have your attention, please. Kitty and I are honored to be in Las Vegas today to celebrate the union of our son, Latham, to this incredible woman," he says, waving his hand toward my younger sister. "Harper, you make Latham a better person with your love and compassion. We're eager to watch you two become husband and wife, as well as blend two families for life. We're proud of you both and wish you a lifetime of happiness. Let's raise our cups and glasses to Harper and Latham."

I hold my coffee cup and salute my sister and her fiancé, as my heart gallops in my chest like a stallion. They did it right. They dated, have lived together, fell in love. Now, they're pledging their love and committing for life. The right way.

Then there's me.

Getting shitfaced drunk and apparently marrying a woman I can barely stand. Wait, that seems a little inaccurate. It's not that I dislike her, it's the fact we're so different.

A bead of perspiration slides down my spine as Freedom shifts in her chair beside me. Her hand brushes against mine in the most innocent way possibly, yet it feels like a bolt of lightning straight into my bloodstream. A pulse lives and breathes in my veins, like a reckless desire I can't seem to contain.

All from the simplest of touches.

"We brought a gift," Emma announces to the table, standing up and reaching for the gift bag she brought with. "I was going to wait until after the wedding for this, but I recall on my wedding day, I was terribly nervous," she says, as she slowly makes her way to the head of the table to where Harper and Latham sit.

Harper kinda giggles but doesn't really look nervous. In fact, I'd say she looks the opposite. She looks excited. Happy. Content.

"I was so nervous, I snuck out of my parents' room and to the hall closet where my Orvie was hiding."

"Oh God," Marissa gasps, her eyes wide with shock at our aunt's insinuation.

"Yes, that's right, Marissa. I was calling our good Lord and savior just moments before walking down the aisle to say I do."

Harper giggles, while mom covers her eyes with her hand.

"The gift!" Emma hollers, handing the bag to my sister.

Carefully, as if she were afraid of something to jump out at her, she pulls out layers of tissue paper before she retrieves a multicolor blanket. Latham takes it, and together, they stand up and unfold the large blanket. Several gasps echo throughout the room, and not necessarily from our table.

"I learned how to crochet this past summer," Emma boasts, clapping her hands.

"Are those…" Jensen starts, but suddenly stops. His hand goes to his mouth as he tries to hid his laugh.

"What is that?" Marissa asks, leaning forward to get a better view of the intricate detail of the blanket.

"Holy shitballs, Sammy. That's a sex blanket," Freedom says as she places her hand on my forearm, her nails biting my flesh through my button-down. I adjust my tie to keep from reaching for her fingers.

I don't look at my arm, however. My eyes are glued to the train wreck of a wedding gift because there, delicately crocheted in bold colored yarn is a couple engaging in sexual acts in just about every position known to man. Dozens of positions, some I've never even heard of before.

"What in the world is that thing?" Mom asks, her cheeks pink as she looks at her brother and sister-in-law.

"It's a fertility blanket. It'll help get the juices flowing and baby gods buzzing," Emma insists, proudly waving her hand in front of the blanket like Vanna White.

Harper's ears turn a lovely shade of red, and I have to look away. While I'm well aware my sisters and their significant others are…adults, and engage in…adult things, I can think of a dozen things I'd rather be doing right now than thinking about my sisters and…that. Root canal with no pain meds. Run over my foot with a semi. Rip my arm off and beat myself to death with it. All things I'd rather do than allow a sexual thought featuring one of my siblings to enter my brain.

"Do you see that reverse cowgirl, Sammy? That's amazing needlework," Freedom coos, as if this obnoxious blanket is the greatest thing since sliced bread.

"Are you serious?"

She turns those dark eyes my way. They're dancing with humor and enthusiasm. "Definitely! Do you not understand how critical a good reverse cowgirl is, Sammy?"

"Very important!" Emma hollers, ensuring all eyes—every single pair in the restaurant—is on me.

"True, Samuel. There's nothing like watching the bounce of a beautiful cowgirl." This from my eighty-something-year-old uncle. Vomit burns my throat, and I'm one-hundred percent sure I'm going to have to give myself a head injury to rid the image his comment just conjured up. "That's good stuff," Orval replies, raising a hand in toast.

I'm starring in the *Twilight Zone*. That's the only reasonable explanation as to why we're discussing sex positions during brunch, mere hours before my sister's wedding. It's not real. I'm still in bed, sleeping off my hangover. I'm not surrounded by my family, by inappropriate conversations and gifts. I'm not stuck listening to my aunt and uncle overshare stories of their marriage. I'm not married.

But I am.

It's all real.

My reality.

Chapter Eight

Freedom

We're getting ready in a suite bigger than my apartment. I don't know how they secured this baby, but kudos to Latham for going all out on the honeymoon suite. The bed in the other room is big enough to comfortably sleep a family of four, much bigger than my postage stamp bed back at home. Not that you'd invite a family of any size to join you in bed, especially on your wedding night, but you get my point.

Marissa tops off my champagne and I catch the sparkle of the diamond on my finger. If anyone has noticed it, they haven't said, which I'm grateful. Not that I'm embarrassed or upset I'm wearing Samuel's ring. Oh, no. Just the opposite, actually. But I don't want what has happened between us to overshadow or cause pain to my bestie. It's her day, after all. We're here for her and Latham, to celebrate their love and witness their union in holy matrimony.

"Free, are you about ready?" Harper hollers through the bedroom doorway.

"Thanks," I say to Marissa as she tops off her own glass and heads toward where Harper is getting ready. "Coming!"

I follow Harper's younger sister to the bedroom, where I'm stunned silent at the vision of my friend. She's simply gorgeous in her strapless ivory lace gown that hugs her curves from chest to thigh. It fans out subtly at her knees and cascades around her sexy ivory pumps. Her long, auburn hair hangs in big soft waves down her back, three rhinestone jeweled flowers pinning some of those curls from her face.

"Holy shitballs, Harper. You're…wow!"

My best friend smiles widely. "You think?" She glances down at her dress, softly touching the lace at her sides.

"Oh, Latham is going to shit a brick when he sees you," I confirm, making my friend laugh.

"Well, I kinda hope not, but I do hope his reaction is as big as yours."

"No worries there," Marissa adds, emptying the champagne bottle into her sister's glass. "He'll swallow his tongue."

"Well, as long as he coughs it up so he can use it later," Harper says, a sly grin showing over the rim of her champagne glass. "His tongue is one of my favorite attributes."

"I'm not sure I want to know what I walked in on," Mary Ann, Harper's mom, says as she enters the bedroom. "Oh, Harper." She stops and covers her mouth with her hands as tears brim in her eyes.

"You like?"

Mary Ann approaches her daughter and takes her into her arms, holding her tightly in a hug. "You're beautiful," she says, those tears no longer contained. They fall freely, and I admit, they even choke me up a bit.

Mary Ann has always been a surrogate mom to me. The mother I always longed for. My own parents took off when I was in grade school, leaving me in the hands of my maternal grandma. When I became friends with Harper, I sort of adopted her mom as my own. We had sleepovers, ate dinner together at each other's houses, and essentially spent all of our free time with one another. Through it all, I've sat by and watched the dynamics between mother and daughter. Not just with Harper, but with all of her kids. Mary Ann is an extraordinary mother, and I am fortunate to have that in my life.

Their whole family, actually. While I appreciate what my grandma did for me, it was the Grayson family that really made my childhood what it was. From moving around, living in spiritual compounds to finally having a home with a real family. That's what they mean to me. Not just Harper, but the entire family.

My family.

Mary Ann is wearing a blue pantsuit with nude pumps, and she's totally hot. Marissa looks a lot like her mom, a bit on the shorter side with dark hair and green eyes, but there's no denying the relation. Harper, on the other hand, favors her dad's look. Tall, slender, stunning blue eyes, and gorgeous auburn locks. Plus, throw in the brains. She has a business sense to rival any big corporation in the area, and does it while selling silky nighties.

My bestie is beautiful, inside and out.

And about to marry Latham.

I knew back in school we'd be right here someday. They did everything they could to get under each other's skin. It was like foreplay. A dance. A seduction that spanned more than a decade. The moment Latham walked into Kiss Me Goodnight, after being gone for ten years, the world finally righted itself. And now, they're getting married.

I couldn't be happier for her.

Spinning the unfamiliar object on my ring finger, I debated on whether or not to take it off. It's foreign on my left hand, considering I haven't worn a ring since the mood one I sported in high school, but there's something so very right and…familiar, all the same. It's like good juju finally settled around me. I don't know how to explain it, but I'm not about to question it either. That's why the ring stays on my finger. If someone asks about it? Well, I guess I'll figure it out then.

"How are you doing?" Mary Ann's soft voice startles me from my own thoughts.

"Oh," I reply with an immediate smile. "I'm good."

She just grins that knowing motherly smile. Like when Harper and I were in high school and skipped PE class to go get milkshakes. Without so much as a phone call, she knew. How? I'll never know, but she did. "I'm happy you're here, Freedom. For Harper."

"Thank you, Mrs. G. Nowhere else I'd rather be."

That's when she glances down at my finger as I'm nervously spinning the double rings adorned there. My heart stops. Literally. It just stops doing its only job, beating and pumping blood through my body. I can't breathe, and I'm pretty sure I'm going to drop dead any second from lack of oxygen to my brain.

But she doesn't call me out on my finger bobble. Instead, she smiles, soft and gentle. She wraps me in a hug and whispers, "You're a part of this family, Freedom. Always." Then, she kisses me on the cheek and backs away, giving my left hand a light squeeze before she returns to where her daughter stands in the center of the room in her wedding dress.

There's a slight tremble to my fingers as I bring my glass to my lips and drink. If only Mary Ann knew what her words meant to me. Actually, maybe she does know and that's why she shared them. Either way, my eyes hold slight tears as I look around the room, taking in this family I've come to love.

My family.

They've always accepted me, weirdness and all. I've always known I was different, even as a young child. You're not raised by hippies and named Freedom Rayne without being even a little weird. But they've never made me feel like an outcast, like I wasn't allowed to be whomever I wanted to be. Even Samuel. He may not understand it, and Lord knows anything not black and white is a struggle for him, but he's never made me feel anything less than accepted.

Even now.

Even as he struggles to come to terms with the turn of events in our lives, he makes me feel alive.

Wanted.

That's all I can ask for in a world where you're so easily cast aside for being different. A world where they do doubletakes when you enter a room because your jewelry is gawdy and maybe a little noisy. A world where they roll their eyes every time you get excited about the benefits of healing powers. A world where they shun you for speaking your mind when faced with prejudice and adversity.

A world where differences aren't always accepted.

But not this family.

They accept me.

Strangeness and all.

***

I'm not a crier, but I openly admit my eyes get a little misty when I turn to see my bestie walk down the short aisle on her oldest brother's arm. She's radiating sunlight as she walks toward Latham, who can't seem to take his eyes off the woman he loves.

And let's take a moment to talk about Samuel. He looks confident and stunning in his suit, but honestly, he always does. As he gives his sister away, there's something different about him. He looks completely relaxed, sure, but there's a hint of sadness there. As if a longing he can't seem to contain is fighting to get out.

When they reach the end of the aisle, the minister asks, "Who gives this woman to wed this man?"

Samuel confidently and proudly states, "I do." Then he turns to his younger sister, hugs her tightly, and passes her hand to the man she's about to marry.

As he walks to the front row to take the empty seat between their mother and his siblings, I catch his eyes raking over my body.

I'm wearing a taupe dress with tiny aqua flowers around the waist, the hemline just below my knees. To be honest, I rarely wear a skirt that isn't ankle-length, but when I saw this one, I knew it was perfect for tonight. Simple, yet elegant, and if the way Samuel's eyes devour my curves, I'd say I made a good choice in dresswear.

Good.

I'm in the second row, alone, and suddenly, he stops. He doesn't take a seat. He glances down the row to his two siblings and their fiancés, and then back to his mom. There's indecision written on his face, but it's quickly replaced with acceptance.

Samuel walks around his family and joins me in the second row. Marissa and Mary Ann both glance back at me when they see where he's going, his mom giving me a wink and a smile. I feel his body heat, his presence as he takes the empty seat beside me. His leg brushes against mine, and I have to stop myself from reaching over and taking his hand. But I don't.

I watch in rapture as my bestie for life professes her love to the man of her dreams. I'm not sure when I started to cry, but when Samuel hands me a handkerchief from his inside coat pocket, I smile. Dabbing my wet eyes, my heart beats wildly in my chest, so full of love and elation for my best friend and the life she's making.

A life I secretly want.

Not with Latham.

With someone else.

Warmth wraps around my left hand as he laces his fingers with my own. The act only makes the tears come even quicker. I'm lost in the sensations of his soft skin against mine, the comfort that silent act provides. My eyes bounce between the couple at the front of the room and to the hand holding my left one. I think witnessing the combination of declaration of forever and friendship and understanding beside me is almost too much.

It just makes the tears fall even faster.

When the ceremony is done and they're pronounced man and wife, Latham kisses his bride with everything he has, claiming her as his own. Forever.

We all stand, Samuel releasing my hand so we can clap with the rest of the family. I dab at my eyes one final time, praying those pesky tears are gone, at least for now. "Thank you," I whisper, handing him back the handkerchief.

Samuel clears his throat, his blue-green eyes locked on mine. "You may keep it," he offers, holding up his hand as I try to give him back the square of material.

I glance down and snort. The hankie is wrinkled and wet, and Samuel's brain is probably about to explode. "Oh, right. It's got my snot on it. I'll wash it first," I tell him, shoving the material in my small clutch purse. Now it's my turn to clear my throat. "Uhh, thank you for sitting by me."

I leave out the part where I thank him for just being him.

"You're welcome. I didn't want you to be alone."

My throat tightens once more with emotion. Frankly, I'm used to being alone. Even though I have Harper and her family, I've been alone for a long time. My grandma tried, but she struggled to raise a young girl who was influenced by tree-huggers and rain-dancers who changed their last name to Rayne because it was "more suiting." What I'm not used to is having it brought to the forefront of my mind, acknowledging it, and then being comforted.

"We're going to take some pictures," Mary Ann says, interrupting my thoughts. It's a welcome reprieve.

For the next twenty minutes, we go through the motions of taking wedding photos. The couple, individuals of the bride, and then family. I sit back down, a smile on my face as they all interact with one another. Their laughter is real, the smiles genuine, the love unwavering.

"Freedom Rayne, get your ass up here," my best friend hollers from the altar. The photographer turns my way, tapping his foot as he waits for me to join the party.

"That's for family," I tell her, smiling awkwardly as the entire group stares at me.

Including Samuel.

"Silly girl, you *are* my family. Get up here!" she says, her pearly white teeth showing as she grins at me.

I make my way to the front, trying to slip in the back. Maybe behind Jensen or even Rhenn. He's broad enough to hide me for sure. However, before I can shimmy my way to the back with the tall kids, Mary Ann grabs my hand and pulls me to stand beside her. Directly in front of Samuel. I can feel his body heat pressed against my back, and suddenly, I'm feeling a little flushed, especially when a hand rests on my hip. The warmth of his hand burns my dress and spreads through my blood.

"Thank you, everyone," the photographer says, snapping a few more pictures before releasing us to the next part of the evening.

I hang back, letting the bride and groom finish up with the minister, all while keeping an eye on Samuel. He's wearing a classic black suit with an aqua colored tie. It's actually the first time I've noticed his tie matches the flowers on my own dress. Without even trying, we're all matchy matchy.

"Oh, Freedom," Harper says, waving me over. "We need your signature."

I stop in front of the podium and glance down. "Really? You want me to sign your marriage license?" My shock is real. When Harper and Latham decided to get married in Vegas, they forwent many of the standard traditions, including maid of honor or best man.

Instead, they opted to stand in front of a small group of family—and me—without anyone standing up with them.

"Of course I do," she insists, handing me the pen. Then, she pulls me into her arms and whispers, "You're my sister from another mister. And I love you."

So, with tears in my eyes and a heart overflowing with love, I sign my name on the marriage license. As soon as I'm done, Samuel steps up and takes the pen, signing his own name below my name.

Suddenly, a flashback.

Signing another certificate.

He swayed on his feet, but eagerly scratched his name across the line before I had a chance to write mine.

He dropped the pen and pulled my lips to his, feasting on me as if I were his last meal.

Then I signed my name.

"Earth to Freedom," Harper says, snapping her fingers in front of my face.

"Oh, sorry," I laugh, feeling the burn of a blush tip my ears.

When I glance at Samuel, the pen is poised directly over the paper, but his eyes are wide in disbelief. As if he's seeing a ghost. He lifts them, slowly meeting my own eyes, and holding my gaze. "I remember this," he whispers, glancing around to see who's watching.

Harper smiles as Latham pulls her into his arms. He kisses her forehead as she looks over at me, a knowing smile on her face. It's as if she knows he just recalled a piece of the messy puzzle from last night—or this morning.

"Ready to go?" Mary Ann says, coming over to make sure the license is signed.

"All set," Harper says, as her older brother signs his name to the other line.

When he drops the pen, he glances up at me and my heart dances in my chest. There's a parade of emotions there, ones I'm not equipped to dissect this evening. I'm exhausted, really. From the tear-filled wedding to all the crap in my own life, I'm just not ready to dive into the looks Samuel keeps giving me. The ones he's going to do something to rectify the whole marriage situation the first chance he gets. He's going to fight me.

Us.

So, I deflect to the one thing I'm good at.

The one thing that drives the man absolutely crazy.

Sarcasm and humor.

"Ready to go, Sammy? I'll let you buy me a drink or two before dinner," I tell him, patting him on the chest for good measure.

He sighs deeply and straightens his necktie. "It's Samuel," he reminds me, and I inwardly smile. It's a game at this point. I've known my entire adult life he hates the nickname, yet I use it every chance I get because I love to get a reaction out of him. It's pretty much the highlight of my day.

"I know, Sammy," I tell him, wrapping my arm around his. "Let's go get some booze."

"I think I'll pass on the alcohol," he mumbles as we follow behind everyone else to exit. "Forever."

"You're no fun."

Again, he sighs. "I think I've had plenty of *fun* to last a lifetime."

"And to think, we're just getting started."

He groans, a mixture of shock and pain. The shock I can understand. His systematic world has been turned upside down. Actually, the pain I get too. It's the same. He's a simple man. Black and white. Everything has its place. Order. He loves his job and does it to the best of his ability. Sure, it's a weird profession, but if anyone understands weird, it's me. I appreciate it, revel in it. It's my thing, and that's why I understand how Samuel can fight this *thing* that's landed right smack dab in the middle of our lives. To me, it's like fate brought us together, one drunken, crazy night. The stars aligned and put me right where I was supposed to be. To him, it's like someone threw a bright red crayon into the dryer with his clean tighty-whities. He doesn't know what to do with it or how to fix it.

So he panics.

Well, I'm not going to let him panic.

I'm going to show him he can still have fun with a red crayon.

After all, red is my favorite color.

***

We have a small, intimate dinner in the hotel restaurant to celebrate Latham and Harper's marriage. I'm not surprised they can't keep their hands off each other. They're deliriously happy, their smiles real and eager. When the plates are cleared, the staff brings out a champagne toast and chocolate drizzled cheesecake. As we raise our glasses to the couple and enjoy dessert, I can't help but feel a little envious that they're so open and public with their love and affection. After all, I'm sitting next to my husband, and no one knows.

Well, except Harper.

And apparently, she's not telling anyone, considering no one is freaking out the oldest Grayson got married one drunken night in Las Vegas.

I dive into my cheesecake, even though it's not really my thing. I don't usually eat dessert with this much real sugar, but I'll admit, it's good. Really good, actually, and I find myself scraping my fork along the plate just to make sure I don't miss a single crumb of that buttery crust. It's heaven in my mouth.

"You going to eat that?" I ask, pointing to Samuel's plate with my fork.

"No," he says, looking about as uncomfortable as a man in a gynecologist's office.

"Why? It's good," I tell him with a mouth full of food.

Samuel looks down at my empty plate and points to his. "Have at it."

I move his dessert in front of me, having no intention of actually eating it. I'll put myself in a sugar coma for sure, but he doesn't know that. Instead, I take a small forkful, swipe it through some of the chocolate drizzle on the plate, and move my fork to his face. "What?" he asks, glancing down at the fork as if it were about to bite him.

"Eat it."

"No, thank you."

I move the fork around and make an airplane noise, softly, so no one hears. "Eat it," I sing, touching the tip of the fork to his closed mouth. The result is a small glob of cheesecake swiped across his full lips.

Now all I can think about is licking that dessert right off his face.

"Stop it," he mumbles, his tongue darting out and licking the white and brown dessert from his lips.

I wave the airplane fork in front of his face once again, this time plopping the cheesecake on his lips with more force. "Eat it," I sing again, forcing myself not to smile at the outrage on his face.

"Freedom. Stop. It."

My body shivers when he says my name. So full of authority. So deep and husky. So full of irritation. Yet, I want to crawl on his lap, wrap my arms around his neck, and kiss him with everything I have.

I watch in rapture as he licks the rest of the cheesecake off his lips a second time, my body humming with desire. Do you think it's appropriate to ask for the cheesecake to go?

Moving my fork a third time, I can tell by the look in his eyes he's not going to let it happen a third time. Yet, I still move my hand, waving the fork in front of his mouth and making the airplane noise. His eyes zero in on the dessert as his hand moves to stop me. Big, warm fingers wrap around mine as he halts my movements. I push against him, the fork inching closer to his mouth. We battle for control, neither of us really achieving it. So when the fork hits his cheek, it's messy, his grunt loud.

"Dammit, Freedom," he mumbles, his eyes wide with surprise.

My smile is instant, my giggle explosive. I fully prepare for him to grab his napkin and wipe away the cheesecake, but he doesn't. Instead, he swipes his finger through the dessert and quickly slides it along my own cheek. I'm so shocked by this sudden playful side, all I can do is stare at him. Even when he touches my nose, leaving cold remnants of creamy cheesecake and crumbly crust in the wake.

"There." A hint of a smile plays on his lips, and all I can think about is kissing them. Samuel has never engaged in a food battle, let alone in a public place. I wonder if he's forgotten where we are. Yet, even though I know all eyes are on us, I can't look away from his gaze. I'm trapped, like a moth to a flame.

"That wasn't nice, Sammy." I sound breathless, excited.

"Tit for tat, Freedom," he replies, still not making a move to grab the napkin at his lap.

The juvenile in me giggles. "You said tit."

He rolls his eyes dramatically. "It's an expression."

"A funny one," I tell him, snaking my tongue out to lick my cheek.

His eyes darken and follow my movement as my tongue tastes a piece of cheesecake. Samuel's throat bobs heavily and his mouth forms the slightest O. With him distracted and looking like he wants to eat me for dessert, I touch a single finger to the end of my fork and graze it along his bottom lip.

Dark, hungry orbs slam into mine as I run my finger along his skin. My body burns, and those pretty blue and pink panties I'm wearing are rendered useless. I'm so turned on suddenly, I'm afraid my nipples are standing up and saluting. Actually, I'm sure they are. Everything is so…tingly.

"Hot damn, Sam." Orval's words are like a cold glass of water being thrown on us.

Samuel blinks, his eyes clear, and he pulls back, dislodging my touch from his skin. I glance to my side and find all eyes—every single pair—focused on us. Most of them are full of question, but there are a few packed with humor too. Like they can't believe they just witnessed stiff ol' Samuel Grayson play with food.

I feel slightly victorious in the moment.

He looks like he'd rather be anywhere else than right here at the moment. Samuel's so uncomfortable he doesn't even correct his uncle when he uses the shortened version of his name. The tips of his ears match his cheeks as he wipes away the cheesecake and clears his throat, completely averting his eyes from everyone at the table. Including me.

"Well, then, if you'll excuse me," Emma announces and dramatically stands up. "I'm going to go smoke after that."

Me too, Emma.

Me too.

Chapter Nine

Samuel

"Come on, big brother. You owe me a dance," Harper says, as she grabs my hand and pulls me onto the dance floor.

"I'm not so sure, Harper," I argue, as she leads me to the dance floor.

"I'm sure. We're doing a different take on the father/daughter dance, Samuel. Come dance with me," she insists, as she places her hands on my shoulders and slowly sways to the music.

The moment our dessert dishes were collected, our dinner party moved to the dance club attached to the hotel. Harper and Latham were able to have their first dance as husband and wife, and now he's dancing with his mom, while I'm trying to spin my sister around the packed dance floor. It's a seductive number. Couples are practically making out like teenagers as they sway—err, grind—inappropriately to the music.

And here I am, dancing with my sister.

"You and Free seemed awfully cozy at dinner," she says, a knowing smile on her face.

"It was nothing," I insist, hating how my heart starts to gallop wildly in my chest when I recall the whole cheesecake incident after dinner. Usually, I'd be appalled by her actions, the concept of dirty fingers in my food making me gag, but for some crazy reason, it was a bit…arousing.

"Mmhmm. Sure didn't look like nothing."

I reach up and pull on my tie. "You know how Freedom is." I'm deflecting, sure, but honestly, I don't know what to say. The entire situation is so very foreign to me, let alone the fact I seemed to actually enjoy our playful banter.

"I do. She's the best," Harper says as the song comes to an end. "Listen, Samuel, I don't know what happened last night and I don't really need the details, but I want you to know we'd all support you. You know, if you were to actually tell everyone that you two. Got. Married."

Again, my heart is starting a little freak-out in my chest. "That wasn't supposed to happen."

She stops moving and just looks up at me. "Probably not, but it did. And that's okay. You two are actually great together."

I can't help but gape at my sister. *Great together?* We're not even...together.

"Don't look at me like that. I'm being serious. She might be just what you need," she says with a shrug.

"Need for what?" I ask, unsure where she's going with this.

"Need in life."

Now I know I'm just staring at my sister. I know she just got married and thinks everyone should be as happy as she is right now, but the concept of Freedom and myself being...well, that, is a little farfetched. "I think you're just deliriously happy right now and not thinking straight."

She lifts a single shoulder. "I am deliriously happy, but I'm not blind. You two have been dancing around this for years."

"We've been dancing around nothing," I insist, hating the tightening in my gut that calls out my lie.

Harper just smiles. "Whatever, big brother. I just want you to be happy, okay? And if that's with Free, then I'm even more ecstatic because she's amazing."

I swallow over the large lump in my throat and start to move to the music again. When the song ends, she leans up on her tiptoes and kisses my cheek. "She brings out something different in you, Samuel. Don't ignore that." Then she steps back and turns, finding her husband on the dance floor.

I'm left dumbfounded by her comments. Sure, she brings out something different. She drives me crazy, and not always in the good way. She's maddening, frankly. No one gets under my skin the way Freedom Rayne can, and that's saying something, considering I have younger siblings. But even when we were children, I had an abundance of patience for Harper, Jensen, and Marissa. Especially Marissa. Yet Freedom just walks into the room and suddenly, I'm like a caged animal on the defense.

Speaking of, I glance to the side of the club and find her talking to a man. He's tall and bulky, like he spends way too much time in the gym. Hell, he probably works in a gym and spends all day long flexing in the mirror. His hair is longer on top and his smile alarmingly white as the neon lights flash off them.

I hate him.

I hate the way she laughs, so easily and free.

I hate the way he puts his hand on her arm and motions to the dance floor.

I hate the way she seems to actually be considering his offer, even though she shakes her head.

I hate the way this jealousy reappears, much like it did last night.

I've never been jealous, let alone of someone like this gym rat, who's showing way too much interest in Freedom.

In my wife.

His eyes scan her dress, the one that hits just below her knee and flares just a bit when she walks. There's no missing the interest flashing in his eyes, or the way they linger a bit too long on the sliver of cleavage she's displaying with that tasteful, yet sexy dress.

My feet are moving before I can even stop myself. The pulse of the music thumps right along with my heart. Approaching where they stand, she notices me before Mr. Gym Guy, her eyes flashing with something that looks like excitement.

"Are you sure?" I hear him ask.

Before she can answer, I slip my arm around her waist and pull her into my embrace. Freedom moves willingly, her hand gripping the back of my dress shirt. "Hey, you," she whispers, her voice sounding all breathy. It reminds me of sex.

Suddenly, I have a flashback.

Freedom pinning me with a look of pure rapture as I slide inside her body.

"Are you okay?" Her words pull me from the memory, the concern in her eyes binding me where I stand.

"Oh, yeah," I reply, clearing my throat. Even though I know the gym guy is still standing there, I pay him no attention. I can't. Freedom's hands are now on my chest, her fingers fumbling with the knot of my tie.

"Sorry, I'm begin rude. Jason, this is my husband."

Her husband.

My mind flashes back to the moment I slid the ring onto her finger and the smile in her eyes as she watched.

"Dance with me." I don't know who says those words, but they apparently slip from my own lips.

Freedom takes my hand and pulls me onto the dance floor, gym guy completely forgotten. She stands directly in front of me, her much shorter body still lining up perfectly with my own. We get lost in the crowd, bodies surrounding us in a sea of dancers.

I'm not a dancer. Far from it. It makes me uncomfortable, especially in a situation like this one with other bodies all packed together in a tight space. But as I watch Freedom start to move her hips and sway in time with the music, suddenly, dancing feels like the only thing to do. So, I place my hands on her hips and let her take the lead. Also, something else I'm not familiar with.

My family is near, but I pay them no attention. Even without the effects of alcohol in my system, I'm lost in the moment, in her. This woman. The only one who can drive me crazy with indignation and make me want to kiss her lips at the same time. I've fought it for years. Years. Family gatherings, holidays, randomly running into her at the grocery store. Years I've tried to appear indifferent, all while this bubble of yearning settles in my chest, alive and breathing.

I haven't wanted to be attracted to her. Oh, no. I've fought it. I've told myself it can't happen—*won't* happen. Yet that didn't stop my brain from conjuring up images of her wild hair and her bare feet. Those damn bracelets that annoy the crap out of me. That smile that beckons me closer, most likely to my doom.

Yet, here I am. Dancing. With my hands on her hips and my own body swaying to the seductive pulse. The scent of her shampoo and lotion permeating my senses and all I can feel, all I can smell is her. My wife.

Guilt is a powerful beast, and it chooses that moment to rear its ugly head. How can she be happy? This entire mess has been just that. A mess. No way is this how it's supposed to go, how she's supposed to spend the rest of her life. It can't happen. I won't let it happen. No one wants to get married while so intoxicated you can't even remember it. No one should spend the rest of their life with someone just because of that mistake.

And that's what we made.

A mistake.

One I can rectify.

I pull back, my eyes meeting hers for a few seconds. I almost say forget it and press my body against hers once more. But I can't let it happen. For her *and* for me. Freedom seems to understand my hesitation. With the softest smile, she takes me hand and leads me off the dance floor. We make our way to the table where part of my family rests, no one seeming the least bit affected by our nearness, our hands linked, our borderline inappropriate dancing. Maybe they just couldn't see it. Or maybe they're choosing to ignore it. Either way, no one so much as bats an eye when we stop at the table.

I guzzle my water, wishing for the first time in a long damn time, it were something stronger. Freedom brings that out of me. That desire to drink. No, that's not exactly a good thing either. She's frustrating and vexatious and so damn outrageous she makes my brain bleed. She's also smart and gorgeous and so damn sexy. I usually just try to ignore those qualities in favor of the ones that don't give me hard-ons in public places.

After a few more songs, the bride and groom join us. "We're heading out," Harper says, a look in her eyes when she glances at her husband I don't want to think about.

Freedom throws her arms around her best friend's neck and squeezes tight. The both whisper-yell over the music, my sister's face blushing. Yeah, I definitely don't want to know what they're saying.

Instead, I turn my attention to my new brother-in-law. I hold out my hand, which he takes easily, his smile full of everything I'd ever hope for my sister. You know, considering I wasn't too sure about Latham Douglas in the beginning, I'm pretty pleased they're together now. He adores her, makes her happier than I've ever seen her before. As long as he keeps treating her right, he'll always have an ally in me.

"Be good to her," I feel the need to say, even though I know he will. Call it that big brother instinct. Some things just need to be said, and it wouldn't be the first time I've said almost the exact same words. In fact, Rhenn has heard them too.

He grips my hand firmly and keeps his eyes locked on mine. "I will." He glances at his new wife, his eyes softening as he says, "She's the best thing to ever happen to me."

They hug the rest of the family before making their way toward the exit. Rhenn and Marissa aren't too far behind them, the looks on their faces saying way more than I care to know too. I'm happy my sisters are so happy, but that doesn't mean I ever want to think about the *other* part of their relationships.

Mom and the Douglases head out next, with Jensen and Kathryn hot on their heels. "We're going to call it a night too," my brother says, his hand wrapped around his fiancée's. Their wedding will be next, followed quickly by Rhenn and Marissa. Then, I'll be the last single man standing.

But, I'm not really single.

Though, I should be because I didn't do it right.

Freedom looks up at me, her eyes shining with something bright. "Wanna get out of here?"

No.

Yes.

"Sure," I finally reply. Clubs definitely aren't my thing, and the longer I'm here, the more I want to pull her back onto the dance floor and wrap my body around hers. Plus, it won't be long before I need to use the restroom, and there's no way in hell I'll be using a public club restroom. I'll give myself hives just thinking about it.

As we head to the exit, Freedom slips her warm hand in mine. The contact sends zaps of electricity through my limbs and my feet stumble slightly. I'm able to right myself before falling just as the cooler air hits me. The sidewalks are packed, and soon we're swallowed up by the masses. I don't ask where we're going, just keep her hand in my own and follow. That should be telling in itself, the fact I'm willingly going wherever she's leading without so much as a glance back.

We're both silent, walking for several blocks before we find ourselves in front of the famous Bellagio fountain. The water show is just starting and we push our way through the crowd to get closer. The whole time I try not to think about the number of individuals touching me. I keep my head down and my hand locked on hers so we don't get separated.

She stops a few rows back from handrailing and we watch the show. Freedom is quite a bit shorter than I am, but there's something about the way she seems to fit against me. Her head hits just below my chin, and her warmth presses against my body as she leans back against me. It's under the guise of letting another couple pass by, but after they pass, she doesn't move. She leans back against my chest and watches the show as "Luck Be A Lady" plays from the speakers.

While my heart pounds like a jackhammer in my chest.

I'm certain she can feel it. I'm sure everyone in the vicinity can hear it, but everyone keeps their eyes on the famous fountain, their phones poised up in the air to capture the show. Several couples turn and take selfies in front of the water, and for the first time in my entire adult life, I think I understand the fascination with them. Suddenly, I have a strong desire to take my own phone from my pocket and taking a photograph of Freedom and myself. I want to capture the look on her face as she gazes up at the lights and water in enthrallment and wonder.

When the song ends, the fountains return to their regular display and the crowd starts to disperse. Freedom and I stand there and continue to watch. We watch the people and how they interact with each other, the families buzzing off the bright lights and sugar, the couples stealing kisses and share private moments, even when surrounded by hundreds of people. We stand there and watch, feeling as calm and collected as I ever have, all things considered.

"I've always wanted to come to Vegas," she finally says, breaking our silence.

"Really?" I ask, though it really doesn't surprise me much. Freedom is more of a people person and can make friends about anywhere she goes. I'm the homebody who avoids crowds at all costs.

She nods her head against my chest. "I never left the compound when I was little, but one of the older girls told me she once went to Las Vegas with her dad. She talked about the lights and the people, and it sounded like a fairy tale. Like someplace I could get lost in the shuffle. I dreamed about coming here and doing just that. Getting lost."

My throat is so thick, I can barely swallow. I knew Freedom spent a big part of her childhood in some weird compound with her parents, but she never talked about it. I overheard my mom and Harper talking when they were in high school about it, but neither of them knew too much. All Harper knew is she didn't want to go back to live with her parents.

"There weren't a lot of kids, so we tended to hang out together between classes. We were all homeschooled by a couple of the moms. I'll never forget the first day I walked into a real classroom." Even though I can't see her face, I can hear her smile.

I'm not sure if I'm supposed to ask, but I've never been one to shy away from saying what's on my mind. "What kind of compound was it?"

She sighs. "One with few rules. One where it was nothing to see naked individuals walking around or the occasional free love under the night sky. We didn't eat meat, grew our own vegetables and herbs, some of them questionably legal, and made money by selling goods we made ourselves in a local town. The law didn't bother us, as long as we kept to ourselves. The land belonged to the leader, an older guy with a potbelly and gray mustache, and I remember my mom frequenting his tent at night as part of the rent they paid to live there."

My stomach churns as she speaks. I couldn't imagine living in a place like that, where everyone lived in tents and apparently shared their spouses with others. Where kids were subjected to all of it, their young, impressionable minds soaking it up like little sponges. While I was watching cartoons and eating Cheerios, she was growing pot and selling it.

"He didn't, you know…" I start, unable to even finish the question.

"No," she confirms, completely oblivious to the sudden rage I feel on her behalf. "Master Leonard didn't touch the girls until they were eighteen. It was a rule."

"Christ," I whisper, grateful he never got his hands on Freedom, yet still angry it was even a possibility. "When did you go live with your grandma?"

"When I was in seventh grade. I was miserable there. I stopped eating and participating in class. I had contracted a bad case of influenza B and pneumonia that required medical attention. Most of our medical attention was tended to by a resident nurse, but she told my parents I needed to be in the hospital with antibiotics and IV fluids. They took me to the nearest hospital and left. Civilization like that made them cagey and paranoid. My mom ended up calling her mom to come get me. Even though it was hard living with my grandma, it was the best thing my parents ever did for me."

I wrap my arms around her shoulders, holding her back to my chest. Freedom grabs my forearms and holds on tight, the bite of her nails causing a flashback.

Those nails.

Raking down my back.

As I push inside her body.

I feel myself getting hard. She's too close. Her ass is too close to my dick. Her familiar scent is filling my body, stealing my sense of right and wrong. That's the only reason I can think of as I continue to hold her against me. It's wrong, I know it, but I can't seem to stop myself. She's like a drug I crave, a hit I need, even though I've never taken an illegal drug in my entire life.

"I'm sorry you went through that, Freedom." My words are soft, yet meaningful.

She slowly turns in my arms, those dark eyes locked on mine. I mean to release my hold on her and step back, but somehow, I don't have the ability. My breath halts in my throat as she reaches up and smooths down my necktie, her soft hands sliding along the silk. I catch a glimpse of her wedding ring. The one I put on her finger less than twenty-four hours ago.

"It's okay, Sammy. I'm just glad I was able to go live with my grandma." She smiles up at me. "I met Harper and your family, and I haven't looked back since."

I clear my throat. "You were horribly annoying at that age," I tell her, looking for something lighter to talk about.

Freedom laughs, her long brown hair blowing against my arm. "Yeah, that was because I was thirteen and made it my life goal to annoy the crap out of you," she replies, tapping me on the chest.

"Well, you're very successful," I tell her, which only draws out another giggle.

"I am," she confirms, wrapping her arms around my waist and giving me a hug. I'm not the touchy feely kinda guy, but this is...nice. Really nice, actually. When she pulls back, her eyes seem to light up. "I have an idea."

Groaning, I already know I'm not going to like this. "Does it involve going back to the hotel and sleeping?"

Sleeping. Together?

Yeah, I could get on board with that.

No, no you won't.

"Hell no, Sammy! We're in Vegas. Let's have some fun!"

"Sleeping is fun," I grumble, but know it's no use.

"You can sleep when you're dead," she says, tapping me on the cheek. I should hate it, but I don't. "Let's go to a casino."

I give her most horrified look. "A casino? Do you know how many germs are on those machines and those chips, Freedom?"

She rolls her eyes, probably because she knows it drives me crazy. "Come on, Sammy. Live a little. We'll go play some slots tonight, and then tomorrow, we'll take in the sights and sounds of the city. We'll do all of the touristy things I dreamed about doing when I was younger."

"That sounds horrible," I state honestly.

"Nope, it's going to be amazing," she says, grabbing my hand and dragging me through the newly forming crowd waiting for the next fountain show.

"But…what if I'm getting ready to leave? We can't just go out and have…fun tomorrow," I mumble, as we push our way out of the pack and start heading toward the Bellagio.

"You're not leaving until Monday, Sammy."

I stop in my tracks, halting her forward progress. "How do you know that?"

She just turns and smiles. With a shrug, she says, "Do you think it was a coincidence we were on the same flight out?"

Then, she turns and pulls against my hand until I start walking again.

Son of a…

Of course, Freedom would have known my flight plan, probably courtesy of my sister. What I wasn't prepared for is the fact she's booked on my return flight home. Another flight, most likely seated directly beside Freedom Rayne. There's no escaping her.

Chapter Ten

Freedom

I can feel his entire body tense up the moment we step inside the Bellagio. I mean, if we're going to gamble, we might as well pick a big one, right? The sounds of bells and sirens fills the large entry and people mill about, drinks in hand.

"I'm not sure about this," he huffs, trying to pull his hand from my own.

Unfortunately for him, my grasp is as tight as Kenna Johnson's skirt in French class, and there's no way he's getting out of my grip without Vaseline. "It's gonna be fun, Sammy. Come on!"

I continue to pull him along, while he continues to huff and puff behind me, which I ignore, of course. Samuel Grayson wouldn't know fun if it threw on a brightly colored sombrero and started to do the Macarena in front of him. He'd just stand there in his tighty-whities (confirmed he wears them, by the way) and his starched white undershirt, wearing one of those neckties…

Okay, I kinda like the neckties.

A lot.

But you understand what I'm saying, right? It's practically my solemn duty to show him what fun is. We're in the land of sin, after all. Gambling. Showgirls. Liquor. It's time to set those tighty-whities on fire.

We stop at the first machine that's open, and I fish a handful of bills from my cleavage.

"Jesus, Freedom. Did you just take that from your…" he says, waving his hand in front of his chest.

"Where do you think I keep money in this dress, Sammy?"

He swallows hard, his eyes dropping to the V at my chest. "I… Well, I wasn't… I didn't really give it any thought."

Unfolding the money, I slide my boob five dollar bill into the machine. "It's no biggie, really. I mean, my keycard is on the other side," I tell him, as I bet a series of pennies and press the button.

I can feel his presence beside me as I watch the numbers spin and eventually stop in a line. I didn't win anything, so I up my ante and spin again. Samuel doesn't say a word, just watches as I lose a few rounds of penny slots. Then, Lady Luck finally lands on my side and I hit a whopping fourteen dollars and eleven cents. "Woohoo!" I celebrate, as if I just won a million dollars, dancing around where I stand.

Glancing his way, his face looks tight. Annoyed. "What's wrong? Why do you look constipated?"

Horrified, he says, "I do not. I can't believe the number of men standing around watching you."

When I glance behind me, I find a couple of guys smiling over their beer bottles, watching my celebratory victory dance. "Those guys?"

"Jesus, Freedom, keep it down. They'll hear you."

Shrugging, I turn back to my machine. "So what? It's not like I'm going home with any of them. I'm married, remember?" I say, my voice dripping with sugar.

Samuel clears his throat. "Trust me, I remember."

My heart stops in my chest, and my eyes turn back to his. "You do?"

"Well, no. I don't *remember* remember, but I do recall the fact we…got married," he replies, the last two words barely audible.

"We did," I tell him proudly, slapping him on the chest. And to really annoy him, I reach up and straighten his impeccable tie. No, it doesn't need adjusting, but for some reason, I seem to really like

Lacey Black

touching it. "Come on, Sammy. Let's win some cash," I state, taking another of my boob bills and placing it in the machine next to mine. "Mama needs some new shoes."

Samuel seems lost, like he doesn't know what to do. Or he doesn't want to touch it. Either way, I offer, "Need some help?" as I push the button on my own machine.

"No, I know what to do," he says with another long glance down at the buttons. Finally, after what feels like a decade of waiting, Samuel takes a seat on the stool and pushes the button.

"You know, Sammy, I was thinking, when we get back to our room, I'm going to give you a massage."

He's silent, so when I press my button for another round, I turn his way. He's pale in color, yet his cheeks are flushed with red. He also looks to be sweating a little as he reaches up and loosens his necktie.

"You okay? You're not having a stroke, are you? Because I gotta be honest, I haven't renewed my CPR card since high school. We had to take the classes as part of Home Ec junior year, but I let mine lapse, so if you need CPR, I'm going to have to get one of those dudes over there to do it," I tell him, throwing my thumb over my shoulder to the small group of admirers.

"I'm not having a stroke," he assures me, his voice deep and crackly.

"Heart attack? Do you have a heart condition?"

He sighs. "No, Freedom, my heart is fine."

I win a few more pennies and take another spin at my machine. "Well, I know it's not ED. My vajayjay felt like it was plundered by a Buick this morning when I woke up."

Samuel chokes on air. "Jesus, Freedom!"

"What? It's nothing to be ashamed of."

118

"I'm not ashamed," he says, pressing the button and spending another handful of pennies on the slot machine.

"Good, because I was seven shades of sore this morning. I'm not exactly sure what all we did, but we did it well, Sammy," I say, as I place the max bet and push the button. The moment the numbers spin and fall in line, the sirens start to go off and the word winner flashes across the screen. "Holy shitballs, Sammy! I think I just won!"

"Seriously?" he asks, standing directly beside me and glancing over my shoulder. I can smell his cologne. It does things to me. He gasps. "You won over four thousand dollars."

"Shut. Up!" I look at the screen, and indeed, it says I won four thousand three hundred and two dollars. "Holy shitballs!" I throw my arms around him and squeal, not even caring it's directly into his ears. "We won!"

When he sets me back down on my feet, he's grinning from ear to ear. "We didn't win anything. That's all you, Freedom."

A few people come over and congratulate me, including those three lurkers at the end of the row. "Hey, congrats," one says, eyeing Samuel, while the other two blatantly stare at my boobs.

"Thanks! I'm Karen, and this is my male submissive, Jose."

All eyes are on me.

"What?" Samuel whispers, a tad on the harsh side.

"I've been thinking of making it a party while in Vegas. You boys interested in joining us?" I take a step toward the first wide-eyed guy and pat his cheek. "Have you ever worn a ball gag before?"

"We better get going," one says, practically dragging his friend away from us.

The moment they're gone, I burst into a fit of laughter. "That was fun."

"What is wrong with you?" he asks, pulling at his collar, as I press the cash out button.

"Nothing a good flogging wouldn't fix," I tell him as I take the paper ticket. When I turn back to face him, he's pale again and looks like he might actually vomit. "What?"

"Are you serious?"

"I never joke about flogging, Sammy. Come on, let's go cash this baby in!"

Samuel cashes out his machine and hands me the ticket. I put a dollar in and am getting twenty-four cents back. As we make our way to the cashier counter, his warm hand wraps around mine, and I have to fight a smile.

In line, he turns and asks, "Are you sure you're done? Don't you want to try to win more?"

I shake my head right away. "Hell no. I'm good. I never win, so I don't want to risk losing it all, thinking I can add to it. I put a five in the machine, prepared to lose it. Why risk all the money I just won?" I ask.

When I turn, he looks like he's considering my words. "I guess I just assume most people would want to win even more."

We step forward in line. "Well, I'm not most people, Sammy."

He sighs. "I definitely agree with you there."

***

After a slight detour around the area, we make our way back to the hotel. We step inside the cool air-conditioning and find Jensen and Kathryn exiting the coffee shop.

"Hey, I thought you guys turned in hours ago," Samuel says.

"We did, but then decided to walk around for a bit. We caught one of the Bellagio fountain shows. Have you seen it?" Kathryn asks, her eyes bright with enjoyment.

"Yeah, a bit ago. Then we went to the casino and won some cashola," I say.

Jensen looks shocked, his gaze sweeping between Samuel and myself. "You?" he asks, pointing to his big brother. "Went to a casino? Willingly?"

"Of course," Samuel replies, straightening that necktie.

"And now we're headed up to my room so I can give ol' Sammy a massage," I announce, instantly sensing the onslaught of tension rolling off him.

"A massage?" Jensen asks, completely stunned. "As in, you're letting her put her hands on you?"

Samuel looks like he's going to faint. "We're not... It's not like that. No massage."

"He's tense. He needs a good old-fashioned rubdown," I tell the youngest Grayson male, while patting the oldest one on the chest.

"I think he's definitely in need of a rubdown," Jensen says, unable to contain his grin.

"We'll leave you to it," Kathryn adds, pulling her fiancé toward the bank of elevators. We all say our goodbyes and head to the coffee shop.

"Coffee? This late at night?" he asks when I get in line behind another couple.

"No coffee for me. I'm getting a green tea chai," I tell him before placing my order. "Do you want anything?"

"No, thank you."

With my drink in hand, we head to the elevators. Samuel is doing his best to keep his distance, but he hasn't taken off the way I'd expect him to. I figured at first opportunity, he'd head to his own room, leaving me standing in the coffee shop. But he hasn't. He's stayed by my side, even if he's not really sure why.

We get off on our floor and head toward our rooms. I start digging in my cleavage until I free my plastic keycard. "Seriously, I can't believe you do that."

"What?" I ask, glancing down at the card in my hand.

"Keep stuff...there."

I shrug. "Where else am I going to keep it? It's not like I have pockets on this dress," I tell him as we approach his door.

He stops in front of it and turns my way. He seems to be struggling with what he's trying to say. Samuel opens his mouth before shutting it quickly. When he opens it again, his eyes meet mine and he swallows hard. "You looked very nice today, Freedom."

I have no idea why, but I start to blush. Sure, I've had compliments before, but rarely from Samuel. He keeps his thoughts guarded close, like state secrets. "Why, thank you, kind sir."

"Well, good night."

I reach for his hand and place mine on his as he goes to swipe the card over the lock. A jolt of electricity sweeps through my blood, and if the way he gasps and jerks against my touch is any indication, I'd say he feels it too.

"Don't think you're getting out of the massage," I tell him, sipping my chai.

Samuel sighs loudly. "It's late, Freedom. That's not necessary."

Shrugging, I tell him, "Maybe not, but it's happening. I'm going to head over to my room and change out of this thing." I pull on the skirt of my dress. "I'll grab my oils and come back to your room."

"You're serious?" he asks, shocked, yet intrigued.

"As limp dick on your wedding night. Well, not our wedding night." I wink at him.

"Jesus," he grumbles, rubbing his forehead.

"I'll be back in ten, Sammy," I holler, as I head farther down the hall to my room. Inside, I sip my chai and throw on a pair of yoga pants and tank top. Usually, my go-to is a comfortable skirt, but since it's close to bedtime, I'd rather wear the comfy pants. I pull my long hair up in a high ponytail and grab my small bottle of massage oil from my luggage. I usually take it everywhere with me, just in case.

With my oil and chai in hand, I slip my keycard into my waistband and head to Samuel's room. I knock quietly and am surprised when he opens the door almost immediately. I'd honestly expected him to ignore the knock and keep me locked out. But he doesn't.

He looks nervous as he opens the door wider for me to enter. I can't help but notice he's still wearing his suit, though he did shed the jacket. "I wasn't sure what to wear," he confesses, rubbing the back of his neck.

"Something comfy," I reply, setting my cup on the desk. When I turn around, he's staring at my ass. "My eyes are up here, Sammy."

"Oh!" he stammers, glancing up and then looking away. "I was just checking out your…pants. I've never seen you in anything but a skirt."

I shrug. "It's almost beddy-bye, so I wanted to be comfy." I take a few steps until I'm standing in front of him. Reaching up, I take that soft silk in my hand and carefully loosen the tie. Another flashback hits me in that moment. Me loosening his necktie just before I crush my lips to his. His hands grip my ass and pull me tightly against him, the hardness of his erection pressed between our bodies.

"You okay?" he asks with a choking sound that catches my attention.

"Oh. Yeah," I assure him. When I glance at my hand, I see his tie clenched in my grip, my other hand resting on his pec. Desire swirls in my gut as I gaze up at those blue-green eyes. "I'm good." Clearing my throat, I say, "Let's get you undressed."

Samuel's eyes widen. "Undressed?"

"Well, not naked, but close. I have to be able to rub your skin. Why don't you strip down to your undershirt and briefs?" I glance at the bed. The big, king-sized bed with the perfectly smoothed bedding, all tucked corners and all. It's very Samuel-like.

And I'd love nothing more than to mess them up.

"I'll grab the extra blanket from the closet and use it to protect the bed. This way, we don't get the bedding all messy."

He swallows again, looking both incredibly uncomfortable and incredibly aroused. My inner Goddess preens. "Messy?"

"You know, in case we accidentally have a squirter." Of course, I absolutely mean my oil bottle. Sometimes, I get a little carried away and have squirted warm oil where I don't want it, but I'm not about to tell him that. The look on his face confirms his mind is in the gutter. He's probably trying to figure out if I'm the squirter or if he is.

"Go ahead and strip down to the tighty-whities and undershirt, Sammy. I'm going to warm up the oil in the bathroom sink."

I leave the door cracked open and listen for his movements. It's silent for several long seconds. Hell, those seconds turn into minutes. Finally, when I start to think he's not going to get ready, I hear him kick off his shoes, followed by the releasing of his belt buckle. Smiling, I make sure the oil is to the perfect temperature before returning to the bedroom part of the hotel room. I'm not fully prepared for the picture of Samuel sitting on the edge of the bed. Stopping in my tracks, I take in the man before me. His arms are defined, which I already knew, considering he was able to hold me up against the shower wall early this morning. The blanket is draped over his crotch, but I already know what he's hiding underneath it. My lady bits start to tingle in anticipation.

Down, girl, down.

"All right, let's get you relaxed," I state as I set the oil down on the end table.

"I'm not sure that's possible," he whispers, most likely to himself.

"Do you have your phone?"

He points to his pants, which are folded on the chair. Lying on top of them is his cell phone. "Why do you need it?" he questions.

"I need to set the mood," I tell him as I type in numbers to unlock his device.

"Uhh, how do you know what my code is?"

Turning, I give him a coy grin. "You seem like a birthdate kinda guy, Sammy."

He huffs. "Remind me to change that."

Shrugging, I find the site I'm looking for and press play. Soft, meditation music filters from the phone, intending to soothe and relax. "Suit yourself. Now, lie on your stomach, but stay down toward the foot of the bed."

He does as instructed. "Are you okay with me getting oil on your shirt?" I ask, pouring a bit of warm lavender-scented oil into my palm.

Instead of saying words, Samuel pushes up on his arms and somehow, pulls his shirt up and over his neck. My girly bits weep with joy at first glance of his back. The scratch marks are still there, red and angry down his back, but that's not what has my attention. The subtle bumps and divots of that muscular plane has my undivided attention. My fingers practically tingle in anticipation.

"Ready?"

"I guess," he says, resting his forehead into the blanket.

The moment my hands touch his skin, he goes completely rigid and an expletive slips from his lips. "What?" I ask, my hands still on his back, shocks of electricity jolting my entire body.

"Nothing," he mumbles as he tries to relax.

I take a few deep, calming breaths and let the music wash through me. It's difficult, considering my hands are all over the sexiest man alive. I use my thumb and gently dig into the tense muscles until they let go and he relaxes even more. I work over his back and neck, my firm fingers working their magic on his tight, corded muscles.

My hands move to his lower back. I press into his pelvis, pushing and pulling to work on his hips. He moans in pleasure as I press my thumbs into the globes of his ass like it's my job. Really, I just want to get my hands on his ass once more. I move down his legs, massaging his thighs and calves, every stroke of my hands bringing me more pleasure than if I were receiving the massage. By this point, I'm so worked up I could come just by grazing my crotch against the bed.

When I finish his legs and arms, I take a step back. "Okay, you can turn over."

"Uhh, no, that's okay," he replies.

"Come on, Sammy, don't be silly. I always massage the front too."

"Really, Freedom. I'm fine." His voice is clipped, as if he were in pain.

"Did I hurt you? Did I use too much pressure? Sometimes I forget—"

He grabs my hand and cuts off my words. "You didn't hurt me. I just…I don't think I can turn over right now."

"Why not?" I ask, completely freaking out that I've somehow hurt him with my deep tissue massage. I mean, I sometimes get a little aggressive as I'm working over the muscles, but he didn't really act like it was hurting him. "I'm sorry if it was too much pressure—"

"Freedom." His voice cuts me off and his eyes meet mine. "I'm having a little problem. Down there."

It takes a few seconds, but the lightbulb finally clicks on. I glance down, even though he's still on his stomach and I can't see anything. "Oh!"

"Yeah, oh," he grumbles. "You had your hands all over me," he says, in a weak defense.

"Well, I never shortchange anyone on a massage, so flip over. It's not like I haven't seen it before."

He groans. "No, Freedom, I think the massage is over."

"It's not. Stop being a baby. I can handle a hard-on."

"I'm sure you can, but I'd rather you not *handle* my hard-on."

"Why not? You don't think I can take it?" I ask, placing my hands on my hips.

"That's not what I meant." He scrubs his hands over his face. "Hell, I don't even know what I meant."

"Turn over, Grayson. I insist."

With another huff and a few more curse words I rarely hear him say, he finally rolls over. My eyes zero in on that dick like I'm a missile and it's my target.

"Stop staring."

"I can't help it. It's…impressive."

I grin as he groans. "Let's call it a night."

"Are you kidding? We're just getting started," I tell him as I grab my oil, lube up my hands, and place my hands on his chest, my eyes locked on that hard cock the whole time.

Chapter Eleven

Samuel

I can *feel* her eyes on me. Or, on my groin. In fact, I'm pretty sure the wetness that just hit my shoulder is drool from her lip. I'm trying everything I can to get my erection to subside, but nothing is working. Not with her hands on me. Not with her eyes devouring me as if I were her last meal. Not with her pussy framed in black leggings right by my head.

It's heaven.

It's hell.

It's my reality, both all wrapped up in one petite little woman with the ability to set my blood on fire with desire and my head spinning with aggravation at the exact same time.

She digs her thumbs into my pecs. The pain should be enough to cause my cock to deflate, but all it does is fuel it. My blood is on fire, and I can't seem to stop it. That's probably why I reach behind her and grab her ass, holding her tightly. Freedom grasps and does this little wiggle, aligning her core right at my face. If I were to turn just a little to the left, I could bury my mouth between her thighs.

A choking sound derives from my lungs as she runs her warm, wet hands down my abdomen and stops just outside of my waistband. "I'm not sure what kind of massage you think this is," she sasses, yet presses her ass back into my hands.

My brain screams, *happy ending, happy ending!*

My cock screams… Oh, who am I kidding? It's screaming the same thing.

Cold air hits my groin as she pulls my underwear down and takes my cock in her hand. My brain officially shuts down as she strokes me long and hard, the oil doing wonderful things to assist in the friction.

Suddenly, she stops. Her movements, her ass wiggling, her breathing. She goes stock-still, even when I thrust my hips upward, my cock seeking the glorious rubbing of her palm. "Samuel?" she whispers.

My name.

She said my name.

"What?" I ask, the desire in my body fighting against all rational thought. I want to pull her to my face and beg her to keep touching me, but her next word is like a bucket of ice water thrown on my entire body.

"Hummingbird."

My body freezes, tenses so tight I feel the ache in my bones. I try to push her off me and grab for the blanket beneath me, but she doesn't move very easily. In fact, she doesn't move at all. She's like a damn ninja, her legs scissoring against my arms and her hands holding down my legs. When I stop fighting against her, I feel the softest touch of her fingers against my inner thigh.

"I remember this," she whispers, my entire body seizing under her touch. "I remember a hummingbird."

Clearing my throat, I open my mouth, but nothing comes out.

She moves off me, freeing my limbs. I dive for the blanket, but she holds it down, refusing to let me cover myself. "It's beautiful." Her words are so soft, so angelic I almost don't hear them.

"It's not," I finally say, my voice low and full of tension. "It was a mistake."

When her dark eyes connect with mine, I don't see the humor I've witnessed from lovers in the past. I see beauty. Soft, elegant, unapologetic beauty. Her touch grazes over the image that has marred my skin for seventeen years. The one I've never shown anyone

129

willingly. The one I keep hidden, that reminds me of a time I can't seem to forget, as much as I try.

"How can something so delicate and beautiful be a mistake?" she asks, seeming genuinely curious.

Clearing my throat, I reach for my necktie. The one I use as a shield, only it's not there. I'm practically naked—again—in front of Freedom, and she won't even release the blanket for me to cover up my groin. "I didn't mean to get it."

Her eyebrows pull together as she looks between myself and the tattoo. Yes, tattoo. My biggest mistake in life, until this weekend. She smiles down at the image and traces the faint outline and bold blue coloring. "In Native American culture, hummingbirds are seen as healers and bringers of love, good luck, and joy."

"This hasn't brought me any of those things," I find myself telling her.

When those stunning eyes meet mine, she smiles. "I'm not so sure about that, Sammy. You're surrounded by love and joy. You just have to see it," she whispers softly, her eyes gazing down at the hummingbird and holding a hint of happiness. My heart pounds against my breastbone and my arms long to reach for her. To hold her close. To tell her she brings me joy, along with heartburn.

Closing my eyes, I fight the emotions raging in my chest. I feel her move and when I look up, her back is to me. She's pulling up that tank top, exposing her upper back. That's when I see it. The tattoo. The hummingbird tattoo. The one so very similar to my own inked over her right shoulder blade. And while mine is black and blue, hers is a soft yellow and pink. It looks ten times more delicate than my own, as if it was made just for her skin.

She glances over her shoulder and smiles. Fuck, that smile is…everything. Everything I want, but won't let myself have. She's gazing down at me as if these tattoos hold some sort of power, some special meaning, and in a way, I guess they do. Except, hers was done on purpose, and mine was...well, not.

Sighing, I sit up, cover myself and pull her to sit beside me. I feel like a greased monkey, but that's not something I can deal with now. Now, I need to tell her a story. The one I've never shared with another soul. Even past lovers, I never told them the true meaning of the tattoo. I've been too ashamed. But something in her eyes makes me feel comfortable enough to tell her about my mistake and why I've avoided alcohol since.

"Back in college, I was pretty much the way I am today. Disciplined and focused on my studies and the task at hand. There was no room for fun, no time for parties. In fact, the thought of a party pretty much made me nauseous, much like the crowds today," I tell her, my eyes falling to the ugly carpet pattern at my feet.

"My roommate, Doug, finally convinced me to go out one night. The fraternity he was pledging was having a big Halloween bash, and he wanted me to go. I tried to get out of it, but he wouldn't take no for an answer. So I went. And I drank."

Deep breath.

"I drank too much, and then drank some more. Somehow, we ended up at this late night tattoo parlor. The artist was...well, she was good looking. I remember lying on the table and trying to get her phone number, but I had absolutely no game and was awkward as hell. My roommate and a few of his friends were laughing and encouraging me, even as the blackness of passing out started to creep in.

"I remember her asking me what I wanted, and I guess I pointed at...well, at my manhood."

"You what?" Freedom asks, drawing my attention back to her face.

"Yeah, I apparently pointed there," I tell her, pointing down at my groin much like I apparently did that night so long ago. I take a deep breath and tell her the part I'm dreading with my entire being. "I pointed there and said...hummer. Only it didn't come out hummer. Apparently, I said hummingbird." The familiar shame rockets through my body, rendering me completely spent and exhausted.

Freedom doesn't say anything. She just sits there, the humiliation of my words floating around us like a bomb, ready to detonate. Finally, she takes pity on me and speaks, "So, let me get this straight. You, Samuel Grayson, went out and got schnockered with your roommate. Somehow, you decided to get a tattoo, and while you were there, you asked the artist for a hummer?"

I close my eyes, the burn of humiliation tinging my cheeks. "Yes."

It's silent for another second. Two. Hell, it's silent for about ten seconds before she does something I'm not prepared for. Freedom bursts out laughing. "Holy shitballs, Sammy! That's kinda badass."

"Badass? Are you kidding me right now? It's a horrible story!"

"No, it's a hilarious story, and shows that you're human."

"I'm not human, Freedom. A human would go back to get it covered up, but I'm too afraid of needles to even do that."

Again, she laughs.

"Fine, laugh it up," I grumble as I stand, hellbent on retrieving my clothes and my dignity, and getting the hell out of here.

Except, this is my room...

"Stop," she says, standing up and grabbing my arm. "I'm not laughing *at* you, honest. I'm just happy the impeccably dressed, always has it together, anal Samuel Grayson is proving to be human after all."

"Did you call me anal?"

"Is that all you got out of that?" she asks, her gaze locked on mine. Her hand caresses my thigh, goosebumps peppering my entire body. It's also the moment I realize I'm still standing in my underwear, and she's wearing tight black pants and a tiny little top. Her nipples are poking through the thin material, and my mouth starts to water.

"My eyes are up here, Sammy. All I'm saying is I'm glad to know you make mistakes just like the rest of us," she says.

"Oh, believe me. I make mistakes." The unspoken meaning is evident and sadness flashes in those gorgeous brown eyes, making me feel like shit. Even though I made a terrible mistake, getting drunk and marrying my sister's best friend, I'd never want Freedom to feel guilty or unwanted. There's definitely a want there, it's just not supposed to be acted upon.

"I have an idea. Why don't you go shower and wash off the oil. I'll go down and get you a chamomile tea," she says. When I glance at the clock, it's nearing one in the morning. I've never been a night owl, let alone multiple days in a row. Yet, I can't seem to find the desire to go to sleep.

"I don't think tea is going to help," I tell her, rubbing the back of my neck. Not with her standing there looking like pure temptation in yoga pants.

"Just go shower, Sammy. I'll be back in a few minutes," she says, heading toward the door.

Before she opens it, she pulls a keycard from the waistband of those pants. "Seriously, Freedom?" I ask, rubbing my forehead.

"What? It's not like I have pockets, and this tank would have shown the rectangular card." Then she leaves the room, questions swirling around in my brain. Like is she really going downstairs dressed like that? Or how did I not see that keycard outlined in those tight pants? Like most situations involving Freedom, I don't have any answers. She's an enigma in bangle bracelets and lavender essential oil.

Stepping into the bathroom, I turn on the shower. I strip from my underwear as images of Freedom in that lovely dress earlier today and then hotter in black leggings parade through my mind. Suddenly, my cock is standing at attention once more, my blood flowing straight to one concentrated area.

Exhaling, I get under the hot water, unable to shake the pictures in my mind. Even as I lather up my hair and then scrub the oil from my skin, she's all I can see. It's no wonder when I rub the washcloth over my balls, they draw up as lust races through my veins. That's why I find myself with my cock in my hand, resting my forehead against the cold tile, and stroking myself. Sweet release barrels down on me as I stroke faster, my body burning with the need to come.

"Freedom." Her name spills from my lips. It's a plea, a balm to the ache deep inside me.

Evidence of what I've done washes down the drain as I try to regain my breathing. I slip under the water again, rinsing away the remaining soap, and turn the knob. Reaching for a towel, I dry off my legs as my hotel room door shuts. "Freedom?"

"Yeah, it's me."

"Uhh, how did you get into my room?" I ask, drying off as quickly as possible.

"A key?"

I wrap the towel around my waist and step into the bedroom. "Where did you get a key?"

She just shrugs, as if she didn't somehow lift my room key and let herself in like she was a guest here. I pull a pair of clean underwear from the dresser, along with a pair of shorts. When I glance over, Freedom's lying in my bed, her face void of any makeup and with her hair tied high on her head.

"What are you doing?"

"Getting ready for bed?" she replies, as if it's crazy I'd even ask such a question.

"Why? In my bed?" I ask, hating how perfect she looks lying under the covers.

"Why not? It's late, Sammy. I'm tired, and your bed is right here."

"But your bed is in your room," I tell her, choking the life out of my underwear with my hands.

"It is," she says with a yawn. Her eyes start to droop, and I realize this fight is fruitless.

I head back to the bathroom and throw on my underwear and shorts. I should probably also slip on a shirt, but for some reason, I don't. Instead, I head back to my darkened bedroom and find Freedom snuggled under the blankets. Sighing in resignation, I slip under the sheet, hugging the edge of the bed.

After a few minutes of silence, I feel her hand on my arm. It's startling, but not because of her touch, per se. What's startling is the way I crave it, how much it comforts me at the same time. She moves, lifting my arm and resting her head against my chest. I'm completely stiff, yet I have no control over my arm, as it wraps around her shoulders and holds her close.

"Tomorrow, we're having fun. We're going on the roller coaster," she says in a sleepy voice.

"Uhh, no, Freedom. I draw a hard line at roller coasters. You remember the plane ride, right?" Her hair tickles my neck, but it feels so good, so I don't move it.

She yawns again and burrows into me farther. "Yeah, but you got a tattoo. That means you're a badass, Sammy. You can do anything."

I'm not, but I don't argue with her, mostly because she makes me feel alive and like I just might possess a tiny fraction of the badassery she's convinced I have. It's the reason I pull her close, close my eyes, and breathe in the scent of her skin against mine.

I'm definitely not a badass, but with Freedom in my arms, I'm suddenly feeling invincible.

Chapter Twelve

Freedom

What a weekend. No, it may not have gone exactly as I had planned, but I wouldn't change any of it. Not for a second. Not the part where I woke up married to Samuel. Not the part where we spent time together, including all day Sunday. Not the part where I had my hands all over him as I gave him a massage. And definitely not the part where I took care of that ache between my legs in the shower this morning.

Twice.

Yesterday was fun. No, probably not the word he'd use to describe it, but I had a blast, and there was no hiding the smile he had on his face from time to time. I saw it when we visited the aquarium and enjoyed the Eiffel Tower experience—though, Samuel seemed a little green under the collar. We toured Hershey's Chocolate World and then played mini golf on KISS's course. He even surprised me with tickets to Shania Twain's Let's Go! residency show, which I'm pretty sure was his way of distracting me from the fact the Big Apple Coaster was still on my list of fun things to do.

It didn't work.

When the show ended, we walked down Freemont Street, hand in hand, taking in the sights and sounds of the city. Hell, I even snapped a picture of Samuel with two showgirls. He pretended to hate it, but that smile on his face was genuine. Now, what he really *did* hate was the exotic animals at Siegfried & Roy's Secret Garden and Dolphin Habitat. I have the photo of us with an albino boa constrictor wrapped around our shoulders in my bag as proof.

He looks terrified.

I loved it.

At the end of it all, we waited in line for the roller coaster, Samuel one step away from vomiting the entire time. He didn't vomit, however, even though he screamed like a teenage girl who saw a spider during every plunge, dip, and loop.

It was awesome.

It was also awesome when we got off the coaster and he threw his arms around me, kissing me silly and thanking me.

Now, we're disembarking the plane and getting ready to drive home. Fellow massage therapist, Claire, brought me to the airport on Friday, but I never arranged for her to pick me up. That's why I'm sticking close to Samuel as we make our way to baggage claim. He doesn't know it yet, but he's my ride. If there's one thing I know about Samuel, it's his need for control. There's no way he relied on someone else to bring him to the airport. His trusty, top rated for safety car is parked in the overnight lot, ready and waiting.

After retrieving our luggage, I decide to go ahead and spring it on him. "Can you drop me off?"

He glances my way as we head toward the parking garage. "You didn't get your car fixed?"

"Oh, I did. Cost me like four hundred smackers, but I decided not to leave my car in the lot. Claire dropped me off, so I need a ride home."

Samuel sighs and shakes his head. "Fine."

I smile at his gruffness, at the annoyance he implies with his tone, but I also know he's genuinely a good guy and would never leave me at the airport to fend for myself. Well, at least he wouldn't, even though he'd probably really want to. I mean, my goal in life *is* to madden him to the point of tears. I've come close a few times…

We find his car right where I'd expect it. In the back of the covered lot, as far away from door dings and bumper taps as possible.

"Jesus, Sammy, why didn't you just park at the Pizza Hut two towns over?" I ask as we finally reach his trunk.

"It's safer to park back here, Freedom."

"Not really. I mean, anyone could be lurking in the dark corners of the parking garage, ready and waiting. Have you not seen *CSI: New York*? I've seen every episode. You could have been stuffed in a trunk and butchered into tiny pieces before anyone even realized you were missing."

He stops and turns my way, a horrified look on his face. "Is that what you watch at night? Television about murder?"

"Well, technically, on my phone, but yes. It's about solving the murder, and yes, I do enjoy watching those kinds of shows. In fact, I'm pretty sure I'm the perfect partner to have if you ever find yourself in one of those murder mystery games."

"I'll keep that in mind," he mumbles, tossing his suitcase and garment bag into the back of his car. He then takes my own bag and sets it beside his, careful not to smash his precious suits.

Using the key fob, he unlocks the doors, and we slide inside. The air is much cooler than in Las Vegas, holding a slight hint of salty ocean. Samuel drives exactly the speed limit as we make our way to Rockland Falls, back to reality. Conversation comes easily for me, so I talk about anything and everything. I recount our entire weekend, even though he was very much a part of it. So, it's no surprise when we reach the city limits of town, Samuel chooses to finally add to the conversation.

"So, uh, listen, Freedom. We should talk. About the…thing."

"The *thing*? Is that what we're calling it?" I tease, even though I very much know what he's referring to. He means the big elephant in the room—err, car—in the form of a marriage license and Elvis impersonator witness.

"Be serious, Freedom. We can't stay married."

"We can." And we will.

"No, Freedom, this isn't the way it's done. We can't just get married in Vegas and live happily ever after," he says, as he maneuvers the streets toward my apartment building.

"Harper and Latham did," I tell him.

"But they were in love beforehand. We're not in love," he says, turning onto my street.

I open my mouth to respond, to tell him we're not in love *yet*, but something out of the corner of my eye catches my attention. I turn to my building, shocked to find so much...stuff outside. As we pull up, I realize it's *my* stuff outside. "What the hell?" I find myself saying, as Samuel pulls to a stop in the street.

Jumping out of the car, I take off toward the building, spying my massage table resting against my stove. Sitting on the sidewalk. With my clothes haphazardly thrown in piles beside it. "Holy shitballs," I gasp, my hands covering my mouth.

"What is this stuff?" Samuel asks as he approaches, his hands shoved casually in his pockets.

"It's my stuff! Why is it in the front yard?" I ask, just as Mr. Monet comes out the front door.

"Oh, Freedom, there you are. We've been looking for you," he says, walking around my bathroom vanity, the wood surprisingly swollen and watermarked.

"What in hell's bells happened here? Why is my stuff on the front lawn?" I ask, glancing around before returning my gaze to him.

"Well, there was a slight problem with the apartment above yours," he says as he goes over to my fridge, opens it, and takes a cranberry juice bottle, as if it's completely normal to pull a drink from a refrigerator sitting in the middle of the yard. Never mind the fact it's not *his* fridge.

"What happened?" Samuel asks, sort of stepping in and taking control.

"Well," Mr. Monet starts, scratching both his head on his paunch belly at the same time. "There was a water leak up at the Foremans' upstairs. They didn't realize it because the water was running down the wall to the apartment below."

"My apartment," I derive, cold sliver of dread sliding down my spine.

"Yep, your apartment. It must have started last Thursday night or Friday morning. The water ran all weekend until it started pouring out from under your door this morning. But by that point, it ran down your wall too and soaked the place directly underneath you too. All three apartments. Ruined."

"Ruined?" I ask, the words catching in my throat.

"Oh, definitely. We got all your stuff here in the front yard and George's stuff in the back. And Frank's is sort of mixed between the two places," he says, scratching his balls.

"Swell," I relay, heading over to check out my soaked clothes.

"We got a truck coming to take all the appliances out, but you're gonna have to move all your stuff. Preferably right away. You know, so it doesn't make the place look junky and stuff."

Right.

"How long?" I ask. "How long will I be out of here?"

He scratches his gut once more and glances back at the building. "Three weeks? At least."

"Three weeks? I don't know what to do," I whisper to no one, trying to piece together how I'm going to move all my stuff and where I'm going to put it. It's not like I keep a storage unit handy, just in case my apartment floods and I need to clear it out.

"I've got this," Samuel says, placing his hand on my arm and pulling his phone from his pocket. He steps away and makes a call as

I start digging through my soppy underwear. Mr. Monet lingers, wiping sweat off his brow as he leans against my dresser.

Sighing, I glance at everything I own. Fortunately, I'm a minimalist and not a *stuff* person. I don't keep miscellaneous and frivolous things, just for the sake of filling a shelf or cabinet. I guess you can thank my childhood for that. It's not like we were making paper mâché angels and framing family photos. If we made something, it was with the intention of selling it. It's how we survived.

So, there's no surprise everything I own doesn't really take up too much space on the lawn. I find my hamper and clothes basket and start wringing out the soppy, grass-covered clothes, chucking them inside. Everything in my dresser is still dry, so I leave it be for now. I find my kitchen stuff all haphazardly thrown in diaper boxes—I probably don't want to know where those came from—and my bathroom stuff wrapped up in my bedspread. And my favorite beads—the ones that were hanging from my bedroom doorway—are in a tangled pile, the plastic bar that extended across the doorframe broken.

Yeah, this isn't how I expected my fun weekend away to end.

"Okay, so we're going to take this stuff to Mom's garage. Rhenn didn't have much, so there should be room," Samuel says, shoving his phone back in his pocket.

"I'm staying at the bed and breakfast?" I ask, my heart pounding in my chest.

"Uhh, no. We're storing your stuff there. Unfortunately, Mom doesn't have any availability right now." He glances down at the pile of wet material and straightens his necktie.

"Where am I staying?" I ask, mostly to myself.

"I was getting ready to call Harper."

"I can't stay there! They'll be returning from Vegas tomorrow and be all honeymoon-ish. I won't be a third wheel on their honeymoon, Sammy. That's just gross."

"Well, then I'll call Jensen and Kathryn. They have all those rooms in her big place," he counters, pulling his phone back out.

"Didn't they just start the second-half of a remodel? I thought they were taking down more walls on the second floor and updating the bathrooms. And there's no way I'd be comfortable taking Max's room, which you know as well as I do, that's what they'd offer me." I sigh, my shoulders sagging in defeat. I could call my work friend, Claire, but I know she's in a one-bedroom apartment too. Her place isn't big enough to have me underfoot for the next few weeks. "There's only one option left."

He looks up from his phone, and his face already gives away his uncertainty. "What?"

"I'm just going to have to stay with you."

He swallows hard, but doesn't say anything.

"The way I see it, Sammy, you're about the only person I know who has a guest room available. You won't even know I'm there," I assure him.

Samuel reaches down and picks up a pair of wet panties. He holds them up and gapes at them, as if the sight of them horrifies him. "I find that very hard to believe, Freedom."

He tosses them into the nearest clothes basket as Rhenn and his big truck pulls up to the building. Samuel takes off his suit jacket and carefully hangs it over the back of the driver's seat in his car. He unclasps his cuff links, shoving them into his pocket, before rolling his sleeves up to his forearms. And holy shitballs, what amazing forearms they are. What is it about guys in dress shirts? The moment they roll them up a little, they're like a bazillion times hotter. And considering Samuel is already hotter than the sun, that's saying something.

I gather up my measly belongings and take them to Samuel's car while they place my dresser, bed, nightstand, and loveseat in the back of his truck. "Where's your TV?" Rhenn asks, glancing around.

"I don't have one," I answer.

He looks horrified. "You don't have a TV?"

Shrugging, I tell him, "I watch streaming on my phone." I don't tell him I've never owned one. It's not like we could have them easily at the compound when I was younger. I mean, they were more of a make love and music kinda group. Sure, my grandma had one when I lived with her, but she always watched her soap operas. There was never time for cartoons or those teenage dramas all the other kids watched. And when I got older, I just didn't see the point of purchasing one if I wasn't going to use it.

When Rhenn goes to load my radio, I hold up a hand. "No, that goes in Sammy's car." His eyebrows pull together as humor transforms his face. He knows I'm the only person to use the nickname and that it's done in spite.

"You got it," he says, taking my radio to the back seat of Samuel's car.

"Thanks, love," I holler, picking up the last bit of my discarded belongings.

The back seat of Samuel's car is loaded, and I can tell he's already starting to sweat when he sees the water pooling on the leather. I pat him on the cheek, just to piss him off more, and say, "Let's go, Sammy, before your seats are ruined."

With a deep sigh I feel all the way down to my lady bits, he heads over to the driver's side and gets in. He has no idea what he's in for, or that I'm about to turn his perfectly organized little world upside down.

***

After we got the truck unloaded at Mary Ann's, we make our way to Samuel's home. I've been here before, but never actually inside his place, so I'm anxious to see how the oldest Grayson lives. If I had to guess, I'd say white walls, bland oak furniture, and not a speck of dust in sight. I'm pretty sure his shirts are hung by color and material content.

He opens the door and waves me in. The moment I step inside, I burst into laughter.

"What's so funny?" he asks, glancing around at his immaculately clean house.

"This is exactly as I pictured it, Sammy. I bet your socks are color coordinated in your drawer too, right?" I ask. When I glance his way, his ears turn red, quickly followed by his cheeks.

"I like clean," he grumbles, shoving his hands in his pockets.

"And white, apparently."

Samuel sighs. "Let's get your things into the guest room. We can start with some of your laundry so we don't have standing water anywhere," he says, turning and heading back out to the car.

For the next fifteen minutes, we unload my belongings, including our luggage, and bring them all into the house. The guest room consists of a full-sized bed with basic blue and green bedding and a single dresser and nightstand combo. There's plenty of room along the closet wall to stack my stuff, which is what I do as we bring it inside.

"Feel free to use the dresser and the closet," he says. He glances around the bare room, void of any knickknacks or pictures on the wall or…well, personality. "Make yourself at home. I'm going to unpack and start to reheat the vegetable pot pie Mom sent home for us."

For me.

She put it together as soon as her son called and asked to store my things in the garage. She loaded it with carrots and celery, corn and potatoes. Mary Ann was pulling it from the oven when we finished unloading my furniture, wrapped it in a towel, and sent us on our way. Man, I love that woman.

I take the dry clothes we pulled from my dresser drawers and closet and start to fill the ones in the guest room. Next, I unload my suitcase, tossing my rumpled dress onto the floor in the closet. There's no bathroom in the guest room, so I take my bath products to the one across the hall. The first thing I notice is the scent of his soap. It's familiar and leaves me a little dizzy. Whistling a little tune, I set my pink razor, shampoo and conditioner, and luffa and bodywash beside his expensive brand of bodywash and shampoo. I grab the back and start to read the fine print, instantly pissed off at what I read.

Tossing them in the trash, I head to the kitchen, where I find Samuel at the oven, dishing up the pot pie. "What the hell, Samuel?" I thunder, placing my hands on my hips and tapping my foot on the gleaming tile floor.

"What?" he startles, spinning around and holding a plate. It's also when I notice he's wearing an apron. Sure it says "Kiss the Chef," but it's an apron, for heaven's sake.

"What are you wearing?"

"An apron," he replies, glancing down in question. "Why?"

"Oh, no reason, Martha."

"Martha?"

"Stewart."

Samuel rolls his eyes and turns back to the task at hand. When he has both plates dished up, he takes them to the table, where he's already set two glasses of ice water. "Are you just going to tease me about my apron, or did you have something important to discuss?" he asks, untying the black and white apron and hanging it from a hook beside the refrigerator.

"Oh, I have something very serious to discuss, but why are you wearing an apron? You know you're thirty-six, right, and not eighty?"

Samuel sighs as I take a seat and place my napkin on my lap. "I wear it to protect my clothes from food splatters. This may sound completely foreign and too refined for you, but there's a whole demographic of people who like protecting their clothes," he says.

The moment the words leave his mouth, I drop a forkful of food down my shirt, so I bring the material up to my mouth and suck the vegetables off.

"See what I mean?" he mumbles, taking his fork and a much smaller bite of his dinner.

I moan in pure divine pleasure as I take a huge bite of food. "Jesus, Mary, and Joseph, this is amazing."

"It is good," he confirms. "What is it you were worked up about?"

"Oh! Yeah, I threw out your animal tested body products." I shovel a big bite of flaky crusty pot pie, letting another moan fly as I chew.

"You what? Why would you do that?"

"Did you not hear me? They test that brand on animals."

"But…" he starts, setting his fork down and rubbing his forehead, "that's my shampoo and soap. What the hell am I supposed to use now?"

I shrug. "Use mine."

"Use yours?"

I glance across the table. "Are you just going to repeat everything I say? Yes, use mine. It's all natural, made from shea butter and tea tree oil."

He pulls a face. "Doesn't that smell nasty?"

"It has traces of it. You can't even smell it."

He just shakes his head and continues eating his food, mumbling about changing his shampoo. He remains silent as I tell him all about my schedule for tomorrow, including one Reiki session and two massages. I'm not working at the lingerie shop until Wednesday, so I'll be able to get a lot of laundry done tomorrow, which is good because I'm not sure I have any clean panties.

"You're headed back to work?" I ask as I gather up my dirty plate, grabbing his as I walk by.

"Sure, I was done," he protests, but doesn't come after his plate. I knew he was done. He'd been just picking at a few crumbs while I finished my meal. "And yes, I'm back to work tomorrow."

"Lots of dead bodies awaiting, I'm sure."

He just lifts a shoulder. "It's what I do."

Filling the sink to wash the dishes, I turn his way. "I think your job is kinda cool."

Samuel stops and turns my way. "Seriously? No one thinks my job is cool."

I shrug as I set our dirty dishes in the sudsy water. "Well, I do. I mean, it's totally weird, but completely cool all at the same time. And I hate to be the one to tell ya, but I'm kinda weird."

"You don't say," he deadpans, grabbing the towel to dry.

"I already know I am, Sammy, but my point is your job is different, it's not something just anyone can do, and what you do matters to the living."

When he doesn't say anything, I stop washing my plate and glance his way. He's just staring at me, a look of wonder and inquisition. "Thank you," he says as he clears his throat. "You're probably the only person I know who sees that."

"Well, I'm sure your siblings do."

"My siblings think I'm weird."

"Well, you are," I tell him with a big grin, rinsing off the plate and handing it to him. "And your siblings just love to tease you."

He dries it off and sets it inside the cabinet. "They think I'm boring and anal."

"You *are* boring and anal. But you're pretty cool too," I confess.

He clears his throat as the tips of his ears turn pink. "Thanks."

"You're welcome. Besides, no one else I know is as much fun to hassle as you are, Sammy."

He just sighs and finishes drying the dishes. Truth is, he's not only fun to hassle, but fun to be with all the other times too. And now we're roommates. At least for a few weeks. Married roommates. It's like the stars started to align for me, and now I'll have unbridled access to Samuel. No better way to prove to him our marriage is headed to forever than if we're shacking up together, right?

Right.

I have so many ideas to prove it to him, too. It's going to be fun.

Chapter Thirteen

Samuel

My first day back after the long weekend is stressful and troublesome. Elma isn't feeling so well, but insisted on staying to help me get caught up. There were two deceased individuals brought in this past weekend, and nothing really done. Not that I'd expected Aaron to do too much work on his weekend on-call. He's more of a leave-it-for-Samuel kind of guy. But the entire downstairs looks as if a small storm blew through it. The embalming machine was left out and plugged in and the sink and countertop littered with latex gloves. This is exactly why I choose to do things myself, because I can't always count on young Mr. Hanson to get the job done right.

Or without trashing the entire business in the process.

After the second family comes in to discuss funeral arrangements, I finally convince Elma to go home. It was bad enough she sneezed and coughed all over the conference room, but she left a trail of used tissues in her wake.

I guess like grandma, like grandson.

When I get the office cleaned up—and ran Clorox wipes over everything that would stand still—I finally close up shop and head home. I'm in desperate need of a shower, although, I should probably stop by the store and grab some new bath products. This way, I don't have to use Freedom's. I mean, it's not like they smell bad or anything—quite the opposite, actually—but more of the fact I don't need to be using her stuff. It already completely freaked me out when I saw her pink razor hanging beside my blue one, but the constant scent that's so very Freedom has been lingering on my body the entire day, which is doing inappropriate things in my groin, especially when gathering with bereaving family.

But I can't help it.

I smell her.

I want her.

My car pulls into a small pharmacy lot, practically on its own. Inside, I head straight for the soap aisle, and the first brand I find is the one she uses. I spy my former brand too, but I quickly bypass it so I don't upset Freedom anymore. I'm not really a guy who follows animal testing and such, but I don't want to willingly use those products. If she says it happens, I'm sure it does. Freedom wouldn't lie about something like that.

There are a few other name brands for men, and after a quick scan of the print on the back to confirm they weren't lab animal tested products, I settle on a shampoo and a bodywash in a clean, ocean breeze scent. I don't really know what an herbal blend ocean breeze smells like, but it must be decent if they bottle it up and sell it for ten bucks a pop.

It's after six when I finally pull into my driveway. The front porch light is on, but the lights appear to be dim inside. Freedom's car is parked along the street, and to be honest, I'm not sure how she got it here. I assumed I'd have to run her to get her car tonight, but apparently someone else beat me to it. There's also a second car there, a nondescript Buick I don't recognize. I'll have to ask Freedom about the car when I get inside.

After a quick stop at the mailbox, I insert my key into my lock, open the front door, and stop dead in my tracks. "What the hell?" I ask, completely stunned at the scene before me. Freedom is standing there, a woman wearing a sheet from the waist down lying on the massage table, as soft sounds of nature filter through my speakers.

"Oh, hey," Freedom says, offering me a warm, welcome home smile, before turning back to her task at hand as if it's perfectly normal to give a naked lady a massage in the middle of my living room.

"Freedom?" I ask, keeping my back against the wall as I try to look anywhere but at the scene in front of me. The lady is completely covering any vital parts, but it still makes me feel a little uncomfortable as Freedom rubs big circles across her oily back. "A word?"

She glances at the clock. "I've got ten minutes left here. Please wait in the kitchen."

Ordering me around like she owns the place.

Typical Freedom.

I keep my back as close to the wall as possible as I make my way through the living room and to the kitchen. Once there, I practically sprint to the fridge and grab a bottle of water. Then, I set it back inside and pull out a beer. I'm not a big beer drinker, but I'll have one every now and again. Usually, at my mom's with my siblings, but today, with Freedom on the opposite side of the wall giving a strange woman a massage, well, I say that constitutes a special beer-drinking occasion.

"Make sure you drink plenty of water," I hear Freedom say. "Go ahead and get dressed in the bathroom, and I'll meet you back in here."

I hear a door shut, followed by Freedom breezing into the kitchen as if she hasn't a care in the world. "Good evening, Sammy."

"What the fuck, Freedom?" I practically growl, setting my beer bottle down on the table with a little too much force.

"Excuse me?"

"Why are you massaging a strange woman in my house?" I whisper-yell so said strange woman doesn't overhear.

"What are you talking about? Priscilla isn't a strange woman. I've been massaging her for years."

"In my house?"

She crosses her arms, and I can't help but notice the way her top dips down low. "No, in *my* house. But since I currently don't have an apartment, I'm doing it here."

"Without asking?" I ask, rubbing my forehead and willing the headache forming to go away.

"Umm, did you not tell me to make myself comfortable?"

I throw my hands in the air. "Well, yes, but that was in your bedroom. You know, like put your clothes in the dresser drawers and your books on the nightstand?"

"Well, I only did what you offered me to do. This is how I make money," she tells me, lifting her eyebrow, as if daring me to argue more.

"I get that," I grumble, glancing down at my shiny brown leather shoes. "I just thought you went to the massage parlor for, you know, massages."

She shrugs and heads to the fridge, retrieving a water bottle. "Usually, I do, but some of my clients that I've had forever have always come to my place. Priscilla is one of them."

"One of them?"

"Sure, there's Sally and Garth Peterman and Emmie Snodgrass, who refuses to wear underwear. Plus, Phyllis Jones and Angel Cays. They both come once a week," she tells me, making my eye twitch.

"Okay, okay, so I get that you need to work, and apparently, some of that is from home. I think we just need to set some ground rules," I concede.

Before she can reply, the bathroom door opens. "Hold that thought, Sammy," Freedom says, patting me on the chest and heading back to the living room.

I follow, but linger in the doorway, leaning a hip against the wood trim. Freedom goes over post-massage details, even though I know she doesn't need to, and gives her client the bottle of water on her way out the door. Once she shuts the door, Freedom turns and busies herself with picking up the sheets and setting them in a pile to be washed, all while humming along to the sounds of the ocean waves rolling through the speakers, as if you can somehow hum to unheard music. But she does.

When she grabs a Clorox wipe and starts cleaning her table, I say, "Freedom."

She glances up and smiles. And my heart pounds heavily in my chest. That one simple gesture is enough to bring me to my knees. To beg her to stay. The concept is so foreign to me, I'm not sure what to do with it. Before I even realize what's happening, she's standing directly in front of me. Her wide brown eyes gaze up, innocence and desire battling for dominance.

"What?" she whispers, the mintiness of her breath tickling my chin.

Clearing my throat, I try to push all inappropriate thoughts of kissing her—or worse, making love to her—from my mind. That's not going to happen.

Even if we are technically still married.

Freedom slides her hands up my arms, and even through my dress shirt, I can feel the burn of her touch. My brain starts to malfunction. I can't seem to think about anything but her. Wanting her. Tasting her. Needing her.

Freedom.

I'm not sure who moves first, but suddenly, my lips are on hers, a hunger I've never felt before. No, I take that back. It feels familiar, yet new at the same time. A sudden flashback of kissing her in the shower with the same fervor parades through my mind. My hands on her ass as I press her against the wall, press my cock into her body. It's the slightest glimpse of a memory, but it's there, flashing like a neon sign and refusing to leave.

I wrap my arms around her back and pull her against me. My body completely takes over. Desire and demand crash together like two cars in a demolition derby, both fighting for dominance. Freedom goes up on her tiptoes, her chest pressing tightly against mine. She purrs, like a kitten. A sexy kitten in a long blue and paisley skirt and tight pink top.

"This isn't exactly the ground rules I was planning to discuss," I grumble, gasping for air.

She's still in my arms, her nipples hard and pressed against the material of her shirt, pretty much confirming she's not wearing a bra. Her eyes are even darker, full of her own desire. So, when she places her lips against my ear and whispers, "Fuck the rules," well, I pretty much lose all ability to think rationally. That's the only logical explanation as to why I reach down and grab her hips, lifting her small body and carrying her to my bedroom.

Her hands dive into my hair, and for the first time in forever, I'm a little glad to have missed my last haircut. She tugs, pain shooting down my neck and spine and landing in my groin. That little burst of discomfort only seems to fuel the craving I feel right now. That deep down yearning for something I shouldn't want, yet can't seem to stop myself from caring.

When I step inside my room, I head immediately to my bed. Freedom's legs slip out from under the skirt as she brings them up and hooks them over my hips. Setting her down on the duvet, my mouth finds hers once more, my tongue dipping into her mouth and tasting.

Her hands are clawing at my shirt, pulling at my tie and grasping at the buttons. "Take this off. Now."

I quickly stand up and start to unbutton my shirt. Freedom crouches on the bed and carefully removes my cuff links, tossing them onto my nightstand. "Be careful. Those are antique."

She rolls her eyes and I swear I can feel it all the way down to my balls. "Oh, they're fine, Sammy. But you won't be if you don't get this shirt off immediately." Freedom practically grabs the material and pulls it apart, pawing it as if it wasn't custom tailored to fit. I'm able to save the buttons by getting them released right away as she loosens my necktie. "I like this," she whispers as she smooths the black and gold silk.

"I like this, but it needs to go," I tell her boldly as I reach for her top. She instantly stops and extends her arms over her head, waiting for me to remove it. My fingers graze against warm, soft skin as I lift. My mouth waters as I expose her small breasts, the ones I've held in my hands before, yet barely remember.

But I'll remember tonight.

Even though we should stop, even though I should send her to her own bedroom and forget about this crazy lust consuming me, I don't. I *can't*. The need for her is too great to fight.

So I don't.

The moment her top is gone, my hands are on her breasts, palming them and pinching her nipples. She mewls, her head falling back in ecstasy. When she looks back up at me, her eyes are blazing as she leans into my touch just a bit. Something almost animalistic sweeps through me, and I know I need more. Picking her up, her body pressed against mine, I lay her back down on the bed and start to lift her skirt. My cock aches in my trousers, but I ignore my own lust, needing more of her.

Bright orange panties with a black lace trim peek from under the skirt, and my mouth starts to water once more. I glance up, seeking permission to remove those delicate panties. Freedom lifts her hips and shimmies as I slide them down her legs. She's completely bare. Not a speck of hair anywhere, and I swear every ounce of blood my body possesses goes straight to my groin. It's painful how badly I want her.

But I continue to ignore my own desire, needing to taste her. I spread her legs and slide between her thighs. The first swipe of my tongue is like touching an electric fence. It's a jolt that stings and is something I won't ever forget. The sound of her moans of pleasure spurs me on as I lick and suck on her sweet flesh. Freedom spreads her legs even farther, giving me full access to her most intimate places.

Using a single finger, I tease her entrance, coating my finger in her wetness before sliding it inside. I can feel the tightness of her muscles contracting around me, which only makes me suck on her clit that much harder. She hollers my name, wiggling her hips and riding my finger and mouth in a frenzy as she barrels headfirst toward release. I can tell she's getting close, so I slip a second finger inside her just to help her along.

Her orgasm slams into her hard, as she bellows my name over and over again. Her hips rock against my face as she takes everything she wants and needs from me. Watching and feeling her come may be my new favorite thing in the whole world. Especially when it's my name flying from her sweet lips.

"Holy fuck," she mumbles as I glance up. She has the most perfect euphoric look on her face, her eyes all glazed over and a seductive and satisfied grin on her lips.

Licking my lips, I rest my chin on her inner thigh and just watch. Freedom Rayne has the ability to completely wreck me. I know this now. She has this power over me, a force I've tried to ignore for years, but here it is, alive and breathing. I don't want to fight it, but I know I have to. Everything about us coming together this way has been a little backward, and I'm not a man who goes the wrong way. Ever.

That's why I have to fix this marriage mess as soon as possible.

Starting with right now.

What the hell am I doing?

I can't sleep with Freedom. I shouldn't have carried her into my room, to my bed. And I *definitely* shouldn't have gone down on her like I was a crazed man. Though, tell that to my cock. He's pretty excited about what just happened and is ready to claim her in other ways too.

"You're thinking too hard," she whispers, her voice as pure as sin.

Freedom gets up, so I do the same. I'm about to excuse myself to the bathroom—to take care of the little problem I'm having down south—when she throws her arms around my neck and kisses me. Her lips are like nectar, sweet and delicious, and I can't stop. My tongue dances with hers as she pulls me forward until we're pressed together.

"Take off your pants." Her breath fans against my face, her words like a direct link to my cock.

I shouldn't, but I do. My hands wrap around my belt buckle, releasing the leather. Still, the rational part of my brain tries to force its way through the thick sex-fog. "I'm not sure we should—" I start but am cut off.

By her lips.

Again.

"Less talking. More sexing," she whispers, sending my brain into orbit in another universe.

Freedom helps me ditch my trousers, my button-down, and necktie. She drops her skirt on the floor. My socks go next, followed very quickly by my briefs. I barely have them around my thighs when her hand wraps around my length, tight and warm. I'm not sure where the loud groan of pleasure comes from, but by the glint in her eye, I'd say it came from me.

By some divine powers that be, I reach into my nightstand drawer and find a condom. The foil package is ripped from my hand as Freedom gnaws at the packaging with her teeth and pulls the protection from inside. All I can think about is how amazing her hands feel as she strokes me, long and hard, positioning the condom at the head of my cock.

"I'm going to suck that, but not now. Right now, I need to feel you inside me," she says, as she slowly rolls the protection over me.

Meanwhile, in my brain, I'm trying not to think about how truly glorious it feels to have her touching me so I don't come before I'm even inside her body.

She spins us around and presses on my shoulders until I'm sitting on my bed, my back against the headboard. Then, she's straddling my waist, positioning my cock at her entrance, and sitting down.

I feel everything. The tightness of her body as I press inside her. The warmth of her arms as they wrap around my neck. The muscles of her thighs as they press against my outer legs. And the squeeze in my heart as we come together in the most intimate way possible.

Completely.

Like someone lights a match, fire spreads through my veins and my hips buck upward, burying myself to the root. Freedom stills, a gasp slipping from her sweet lips. "Shit, I'm sorry. Did I hurt you?" I ask through gritted teeth. My body is begging to move, but I refuse if it's only going to cause her discomfort.

"Holy shitballs, I forgot how big you are," she whispers, her eyes closed.

"We can stop," I tell her, realizing I might actually explode if we do. But I won't hurt her.

"Don't you dare stop." She gasps, slowly lifting her hips and sliding back down again. "So fucking good."

She's right, this is too fucking good to stop. Now or ever.

With my hands on her hips, I let her set the pace. She slowly moves up and down, her hands positioned on my chest for stability, as she adjusts to fit me. I can feel every flex of her muscles, every delicious slide of her body as it grips mine. And holy hell, does it grip. She's got my cock so tight, I'm not sure I'll last much longer.

Her nails score against my flesh as my grasp on her hips tightens. Quite possibly, I'm leaving marks, but I can't seem to stop myself. She rocks and grinds in the same motion, and I'm not sure if I should beg her to stop or plead for more. My brain has officially left the room, probably off to have a cigarette. I'm left with a burning desire to claim her and an ache in my chest where she seems to have rooted.

I'm close, teetering on the edge of sanity and oblivion. With each move she makes, she brings me closer to release, like the vixen she is. This wild and carefree vixen I can't stop wanting. Needing.

She clenches my cock as her hips buck uncontrollably. My eyes start to cross and all I can do is hang on tight. I'm pleading with myself to not come, to sit back and enjoy the ride, but it's impossible. Especially when she says, "I can't get enough of you, Samuel."

My name.

The way she says it, her voice dripping with seduction and confidence, as her orgasm washes through her, triggering my own release like a bomb. There's no stopping or containing it.

My hips thrust upward, hard and fast, until I'm finally unable to move. Freedom's lips claim mine, our gasps for air as tangled as our tongues. My hands finally release her hips and move to frame her face. Hair hangs over her eyes, soft, yet wet from sweat. Our bodies are pressed together, a fine sheen of sweat covering mine, which is something I can't say has every happened before. Sex has never been so...aggressive. Nice, yes. Sweet, absolutely. But this raw, animalistic obsession that leaves me fulfilled and spent? Not so much.

Not until Freedom.

She pulls her lips from my own and rests her head on my shoulder, the slightest tickle from her breath caressing my neck. I hold her tightly against me, wishing we could stay just like this. Wishing things between us could be different. Not the sex. No, I wouldn't change that for anything, but the confusion I feel because of it. My head still tells me to do the right thing, to step away and right the wrong we made in Las Vegas. But my heart? It's telling me I've already found that right.

With her.

My back sags against the headboard as exhaustion sets in. I'm not sure if she's sleeping or just that relaxed, but her lithe little body is practically limp against me. Carefully, I turn us sideways and pull from her body. She whimpers, but it doesn't seem to be from pain or discomfort. Freedom clings to my chest, her breasts pressed tightly against me.

I move us until we're both lying on the same pillow. Her dark hair is a striking contradiction to the soft white sheets, and for once, I seem to find a bit of peace in the paradox. She's the splash of color against my compulsory white world. That thought doesn't scare me as much as it used to.

Knowing I need to get up and dispose of the protection, I slowly pull myself from our embrace. Not by choice, by necessity. Freedom whimpers again, but her eyes remain closed as she burrows deeper into the bedding. With every step I take to the hallway and toward the bathroom, I'm drawn to the vision of her lying in my bed. One I want to return to as soon as possible.

After taking care of business in the bathroom, I grab a warm washcloth and return to my room. I ignore the hammering of my heart in my chest as I approach her. Her wild hair is splayed across her face, and as I gently move it from her forehead once more, I can't get over how delicately soft her skin in. So different from her bold and brash personality.

Her eyes open and focus on me. She doesn't say anything about me standing there, watching her rest, which I'm grateful for. I'm not sure what I'd say anyway. That I like watching her sleep? Especially when she's in my bed? Yep, both of those things are true. I don't tell her that, however. Instead, I don't say anything as I pull the blankets back and gently clean her thighs, completely avoiding the intensity of her stare as she lies there.

As I'm finishing, I notice the redness of her hips. "My God, did I do that?" I ask, feeling instant guilt over the markings on her skin.

Freedom glances down and notices the finger imprints around her narrow hips. She doesn't say a word, just reaches for the washcloth and tosses it on the floor. She takes my hand and pulls me back to bed, wrapping her leg around my hips and her arm around my stomach, her front pressed to my back. "Get out of your head," she demands, her voice gravelly.

"What?" I ask, trying to turn so that I can see her.

She holds on tight, not allowing me to shift our positions. "You didn't do anything to me I didn't like."

"But I hurt you." My entire body seems to deflate.

"No, you didn't. You didn't hurt me at all, Samuel. You made me feel better than I've ever felt before. And those marks? They weren't put there in punishment or for pain, right?"

Adamantly, I shake my head. "Of course not!"

"Exactly. I know that. Please don't diminish what we did because you're worried about a few fingermarks on my skin. I didn't even feel it, and if anything, your grip on me only spurred me on."

I stop and consider her words. She's right, I know it. But that still doesn't mean I don't feel bad for marking her skin. I've never done that before—would never even consider it possible to do. Just another reason why I'm so out of my mind with Freedom. "I'm still sorry," I tell her, relief washing over me.

"Please don't be. In fact, I hope you do it again next time."

Next time.

Will there be a next time? There shouldn't be, but I'm learning I'm not that strong when it comes to fighting whatever pull is between us. I don't seem to be capable of making sane, rational decisions where she's concerned.

I hate that.

Instead of arguing, I find myself being pulled toward sleep. My body is exhausted, my mind reeling from what happened earlier. Even though I know I should shower, because I always shower at the end of the day, especially if sex is involved, but for some reason, I'm perfectly content to be wrapped in Freedom's arms and lulled to sleep.

She sighs, her body relaxing around me. We're in sort of a reverse spoon position, and I can tell the moment she drifts off to sleep. Her hand stops caressing my chest and her leg lies limp over my hip. Her breathing evens out against my ear as she murmurs my name.

My name.

Not Sammy.

Samuel.

It's not the first time I've heard her say it. Sure, I heard it earlier when her orgasm was ripping through her body, but that wasn't the first time.

Like a flash of lightning to my memory, I remember her saying it one other time.

When we said our vows.

In that little chapel in Las Vegas.

She looked me in the eye and whispered, "I, Freedom Rayne, take you, Samuel Grayson, to be my husband."

It was the sweetest sound I've ever heard.

Chapter Fourteen

Freedom

Night has fallen when I slowly open my eyes and blink. It takes me a few long seconds to get my bearings, but when I do, I relax. I know where I am. The familiar scent of Samuel's detergent tickles my senses and brings a warm and comforting sensation to my already overly sensitive body.

I realize I'm wrapped around his back, my leg thrown over his and my arm around his chest. His hair—which is still longer than I've ever seen it—prickles my nose, but that doesn't cause me to move. Oh no, I don't want to move.

Ever.

There's a soreness between my legs that makes me smile and want to slide against him like a cat in heat. We're both as naked as the day we were born, and all I can feel is the heat of his skin pressed against mine. It's tantalizing. Intoxicating. Hormone-inducing. Because all I want to do is hump him.

Again.

And maybe again after that.

My stomach growls, reminding me we didn't eat dinner before arguing over my use of his living room for massage clients, and I'm regretting that now. Not the sex. Oh, no. Never the sex. I'm regretting not fueling our bodies beforehand for round two.

"Was that your stomach?" he whispers, his voice like whiskey and sex.

"'Fraid so, Sammy. You didn't feed me before you plundered me with your summer sausage."

He goes completely rigid in my arms. "Seriously, Freedom?" he asks with a deep exhale, slowly turning in my arms. This time, I let him.

His blue-green eyes are a little hesitant as he faces me, and when they finally do, I see a whole plethora of emotion. Guilt— probably still from his fingermarkings on my hips—desire, and even shyness. That last one's my favorite.

"I'm starving. What time is it?" I ask through a yawn.

"After eleven," he replies, stretching his arms and treating me to a delicious view of his chest. The blanket dips down and I spy a peek of something else down below the waist. It's big and hard and raring to go for that round two I've been thinking about. My lady parts start to weep with joy. Samuel notices where my eyes have fallen and slowly puts his arms down, covering up his impressive hard-on. I mean, seriously. Some guys have been just blessed in that department, and Samuel is one of them. How he hasn't had a line of waiting women a mile long is beyond me.

"I don't usually eat after seven o'clock. Studies show it increases the risk of heart attack and stroke and keeps your body from winding down," he states, and the truth smacks me upside the head. Samuel is very black and white. There are rules that must be followed, or it doesn't add up to him. I've known this, pretty much my entire adult life, but seeing it now, in the dark of night and while lying in his bed, is a stark reminder of how very different we really are.

Rolling my eyes, I say, "Live a little, Sammy. I'll make you some eggs."

His stomach growls like mine, and that's probably the only reason he relents. "Fine, thank you. I think I'm going to grab a shower," he says, standing up and trying to hide his erection from me as he practically runs from the room.

A snicker bubbles from my chest as I slip from the bed and look for my clothes. They're a wadded up mess on the floor, which usually doesn't bother me in the least, but I opt for another piece of discarded clothing. I slip on his button-down and secure most of the buttons. The shirt is huge, but it smells absolutely delicious, like woodsy cologne and fresh deodorant.

I head to the kitchen and pull out the carton of eggs. The bread is in the pantry and I'm able to find the toaster in one of the cabinets. In the fridge, I spy a small carton of fresh mushrooms and a brick of white cheddar cheese. As the skillet heats up, I pop a few slices of wheat bread into the toaster and slice up the mushrooms.

When the skillet is ready, I scramble half a dozen eggs and add the chopped shrooms, stirring it occasionally to keep the eggs from scorching. When the mixture starts to fluff, I drop the bread and add the cheese and a lid to the skillet, all while humming whatever tune is stuck in my head.

"Something smells amazing," he says behind me.

Spinning around, I find Samuel standing in the doorway, his shorts hanging low on his hips and a bright white T-shirt molded to his torso. His eyes meet mine, then suddenly drop, right along with his mouth. He slowly takes in my appearance from my bare feet, up my legs, and to the large shirt hanging loosely on my petite frame, the sleeves rolled up a bit, so they don't hang in the food.

"I hope you don't mind, I borrowed your shirt," I tell him, spinning back around as the toast pop up to slather yogurt butter on the top.

"Uhh, no. Not at all," he answers. I can picture him running a hand through his hair, which makes me smile.

I feel his presence beside me as he grabs a pair of plates for the eggs and takes them to the table. He sets out a fork and napkin for each place setting, making sure they're properly positioned on the placemat. I join him, flopping the pan down in the center of the table, much to his dismay. Samuel quickly grabs a potholder and places it correctly beneath the pan of eggs.

"Smells delicious," he says as he takes a seat across from me.

"Right? I'm so hungry I could eat the ass end out of a cow," I state bluntly, scooping up a forkful of fluffy eggs.

Samuel chokes. I glance across the table and witness him pulling his fork out of his mouth and trying to swallow the food he just inhaled. "Jesus, Freedom."

"What?" I ask, reaching over and banging on his back a few times.

"Do you have to be so…crude?"

It takes me a second to realize what he's talking about. "Huh, you know, I don't know why I say that. I mean, I don't even eat cow, let alone cow ass," I chuckle.

When he doesn't reply, I look back his way, our eyes locking once more. He doesn't reply, but I can see the hint of a smile on his face as he takes a much smaller bite of eggs. We eat in silence for a few minutes, which might be a record for me, but there's something so easy and natural about sitting here with Samuel.

"So, what's it like to work at a funeral home?" I finally ask, unable to take the silence any longer.

He looks my way but doesn't reply right away. It's as if he's a little skeptical about answering. "Why?"

"Why what?"

"Why do you want to know about the funeral home?" he asks.

I shrug. "I guess it looks interesting to me, you know? I mean, you see people at their absolute worst, but have to still make the best out of the occasion, right?"

Again, he just stares at me. After a few long seconds, he clears his throat. "Yeah, actually, that's very accurate. My job isn't very glamorous, but it's a necessary part of the life cycle, and my goal is to do it with dignity and compassion."

"You sound like the front page of the website," I snort.

"Well, I did design it," he states, matter-of-factly.

I push my plate forward, my belly full of delicious eggs. "So…you see them, like, naked?"

He gives me an exasperated look. "Really?"

"Well, it's true. They're all nudey and you have to touch them. It's not that different from my job," I reply with a shrug. "Except mine are still breathing when I put my hands on them."

"I guess," he says, finally finishing his food.

"It's really cool that you do what you do. Not a lot of people could actually deal with death and bodies all day, Sammy. And I'm always hearing about how wonderful you are to work with. Families choose your funeral home because of you, not because of the Hansons. You're amazing at your job, Samuel."

When silence falls on the room again, I peek his way. "I don't know what to say."

I lift a shoulder and reach for the plates. "You don't have to say anything."

He reaches out and grabs my hands, halting my progress. "Thank you."

My breath catches in my throat as my heart pirouettes in my chest, and I swear his thumb dances along my hand. "It's the truth," I tell him, my voice sounding like someone else's, even to my own ears.

We stare at each other, caught in a trance where it's only him and me. Like we're the only ones in the world. "I, uh, I'll get the dishes. You cooked," he says, as he takes the plates from my hand and heads for the sink.

"Thanks." I gather our glasses and napkins and meet him at the counter. "I think I'll go take a shower," I add, waving a thumb toward the doorway.

Just as I get to the hallway, I hear, "Hey, Freedom?" I glance over my shoulder. "No one has ever asked me about my work before. Hell, I'm pretty sure my family doesn't even understand the importance of what I do, both to my employer and to me. So, just…thank you."

I nod once and give him a smile. I'm not sure what to say, so I don't say anything at all. It's not that his family doesn't think his work is valuable or important, but it's the fact they don't understand fully. No one thinks about the people who actually direct funerals. The person who goes to the hospitals, the morgues, wherever to retrieve the bodies. The condition they may encounter. The scene. The smells. All they see is the final result, not what it takes to get a deceased individual to that point. Samuel's job is probably harder than any I know, and the respect I have for him is tremendous and unwavering.

"You're welcome." With a smile, I turn and head for the guest room to gather my things for a shower.

My body is still humming as I slip under the spray of hot water. I pull my hair up on top of my head in a messy bun, just because it takes so damn long to dry, but wash every other part of my body, using Samuel's bodywash. As I run the cloth over my hips, I wince at how tender they are. There are definite fingermarks, but that only makes me smile more. I feel…marked by him.

And I love it.

When I'm finished, I grab one of the big, fluffy white towels that smell like sunshine and spring rain and wrap it around my body. I moisturize my face and draw a smiling face in the fog on the mirror—oh, he's going to hate that—and head back to my room.

When I reach the hallway, I notice his door is only slightly ajar and the room dark. Apparently, he went back to bed after he washed our dishes.

I slip quietly into the guest room and pull a fresh T-shirt from the drawer. It doesn't smell as good as the button-down I wore earlier, but it's probably not acceptable to head back to the bathroom and take it off the floor. But when have I ever been worried about something being socially acceptable?

That's exactly why I slip out of the room, naked, and retrieve the discarded white shirt Samuel wore today. Quietly, I make my way back to my temporary room, throw my arms in the shirt and secure the buttons. I find my hairbrush on the dresser, remove the hair tie, and try to untangle the mess I call hair. When it's finally brushed out, I flip off the light and climb into bed.

The first thing I notice is the cold sheets. They smell clean, but they lack any…heat. Any familiarity. I hate it. But I snuggle into one of the pillows, curl up on my side, and try to go to sleep.

It doesn't work.

Even though the clock reads midnight, I can't sleep. I toss. I turn. I count sheep. Nothing works. My mind wanders right back to the feel of his arms around me, the way his lips molded to my own, the way his cock moved inside me. My nipples start to tingle and I'm pretty sure I'm getting wet already.

Sighing, I flop onto my back, wishing I was back in his bed. In his arms. Surrounded in his heat as I drift off to sleep.

That sounds a thousand times better than lying here, alone, and wishing for sleep to claim me.

That's probably why I find myself getting out of bed and padding quietly to the door. I'm noiseless as I slip across the hall, his door barely moving as I enter his personal space. Instantly, I'm wrapped in everything the other room is lacking, and as I climb into his bed, there's a smile on my face.

I try to move quickly and silently, and I'm grateful Samuel doesn't seem to notice he has a bedmate. As soon as I relax against the pillow, I feel the weight of the day just drain from my body. I'm exhausted and finally feel like I can fall asleep.

Just as I close my eyes, I feel his arm swing over my body and pull me toward him. The heat of his chest is pressed against my back, and all I can do is wait. Wait for him to bust me. Wait for him to ask me what I'm doing. Wait for him to boot my ass from his bed.

But he doesn't.

Instead, he relaxes against me, spooning my back with his much larger chest. I can tell he's still wearing his undershirt and shorts. The hair on his legs tickles my own legs, but I only seem to burrow in farther. My eyelids finally start to droop as sleep finally calls.

Just before I succumb to the darkness, I feel his arm tighten around me and his lips rest on my shoulder. "Good night, Freedom," he whispers.

I don't answer. Instead, I fall asleep with a smile on my lips.

Chapter Fifteen

Samuel

As I embalm the lady who owned the bakery in downtown Rockland Falls, my mind keeps flashing to waking with Freedom in my arms for the last three mornings. I've learned in a short time she's not a morning person. She requires an ungodly amount of coffee just to function, and she loves to dance in the kitchen when she thinks no one is watching. Or maybe she knows I'm there, observing, and is doing it just for me.

I've also noticed how my house suddenly feels different. Sure, there are splashes of color in the living room I've had to adjust to—throw pillows and some potpourri shit that smells like lilacs—but it's more than that. It's the panties I find drying on the shower curtain rod, the chipped coffee mug in the sink that I would have long thrown away, and even the tofu and kale in my refrigerator. It's all part of her, part of her quirk, her passion.

I like it.

A lot.

I'm also completely torn as I flip the switch and the embalmer starts to do its job. I'm even more confused by the crazy pull I feel toward Freedom than ever before. It's like I'm not really me anymore. Well, no, that's not exactly true. It's like I'm a different version of me, and I believe I might like this new version too. Maybe even better than the old me.

I pull off my gloves, toss them in the trash, and wash my hands. Once they're dry, I dig my cell phone out of my trousers front pocket. It takes me a few seconds to find the name I'm looking for, but when I do, my finger hovers over the call button. Part of me wants to shove my phone back into my pants and move on with my day, with my life. But the other part is like a flashing reminder of how wrong we've gotten it.

How wrong I've gotten it.

You can't get married in Las Vegas and expect to live happily ever after for the rest of your life. Not with your sister's best friend after a night of too much drinking. Not when there's no foundation of a real relationship. Trust. Compatibility. Love.

That's why I push the call button and bring the phone to my ear.

"Anthony Hurliman, please. It's Samuel Grayson. Yes, I'll hold. Thank you." Anthony's secretary puts me on hold to see if my attorney can speak with me. I'm really hoping he's available, but if not, I'll leave a message.

"Samuel, it's good to hear from you," my former classmate says when he picks up the line.

"It's been a while," I say, adjusting my necktie nervously.

"It has, but in my world, that's not necessarily a bad thing," he replies with a chuckle.

"That's true," I state, clearing my throat. "Listen, the reason I'm calling is to ask a question."

"Okay, shoot."

"I was hoping you could recommend a divorce attorney."

I'm met with silence on the other end.

"Anthony?"

He clears his throat. "Uhh, yeah, I'm here. I'm sorry, I must have misunderstood you. I thought you were asking about a divorce lawyer."

Closing my eyes, I sigh. "I am."

Again, silence. After several very long seconds, he finally asks, "So, let me get this straight. Samuel Grayson needs…a divorce lawyer? Are you serious?"

"As a heart attack."

Then, the sound of laughter fills the phone line. I knew I should have called someone else.

"Jesus, Samuel, what did you do?"

"Long story short, I made a mistake. In Vegas."

"Am I being punked? Is this some sort of joke? Samuel Grayson got married? In Las Vegas, of all places?"

"Listen, Anthony," I exhale loudly, the weight of my mistake still weighing way too heavily on my shoulders. "I had too much to drink and may have made a mistake."

"May have?"

"I did, okay? Can you recommend a good attorney or not?"

"Settle down, I can help you. I have a colleague who's a real viper in the courtroom. She goes for blood and doesn't stop until she has it."

"I don't need that, Anthony. I just need a quickie divorce," I tell him, hating the thought of putting Freedom through the wringer. Besides, there's nothing to fight over, really.

"Okay, well, I have another guy who should fit the bill. He's hovering past retirement age, but I think he'll take you as a client, if I put in a call."

"I appreciate it," I tell him, a sense of relief filling my chest.

He promises to pass my phone number along to his colleague and hangs up without any fanfare or small talk. Satisfied with the call, I slip my phone back into my pocket and head back to work.

After finishing up my work on Mrs. Gomez, my mind drifts back to Freedom. Specifically, dating her. It's something I've never considered in the past, yet here I am, mentally working out the logistics, as if she were a business proposition. Would she be so obliged to officially enter a relationship with me? I mean, I know we're married, but that's going to end soon.

I need to do this right.

In the correct order.

We need to end our marriage, and then, maybe we can date.

Officially.

Like boyfriend and girlfriend.

Never in my wildest dreams would I ever have thought I'd be excited to date Freedom Rayne, but here I am, full of hope and anticipation and eager to get home so I can see her. It's not enough to fall sleep with her in my arms, which is exactly where she's been since that night I found her massaging some stranger in my living room, or waking up inhaling her hair that's all wild and crazy from sleep. I want more.

When the long day finally ends, I lock up the funeral home and head out, recalling my conversation with Bartholomew Christmas. He assured me it would be nothing to get a quickie divorce. Of course, the fact we're living together—albeit temporarily—didn't make him very happy. That's why I left out the fact my wife is also sleeping in my bed. Despite the odd circumstances, Mr. Christmas assured me he would get a set of divorce papers drafted soon and sent to me. All we'd have to do is sign and go before the judge. Sounds easy enough.

The drive home is fairly short, even after I stop by an Italian restaurant and pick up dinner. Freedom's a huge fan of mushrooms, so I grabbed us each a cheese stuffed portabella mushroom with noodles and garlic bread. It's not my usual, but I'll give it a try. I'm pleasantly surprised I don't seem to miss meat as much as I thought I would. She's never guilted me into not eating it, nor has she refused to cook it, but still. I'm trying to be conscious of her lifestyle and not throw our differences in her face.

The porch light is on when I pull into the driveway. In fact, it looks like every light inside is on too. What the hell is she doing? She's like a kid who forgets electricity actually costs money. I hop out of my car and grab our bag of food, anxious to get inside to scold her about the lights, and fly up the steps. The first thing I notice when I'm on the porch is my front door.

It's…different.

I stand there and stare, trying to figure it out. It's the same door, but it's been…

Painted.

My front door is a vibrant blue.

"The hell?" I whisper to no one as I slip my key into the lock and push open the door.

Inside, I'm stunned silent. It's like I've stepped into someone else's house. In fact, I glance outside, just to make sure I haven't walked into my neighbor's house by mistake. When I look back at the living room before me, I find my couch and television there, but everything else is essentially different.

"Freedom?" I bellow, unable to move at the transformation.

"Oh, hey!" she singsongs, practically skipping into the living room from the kitchen area.

"My…the…what… Oh, God, am I having a heart attack?" I ask, my heart pounding like a freight train in my chest. It's so loud I swear everyone within the block can hear it.

"Here, sit down," she says with authority, her voice full of concern. Her soft hands grasp my arm as she leads me to the couch. Out of nowhere, she has a glass of liquid, practically forcing it down my throat.

I gag at the cold, bitter liquid. "What the hell is this?" I gasp, pulling my face away from the cup.

"It's a liver detoxifying tea with peppermint, lemon, and ginger."

"Why are you detoxing your liver?" I gape at the woman beside me. Her hair is piled on top of her head and her face void of any makeup, yet I've never seen her look more beautiful.

Focus, Samuel.

"You should always detox your organs, Sammy. It'll help boost your immune system and build stamina. Plus, even though you don't need it, they say it's good for your libido."

My head starts to throb.

"Fine, fine," I mumble avoiding the yellowish liquid in her glass. I glance around, once more taking in all the…color. "What the hell happened here?"

Freedom looks around. "What?"

I wave my hands like a crazy person. "This."

"Oh, you mean the room? It really livens the place up, doesn't it?"

"Why? Why did you paint my living room?" I ask, the words barely audible as I take in the pink walls. It's the only color to describe it.

"You said to make myself at home," she says, matter-of-factly, as if completely redecorating my living space is a solid enough reason.

"In the guest room, Freedom. I didn't mean to repaint my living room pink!"

She just stares at me, blinking. "First off, it's not pink, it's Soothing Sunset Coral. And second, why wouldn't I make myself at home in the living room too? There was too much white, Sammy. It was like a hospital in here, and even those have more life than this place. So, I added a few splashes of color."

"Splashes of color? My coffee table is green!"

"Simply Seafoam," she corrects with a smile.

"Hell," I grumble and rub my chest. I really think I'm having a heart attack. Or maybe a panic attack? "How did you do all of this so fast? I mean, my door is blue."

"Just the outside," she boosts proudly. "it's so much more welcoming, isn't it?"

I just groan in response. My entertainment center, my coffee table and end tables, they're all green—or Simply Seafoam—as she so elegantly put it. My walls are pink. The pillows are bright shades of blues, greens, and pinks, and there's a bright yellow rug in the middle of my floor. "How did you do all this?"

She shrugs. "I started when you left for work. When you finish one coat on something, you move on the next. It wasn't hard, really. Plus, I'm used to it. I repaint my walls and furniture at least four or six times a year," she states chipperly.

She's so blasé about it. Like she didn't just completely change my entire living room without so much as a care for my own tastes and wants. What the hell is wrong with white walls and oak furniture? Nothing. Nothing is wrong with it, but now, it's all covered in crazy colors. If I ever want to go back—and Lord knows, I definitely will—I'll have to sand everything down and stain it. It'll take so much time to put it back to the way it was.

"I can't believe you did this," I tell her, my hands on my hips.

Freedom glances around, the slightest hint of a smile on her plump lips. "Thank you."

Clearly, she took it as a compliment. I run my hands through my hair, chastising myself for still not making my hair appointment.

But that's the least of my worries right now. Right now, I'm so mad at her, I could spank her.

When I look her way, her eyes sparkle with desire. "What?" I ask, trying to read the look on her face.

"You want to spank me?"

Did I say that aloud?

She takes a step toward me, her chin raised, as if poised for a fight. "I thought I was helping you."

"Helping me?"

"Making the place look better. Like a home. Like someone lives here."

"Someone *does* live here, Freedom. Me!"

"And you don't like what I did?" she asks, the slightest hint of vulnerability etched in those dark eyes. She runs her hands up my chest, smoothing my lapel and straightening my tie. Electricity jolts through my body, and we're not even skin-to-skin.

"It's not me," I croak.

She shrugs. "I think it'll grow on you." Then, she goes up on her tiptoes, her lips a hair's breadth away from my lips as she adds, "Like me."

I'm not sure who moves first, her or me, but my lips claim hers with a fierceness I've never felt before. Like a man possessed, I plunder her sweet mouth, my tongue diving inside, taking everything I want and need. And she's right there, matching me stroke for stroke, giving as good as she gets, stealing my sanity with her wicked tongue.

"Fuck," I groan as her mouth drops to my neck, sucking hard and nipping at my coarse skin.

"Yes, please," she replies sweetly, reaching around and grabbing my ass. "Now."

"Now?" I gasp, trying to grasp onto any ounce of self-control I can find.

"Yes, now." Then she runs her hand around and grabs my cock, stroking it through my trousers.

It's like someone flips a switch or lights a match. The room ignites. My hands are everywhere, pulling her top up and over her head, so very grateful she's forgone a bra again today. I pinch her nipples, loving how they're these perfect little hard nubs, ripe for sucking. So I do. My mouth is on them so fast, she barely has time to move her own hands out of the way. But the moment I'm in position, lapping and sucking at her breasts, her skillful hands return to my throbbing erection.

It's not enough. I need more. I need to claim.

I spin her around, holding her against my chest so she doesn't lose her balance and fall. The moment she's situated, I apply slight pressure to her back, pressing her forward. She bends willingly, her hands braced on the back of the couch. Freedom glances over her shoulder, her eyes meeting mine with fire and demanding for more.

I'm more than willing to oblige.

I bend down and grab the hem of her long skirt. I don't know what it is about these, but they make my cock so fucking hard, I can barely think straight. Believe it or not, they've always had that effect on me, even way back when we were younger. I think she was nineteen the first time I really noticed her in one of these fucking skirts. Sure I had known her for years, but it was truly the first time I saw her as a beautiful woman. I was home from college and swore I was hard for two days straight. Every time I stroked off, it only seemed to make my problem that much worse, the fantasies that much more vivid.

And here I am, finally living out one of those fantasies.

"Keep your hands on the couch, Freedom," I direct as I bring the skirt up to her waist, slowly exposing long, smooth legs. She's wearing a yellow thong with little suns on it and tiny words that say 'Have a great day.'

Oh, I'm most certainly about to have the best *fucking day.*

Keeping the skirt piled up on her back, I carefully remove the panties. I can feel the dampness between her legs and my cock jumps in my pants, a painful reminder of what he wants. When they're discarded, I slowly stand back up, running my hands up the insides of her legs. When I reach the apex, I'm rewarded with smooth, wet skin. "Are you ready for me?" I whisper, bending over to whisper in her ear as I slide my thumb between her wetness.

"Damn, Sammy," she gasps, rocking against my hand. "So fucking ready."

With one hand still on her pussy, I rip my shirt from my waist. I'm going to need both hands to undress, which doesn't bode well for me right now. But it's necessary if I want to take this further than just fingering her ready body. "Stay right where you are, Freedom. Don't move."

With the quickness of a ninja, I rip off my belt and unfasten my pants. She's watching me over her shoulder again, her eyes devouring my movements, her breath catching in her throat with each article of clothing I lose. I get my shirt unbuttoned, but decide to leave it on. Her long fingers reach back, her nails digging into my chest as she caresses the hard plains of my abs. I tug my pants down, my underwear with them, and kick both out of the way. My cock is hard and throbbing, angling directly to where it wants to go.

"Shit," I mumble, realizing my mistake.

Freedom turns just enough to see my cock and reaches out for it, slowly stroking it in her hand. "What's the matter?"

I moan in pleasure as her soft hand wraps firmly around my length. "I don't... I don't have any protection with me."

"We don't need it," she says as she gives me another long, luxurious stroke that makes my eyes cross.

"We do," I ground out as my hips automatically buck into her hand.

"I'm on the pill." Her eyes meet mine. "Plus, you're the only one I've been with in a long time." There's something so pure, so trusting in those brown eyes, and I feel it square in the chest.

But even though I hear her words, I'm not sure we should take the risk. "I'm not sure, Freedom," I tell her, my duty to protect myself and the one I'm with battling with my desire to take her without the barrier of a condom.

"Please." Her eyes plead, so open and full of faith. "I trust you."

"I…" Clearing my throat, I try to find the right words. "I've always used protection, Freedom. And I've been tested after…everyone. I'm clean," I tell her, leaving out the part that my last test, after my last girlfriend, was just over two years ago.

"Please." She punctuates the word by pressing her ass back against me and wiggling. My cock easily slips through the wetness between her legs.

"Are you sure?" My voice is tight, my body ready, but I don't move. Not yet.

"So fucking sure," she begs, reaching behind her and taking me in her hand once more. She strokes me as she pulls me toward her, positioning my cock where she wants it most.

I position my hands at her hips, much more mindful of the fading bruises there from earlier in the week, and finally succumb to the desire. To the need. The fight just leaves my body. A hot, lava burn replaces it, coursing through my veins and landing in my cock with the force of a thousand cannonballs. I gently push forward, her soft hand guiding the way, and when I'm fully seated in one stroke, I know I'll never be the same.

I'm hers.

Chapter Sixteen

Freedom

There's nothing like this stretch. The feel of him filling me so completely, so fully. The point where I don't know where I end and he begins.

With my hands poised on the couch, I do all I can to hold on and enjoy the ride. And holy hell, is this a ride. His hands grip my hips, but without the pressure of last time. They're more for guiding as he deliberately and precisely moves in and out of my body. It's like I'm on fire, the reckless sensations and overwhelming desire colliding, burning in its wake.

I can feel everything.

"Jesus," he grunts, pressing hard and fast into my pussy and then stopping, as if to just feel.

"So good," I groan, pressing back and wiggling.

"Stop that."

Of course, I don't. "Stop what? This?" I ask, doing it again, pressing back hard, taking him as deep as possible and grinding against him.

"Fuck, Freedom," he groans, right before pulling almost all the way out and thrusting in hard.

"Yes, we are. Don't stop," I beg, holding on for dear life and pressing my ass up in the air.

His big hands slide around, one moving down my body and the second up. He gently pulls me back so that I'm standing in front of him, my ass still pressed back into him. His left hand cups my breast, tweaking and playing with my nipple until it's so hard it's almost painful. His right hand finds pay dirt between my legs, gliding easily through the wetness coating my clit. The moment he presses into it, I see stars.

"You tighten around me when I do this," he whispers against my ear, continuing to thrust his hips forward, filling me to the max.

I don't know what to focus on. The hand on my nipple, the one on my clit, or the fact his bare cock is driving me straight to orgasm. Probably a combination of all of it.

"You're going to make me come," I tell him, needing to lean forward once more. He doesn't stop me as I place my hands on the armrest of the couch and bear down. Arching my back, he seems to hit just where I need him to.

With one arm still wrapped around my waist so he can toy with my clit, I ride his cock hard until I'm flying over the edge, my orgasm ripping through my body like an exorcist on speed. "Fuck," I scream, feeling him tense behind me. To help him along—even though I'm pretty sure he's already there—I reach between my legs and grab his balls, gently stroking them with my palm and fingers.

Samuel roars, my name slipping effortlessly from his lips, as he thrusts hard one last time, emptying himself into my pussy. I don't stop stroking his balls until he's shivering and gasping for air. His sweaty chest presses into my back as we both sag together and fall onto the couch.

"Holy shitballs," I mutter, placing my lips on his forearm.

"Yeah."

We lie together, a mess of tangled limbs on the small, yet comfortable couch, and try to slow our breathing. The only sound is the occasional car passing by and the steady beat of his heart under my ear. I could easily fall asleep, letting the serenity lull me into the darkness, but I don't. All I can think about now is how mad he was when he came home.

"I'm sorry I painted your living room without asking if it was okay first," I tell him, nestling my jaw into the side of his chest.

Samuel sighs. "No, I'm sorry I freaked out the way I did."

"It's just so...white and clinical here. I was trying to breathe a little bit of life into the place."

He's silent for a few long seconds before he responds. "I get that. It's just, well, having you here is already pushing me outside of my comfort zone. These changes, they're just a lot to take all at once." There's a pain in his voice, but I know it's only because he speaks the truth. He's as anal as they come, so me painting all his stuff is probably a hard pill for him to swallow.

I should have realized that before I did it.

"How about we make a deal," he starts, running his nose along my forehead and sliding his fingers in my hair. "You can make small, subtle changes while you're here, but you have to run them by me first, okay? And maybe, start in the guest room?" he says with a chuckle.

Smiling, I reply, "You got it, Sammy. I'll make sure to ask before I buy the purple bath towels I was looking at and the black light for your bedroom."

He stiffens around me. "Black light?"

"You know, all the rage back in the day. You can write messages on the walls and then when you turn on the light, the messages appear. I remember we used them in the compound every once in a while. I'm pretty sure the names on Master Leonard's wall was his sex list, but I tried not to look at it when I went in to gather his laundry. He always left on his black light."

"That's...gross."

"Tell me about it."

"I brought home dinner," he finally says, kissing my forehead. "Why don't we run and get cleaned up and then we can eat."

"Sounds good. I'm ravenous."

And not just for food...

***

The days fly by and before I know it, another week has passed. I've made very few changes to Samuel's house, little almost unnoticeable changes, as to not cause him any additional stress. Elma hasn't been well for more than a week, but insists on going in every day, even though her son, Robert, as well as Samuel have tried to convince her to go home. Personally, I think she's just tired. The woman has been working that funeral business for decades, and what she really needs is some R&R.

Samuel is working nonstop, putting in late hours at visitations and going in early to prepare for the funerals. It's all part of the man he is, the one I've fallen in love with. He's driven and committed, giving more of himself than required to make sure the job is done well, and right. He's so dedicated to his job, but it's hard to watch him wear himself completely out.

That's why I'm stopping in for lunch. I have a basket full of fried chicken, mashed potatoes with gravy, green beans, and rolls. I purchased some additional veggie kabobs for me and even some fresh, warm peach cobbler for dessert.

The low hum of a buzzer sounds when I enter the funeral home. I was grateful not to find extra cars in the lot, so I'm not interrupting funeral planning or something. That would be embarrassing.

Before the door is closed behind me, Samuel appears from the office. "Freedom?" he asks, concern written all over his face. "Is everything all right?"

"Oh, yeah, fine," I tell him, holding up my basket of goodies. "I brought lunch."

"Lunch?" He seems completely perplexed by this scenario.

"Yep, you know, food? I thought you could take a few minutes and eat a good meal," I state as I breeze by him and enter the office. "Oh, Elma, you look absolutely stunning in that shade of blue. It's definitely your color," I tell the older woman, as I set my bags down on the floor in front of her desk.

Elma grins and stands, her cheeks flushed and a tired look to her green eyes. "Why, thank you, dear."

"You know, Miss Elma, a little birdy has told me you've been putting in long hours again," I say, as I come around to her side of the desk. Before she can open her mouth, I continue, "And for someone who has given her blood, sweat, and tears to this business, I think you deserve a break."

"Oh, uhhhh…"

"That's why I brought you a gift! It's a care kit I put together with you in mind," I tell her, bringing the bag up to her desk. "I have lavender and vanilla scented candles for relaxation, some rose and jasmine soaps and bath products, rich in essential oils, and a calming CD with soothing sounds of nature."

"Wow," Elma replies, grinning from ear to ear as she gapes inside the bag of goodies. "I don't know what to say."

I wave my hand dismissively. "You don't have to say a word. This is Samuel's and my way of thanking you for all your dedication and commitment to the business your husband so tirelessly started all those years ago. I mean, three generations? That's amazing."

Elma nods, her eyes sparkling with life and excitement. "Definitely. Ernest gave everything to his business."

"And you too," I add, like a cherry to an ice cream sundae.

I think Elma actually blushes. "Well, yes, I really have."

"You know what, Elma? I think you should take the rest of the day off! I mean, you've earned it. When was the last time you took some me-time?"

She just blinks a few times. "Actually, I don't know."

"Exactly! I insist, Elma! And I have the afternoon off, so I'll make sure to run a tight ship in your absence."

She places her hand on her heart and looks around uncertain. "Oh, well, I don't know..."

"Actually, take tomorrow too! I don't have anything scheduled and would be honored to help here in your absence."

Elma looks at Samuel, as if seeking confirmation. He quickly steps forward and nods. "I think it's a wonderful idea, Elma. Freedom and I can manage the afternoon and tomorrow in your absence."

"Well, if you're sure," she says, glancing down at the bag of goodies I brought. "It *has* been a long time since I took some me-time."

"Exactly," I reply, all bright and full of eagerness.

Before Elma knows what's happening, I have her bags gathered and am practically pushing her to the door. Even though she seems a little shocked by the recent events, she goes willingly. Samuel follows, opening the front door and escorting the older woman to her car. When Elma is secured inside and pulling out of the lot, he returns to the entrance, where I'm standing.

Samuel shuts the door, places his hand around my elbow, and escorts me back to the front office. "I don't even understand what just happened," he says.

"Well, you said you thought she was worn out and possibly wasn't feeling well, so I thought I'd help. Hopefully, she'll take a break and come back next week feeling refreshed and energized." I dig out the food from the basket and start placing it on the small table in the middle of the office.

He's silent for what feels like minutes, so I look his way. What I wasn't expecting was the smile on his lips. Shit, he's so sexy when he smiles. "Thank you, Freedom. For everything."

Shrugging, I reply, "It was nothing. Plus, it was lunchtime so I thought I'd bring you something to eat."

He joins me at the table and shocks when he sees the spread. "Chicken? But you don't eat meat."

"I know. They had veggie kabobs, so I bought some of those for me. But I could eat my weight in mashed potatoes and gravy, so be ready to receive less than half of those," I reply, scooping a little on his plate and a lot on mine.

"Take as much as you want, Freedom. I just can't believe you bought chicken," he replies, taking the seat across from me.

"Well, I know you like it, and even though I don't eat it, doesn't mean I haven't noticed you've changed the way you've been eating on my behalf."

Now it's his turn to shrug and he grabs two pieces of chicken and piles it on top of the potatoes. "Believe it or not, I haven't missed it much."

"No?"

After taking his first bite, he wipes his mouth with the napkin and says, "Well, maybe a little. I do love fried chicken." He gives me a sheepish grin before taking a second hearty bite.

He tells me a little bit about his morning as we eat lunch, as if sitting around and sharing a meal is the most natural thing in the world for us. When I'm finished eating, I start to gather the trash and put lids on the food containers, but Samuel stops me. "I can get the cleanup."

His hand lingers on mine, a fresh wave of heat and longing sweeping through my body. "Thank you," I whisper, just as the phone starts to ring.

Samuel smiles, and I feel it clear down to my fancy little panties.

"I guess, since I'm working here for the afternoon, I better get that," I say, nodding toward the ringing phone.

"Yeah," he says, his own voice sounding thick and raspy.

I head over to the desk and pull the phone from the cradle. "Hanson Funeral Home, how may I help you?"

And with a smile on my face, I get to work.

Working alongside Samuel.

Chapter Seventeen

Samuel

"You actually worked at the funeral home?" Harper gapes across Mom's massive dining room table, her fork halted halfway to her mouth.

"Yep! It was pretty much awesomeness," Freedom tells her best friend.

All eyes seem to bounce between Freedom and myself, making me a little hot under the collar. Reflexively, I adjust my necktie and glance down at my food. I hate being the center of attention, especially at a family dinner. Even as I toy with my mashed potatoes, I can feel their eyes on me.

"How did that go?" Marissa asks, seeming very curious by the conversation.

"It went great! I sent Mrs. Hanson home to rest and spent Thursday and all of Friday there. I even got to help set up and greet people for a visitation that night," Freedom adds, her eyes sparkling like the chocolate diamonds they are.

"And you didn't kill each other?" Harper asks, a wide smile on her face as she looks my way.

"We live together," Freedom reminds my family.

"Temporarily," I add, even though I'm not sure why. I mean, yes, it's a temporary situation, but it's more than that. I actually seem to enjoy having her in my space, despite the fact she repainted and redecorated the living space. But it's the flash of hurt that fills her eyes that gives me pause and makes me feel total guilt.

"Anyway, Sammy was super helpful and showed me all that goes into preparing for a visitation," she tells my family over sautéed vegetables and potatoes.

"She asked me if I have to shave their balls," I mumble, recalling the completely inappropriate conversation after I had Mr. Marton prepped for his visitation.

Everyone laughs.

"Total legit question, right?" Freedom asks Harper, who nods her approval. "The answer is no, in case you're wondering," she adds, telling the rest of the table.

"I'll be able to sleep at night knowing my big brother *doesn't* have to shave their balls," Harper bellows, giving me a wink.

"So how was the honeymoon?" Kathryn asks as dinner progresses.

"It was amazing," Harper singsongs, giving her husband a knowing look I don't want to dissect. "I'm ready to go back."

The way Latham gazes at her lets us all know he's more than willing for a repeat trip. He takes a sip of his beer. "Me too."

"Did Kate tell you she was selected to show some of her art in town?" Jensen asks, proudly grinning at his fiancée.

"What? That's exciting!" Marissa boasts, echoing what we're all thinking.

"It's just a small showing," Kathryn replies with a blush, waving her hands.

"No such thing," Jensen says, bringing her hand up to his mouth. The sparkler on her ring finger flashes as the lighting hits it. "They're wrapping up a display from an artist from New York City, and they're eager to show some of Kate's stuff afterward."

"Kathryn, we're so proud of you," Mom declares with tears in her eyes. Kathryn and her mom haven't had the best relationship, and

Kathryn has really become close to Mom since she returned to Rockland Falls.

Kathryn tries to brush off the praise. "Thanks."

"Do we get to go to a show or something?" Rhenn asks.

"Yes, the gallery is hosting an opening night gala after the first of the year. You're all invited," Kathryn says.

"Really? Like dressed up in fancy clothes and drink champagne?" Freedom asks, seeming to perk up at the idea.

Kathryn nods. "As soon as I have the details, I'll let you all know."

Conversation fills the room as everyone shares what's going on in their lives. I've been here before—many times, actually—sitting around the dinner table and surrounded by laughter, and for the first time, I feel a part of it all. The conversation, the arguments, the merriment. I've always felt like an outsider looking in at these things.

But something has changed.

Glancing to my side, I realize what.

It's Freedom.

Having her beside me, hearing her laugh and carry on with my family, fills a void in my chest. That hollow feeling is replaced with something else.

Love.

I realize, in the midst of everything, I'm falling in love with her. Hell, I probably have been for a while, just too stubborn and stupid to realize it. But we're so different, you know? Oil and water, that's us. Yet, here we are, coexisting at home and even working together the last two days. If I were being completely honest with myself, working beside her at the funeral home has been a bit unbelievable. She brings a sweet chaos to my calmness, and I didn't realize I desperately wanted or needed it.

For the first time in my life, I don't feel alone.

Guilt sweeps in once more. The divorce papers were delivered yesterday. Fortunately, Freedom was arranging some of the flowers that had arrived an hour before. I was happy to let her have the moment, knowing I was going to rearrange them as soon as she was done. Then, the carrier walked through the door and had me sign. The moment he left, I shoved the large envelope into my shoulder bag, where they still are today.

"You okay?" The woman I can't seem to stop thinking about is staring at me, concern written all over her beautiful face.

"Oh, yeah. Fine." Clearing my throat, I glance around and realize everyone is moving. The ladies are headed to the living room, while the guys are collecting the dirty dishes. "I'm going to help," I add, reaching for the stack of plates in her hand.

"The girls are going to overshare and have margaritas on the back deck. I'll see you in a bit?" she says, leaning in but then stopping herself. It's as if she realizes what she is doing, but stops before our lips actually meet.

I stand up tall and nod, quickly making my escape to the kitchen. Rhenn is rinsing the dirty dishes and handing them to Jensen, who places them in Mom's industrial-sized dishwasher. Latham is over scooping the leftovers into bowls, so after I set the rest of the dirty dishes down on the counter, I head over to help him.

"You've been working *and* living with Free, and you're both still alive?" Latham breaks the silence in the kitchen.

"Well," I start, clearing my throat. My hand moves up to my tie, where I adjust the already pristine Windsor knot. "It wasn't easy at first. She repainted my living room."

Silence wraps around me as they all turn and gaze my way. "Seriously? Like a soft beige or, maybe, ivory?" Jensen asks.

"Uh, no. Soothing Sunset Coral."

Rhenn barks out a laugh. "She painted your place pink? The man who hates color has a pink house?" He can't control his laughter. "That's fucking golden. I knew I loved that girl for a reason."

I stand up straight and glare at my future brother-in-law before I even realize I'm doing it.

"Oh! Did you see that?" Jensen bellows, pointing at my face.

"Definitely. I think he was about ready to rumble with Rhenn over Free," Latham chimes in.

"I was not." My argument falls on deaf ears.

"Oh, there was definite anger on that face," Rhenn agrees with a grin. "I was scared a little."

"There wasn't… I wasn't…"

"Samuel and Freedom sitting in a tree," Jensen sings, like the annoying little brother he's always been.

"Shut up," I retort, like the older annoyed brother I've always been.

"Boys, boys, boys, let's not fight. Samuel can't help it he's falling in love with Freedom," Latham replies, making them all laugh. It's supposed to be a joke, one at my expense, but I can't seem to muster the will to laugh along with them.

Mostly because it's not funny.

When Rhenn sees I'm not laughing, nor am I annoyed, he stops snickering and his face turns seriously. "Holy shit."

"What?" Jensen asks, glancing my way.

Rhenn takes a step forward. "You really did. You fell in love with her."

I open my mouth to argue, but I can't.

"Son of a bitch," Latham adds with a big smile and a slap on the back. "You fell for her."

I plan to argue, to deny, but when my mouth opens, different words spill out. "I don't know how it happened."

Rhenn chuckles and shakes his head. "You never see it coming, right?"

Latham grins and nods. "Never. One minute you're ready to pull out your hair and wring her neck, and the next thing you know, you have her pressed against the countertop and can't even form sentences."

"Gross," Jensen gasps.

"It happens to the best of us," Rhenn replies, as he picks up another dirty dish and hands it to Jensen.

They all go about their jobs, washing the pans, drying and putting them away, no one the wiser to the turmoil brewing in my head and chest. The constant tug-of-war between the two organs, neither of them getting the leg up on the other.

"So," I start, adjusting my necktie, "what do I do now?"

The three men I'm closest to—my brother and the two I consider brothers—all turn and look my way. The water is shut off, the towels are set aside, and attention is turned on me. I hate it, but I don't shy away. I asked them for help, the least I can do is hear them out.

"What do you mean what do you do?" Jensen asks, leaning his hip against the counter.

"Well, I mean, we live together, technically, we're married—"

"What?" three men all bellow at the exact same time, and it's right then and there I realize my mistake.

"Shit," I mutter, closing my eyes and wishing the clock would turn back ten seconds. When it doesn't and I know they're still standing there, waiting on me to elaborate, I open my eyes and say, "Freedom and I, we, uh, got married in Las Vegas."

"No shit? How? When?" Latham asks. There's no judgment on his face or in his question, just curiosity.

"That night after the magic show. We left the club and drank. A lot. Apparently, we continued to drink and wound up at some little chapel on the strip."

After a beat of silence, Jensen says, "I never would have thought you'd be the one to elope with someone you're not even dating."

"No kidding, but, somehow, we've been spending all this time together, and even though she painted my living room pink and the oak furniture some seafoam green color, I think I fell in love with her."

They continue to smile at me for several long seconds, and I start to feel a little hot under the collar.

"Congratulations, man," Rhenn says, coming over and patting me on the back.

"What?"

He shrugs. "Love is pretty great. Take it from a man who ran from it and avoided it his entire adult life. It wasn't until I spent those few weeks here, with your sister, that I actually realized what a gift it really was."

"Before you know it, you'll be an old married man like me," Latham adds.

"Actually, I think technically, he beat you to it," Jensen says with a pointed look.

"Shit, you're right. Who here actually thought Samuel would be the first to marry?" Latham teases.

"Not me," Jensen argues.

"Actually, I'm not sure we're going to stay married," I tell them, suddenly feeling a tad nervous.

"What do you mean?" This from Rhenn.

"I've filed."

I'm met with three shocked expressions. "Why?" Latham asks.

"Because we've gotten it all wrong. From the start, you don't get married before you date, guys. That's not how this works."

"Not all stories are the same, Samuel," Rhenn says.

"Besides, it's the shit in the middle that makes the story good," Latham adds.

"So you did things a little backwards. How bad could it be?" Jensen asks before turning around and finishing up the dishes.

How bad could it be?

My heart is telling me it's not the end of the world, but I can't seem to let it go. My brain just isn't wired like that. It's black and white, with no room for gray. And right now, I feel like my whole life is a whole lot of gray.

***

"Do you want some peach cobbler?" Freedom asks from the back door.

"Uh, no, thank you."

I've been sitting outside, enjoying the cooler night, and thinking. Talking with the guys tonight planted the seed that I don't actually have to get a divorce. Yet, here I am, trying to convince myself it's the only way. Start over. Fresh slate. It's all there in black ink, just waiting for me to sign on the line.

The door opens and Freedom blows onto the deck like a light wind. She's wearing one of her signature skirts and has paired it with an ivory sweater that hangs loosely off one shoulder. There's no strap, which tells me she's not wearing a bra beneath the knitted top. My cock starts to thicken at the thought.

"So, I was thinking," she starts, coming over to where I'm seated. Shockingly, she doesn't take one of the other available seats, but instead, climbs up on my lap.

My entire body stills, even though my hands itch to touch. "What were you thinking about?" I ask, clearing my throat. I reach for my necktie but realize it's not there. When we came home from dinner, I took it off and hung it in the closet beside the dozens of other ties. It's weird to not wear one right now.

"I was thinking we should add a little something to the kitchen," she says, curling her legs up on my lap and essentially making herself comfortable.

I have no other option than to wrap my arms around her and hang on. "Define a little something." My heart starts to pound in my chest.

"A theme."

"A theme?"

"You know like farmhouse chickens or vibrant sunflowers," she says, as she leans her head back on my shoulder and gazes up at the stars. "They're so bright tonight. The sky's so clear."

I glance up and take in the majestic beauty of the sky. When was the last time I just stopped and looked at the stars? Ever?

"When I was at the compound, I used to watch the stars. I'd lie on the ground and make shapes and pictures with them. Once, I swear I saw a whale in the sky."

I'm not sure if her comment requires and answer or not, so I just pull her tighter into my chest. All I can picture is a young Freedom, with her long brown hair in the dirt and a smile on her face as she stares up at the sky and finds star animals.

"Anyway, I was thinking you needed a theme. Some matching hand towels, a few pictures on the wall, and maybe a clock. If you're feeling super adventurous, we could even paint the cabinet faces a coordinating color." The entire time she talks, she just stares up at the sky, a serene look on her face.

"Those are solid mahogany cabinets, Freedom."

She turns and our eyes meet. "Are those nice?"

I snort a laugh. "Yeah, darling, they're nice. They were quite expensive to install."

"Huh. Really? I mean, they're okay, but why spend so much on something that's just a plain wood? You could have gotten a cheaper pine cabinet and painted them to fit your mood or theme," she reasons, and I find myself, surprisingly, smiling.

"Maybe my next kitchen."

"So, we don't paint your fancy cabinets then. What about the walls? We could do an accent wall?"

The no is on the tip of my tongue, but for some reason, I don't say it. Instead, I find myself agreeing. "That might work. What theme were you thinking?"

Her eyes widen with delight as she tells me all about the different ideas she has. I don't really pay that much attention. I'm too transfixed on her eyes. At the delight. At the sparkle. At the light that seems to radiate from her soul. I don't know why I didn't see it before. Freedom is a true ray of sunshine, packed in a tiny, eccentric woman.

"Oh! What about some Aztec pottery? Did you know I used to make bowls and things to sell at the market?"

"Really?"

"Yeah, when I was seven, they showed me how to bake pottery over a fire."

My heart stops in my chest. "At seven?" I ask, trying to picture young Freedom working by a large fire she had no business being around.

"That's how I got this," she says, holding up her arm and showing me a faint scar across her wrist. "One of the pieces we were baking fell over and touched my skin. It burned horribly," she says, holding up her arm to my face.

I find myself bringing my lips down to the skin and skimming over the soft area. "I'm sorry you were burned."

She shrugs. "They put some cream on it, and it was better a few days later. But this mark never went away."

My eyes are glued to hers, and I swear I fall further in love with her in this moment, with her sitting on my lap and my arms wrapped protectively around her body. "I think adding some pottery to the kitchen would be a great idea," I tell her. My heart swells with happiness as she beams a bright smile at me.

"Okay, well, I'll check around and see what I can find."

"Okay."

We sit together, staring up at the sky, and lost in our own thoughts. I'm thinking about the woman in my arms, about the difficult childhood she must have endured. I'm sure she didn't realize it at the time, and maybe difficult isn't the right word. Different. Like me. Her upbringing was different than mine. But that's not necessarily a bad thing. She learned so many important lessons we may not have learned until an older age, if ever.

Maybe that's what I need in my life. Not a piece of normal, but a slice of different.

Someone like Freedom.

Glancing up, I smile. "Do you see those stars there?" I point to the dozen stars all clustered together. "It looks like a taco."

Chapter Eighteen

Freedom

The days fly by, and before I know it, I've been staying with Samuel for almost four weeks. We've successfully learned to coexist in a small house, without killing each other. If you would have asked me months ago, I would have sworn one of us wouldn't have survived this excursion. But here we are, with splashes of color all over his drab, white house.

Except his bedroom. It's the only room he hasn't allowed me to decorate.

Yet.

I'm anticipating the call my apartment is ready any day. I'd rather just stay here, but I know that's not going to happen. Although he's allowed me to bring a little life to his home doesn't mean he's ready for a permanent roommate. And he's welcomed me into his bed pretty much the entire time. He also seems more relaxed, maybe even a little happier than before. None of that means he wants me to stay.

He hasn't brought up the whole divorce thing, not since early in our roommate arrangement, and I'm not about to say anything. Instead, I've tried to show him, day in, and day out, how great of a team we make—together—and I think he may finally see it too.

I smile as I grab the container of treats I made and head out the front door. Today, I'm scheduled to work with my bestie at Kiss Me Goodnight. I'm so excited to spend the time with her. It seems Elma Hanson enjoyed her time away so much, she actually started scheduling herself less hours and asked me to fill in for her. So I added another job to my already busy schedule.

But I don't mind. I love being so busy, doing a wide variety of jobs.

The drive to the lingerie store is short, and I'm singing Backstreet Boys as I pull into the alley behind the shop. I smile when I see Latham milling around out back by the lumberyard behind the hardware store and pull into the space closest to my bestie's sexy store.

When I get out of my car, I spot Latham heading in my direction. He waves and smiles when he spies the container in my hand. "Any chance that might be some of your banana bread again?"

Smiling, I open the lid. "Not banana bread, but cranberry and mandarin muffins."

He glances down, grimacing. "Will I like it?" he asks, hesitantly taking a treat.

"Does a bear shit in the woods?"

Latham snorts and takes a bite on the top of the muffin. He chews slowly, pulling a face. "Are there nuts in there?"

"Oatmeal."

He takes a second bite, again carefully chewing, before he reaches in and grabs a second from the pan. "I'll just take another for later," he says before throwing me a grin and a wink and turning to head toward his side of the business. We all know 'later' really means like five minutes.

"Enjoy!" I holler, grinning as I close the container and make my way to Harper's side.

"Thank you, Freedom!"

"You're welcome, Latham!"

"Were you talking to my husband?" Harper asks when I pop in the back door.

"I was. He stole two muffins," I tell her, taking my phone out and setting my purse in her small office.

"Only two? He's always hungry," she says, shaking her head and grinning like a loon.

"Hungry for your cookie?" I tease, recalling one time I showed up to help with inventory but found them in a very compromising position in the dressing room.

Harper laughs. "That too…"

I follow her to the counter and grab the coffee cup that doesn't have the lipstick mark on the top and take a sip. "Mocha?"

"Sugar free," she adds with a wink.

"So, good," I draw out, groaning in happiness as I take my first sip.

"We have fifteen minutes before I have to unlock the door. Tell me all the deets of living with my brother, but leave out the icky stuff," Harper begs, her bright blue eyes wide with excitement as she takes a seat on the stool behind the counter.

I shrug. "There's nothing to tell, really."

"Bullshit! You painted his front door. I still haven't heard how you got away with it." Harper grins over the lid of her coffee cup.

Again, I shrug my shoulders. "His place was in need of some serious color," I tell her, even though she already knows.

"No shit! Did he flip his lid and start spewing statistics about burglary and crime rates to houses with painted doors?"

I chuckle. "No. I mean, yes, he flipped his lid, but mostly because of all the other stuff I painted too, remember? I've learned since then he's not so bad if I just ask for his input before I do it."

I can feel my bestie's gaze from across the counter.

"What?"

"You love him."

I open my mouth to argue, but nothing comes out. Instead, I go with the truth. "Totally."

"So? What are you going to do about it?"

I sigh. "Well, he hasn't brought up the whole divorce thing for a while, so I'm kinda hoping he just wants to stay shacked up with the ol' ball and chain."

She smiles. "And if he doesn't?"

The thought makes me sadder than I ever thought possible.

"I guess I'll just have to change his mind with *the sex*," I tell her, going for comedy relief instead of facing the real issue.

Harper snorts and shoves half a muffin in her mouth. "I'm so glad you're having *the sex*, even if it's with my brother," she says through an open, full mouth.

"I can see what Latham sees in you, being all refined and ladylike," I tease, as she continues to chew through her massive bite.

The moment she swallows, she says, "It's my boobs."

"Hell yes," Latham chimes in as he enters the boutique side of their business. When he reaches his wife, he adds, "And her ass too," as he gives her a hard slap that makes her yelp.

"Please don't get all kinky right now. We're about to open, and I really don't want to have to explain why you're demonstrating the flogger to the first lady to enter."

"You have a flogger?" Latham asks his wife, his eyes eagerly searching her lingerie boutique for the dirty goods.

"No. Well, not here anyway," she replies with a grin and a wink.

There's no missing the fact Latham adjusts his crotch before kissing Harper on the lips. "See you at lunchtime. Love you."

"Love you too," she tells him, smiling like a schoolgirl with her first crush.

"Bye, Free."

"Later," I tell him as he disappears into the hardware store. "You two are so cute."

She snorts. "I know. And we're banging like monkeys right now. Total honeymoon phase. I kinda don't ever want it to end, but then again, my vag could use a day or two of R and R."

"You can take a break from beaver bumping, you know. Just because you rest the cooch, doesn't mean you're not in the honeymoon phase anymore," I reassure her.

Harper flips the closed sign to open and makes sure all the lights are on. "That's true. I mean, I could practice my stellar blowie skills for a night or two," she says, her face tight in concentration, as if she were in deep thought.

"That's true. No man every passes up a blowie."

I spend my morning working the floor, helping the customers who come in, and restocking product. Harper is in her office most of the time, working on paperwork and orders, so I take the opportunity to browse the merchandise. I find this gorgeous light green bra and panty set with little white eyelets on it. What's best is I find my size almost right away. Since my girls are a little on the smaller side, I always have trouble finding bras that fit right. Harper knows this, and always makes sure she stocks plenty of product in all shapes and sizes.

When the clock hits noon, Harper comes out of her office and stretches. "God, I hate being cooped up in there. But I got all of my new spring products ordered, and most of the bills paid, so I'll call it a success."

"Definitely," I tell her setting the bra and panty set on the counter.

"Are those for you? That color would be gorgeous against your fair skin," she says, toying with the lace on the bra cup.

"I thought so too."

"I'm going to meet Latham next door in his office for lunch. Will you be okay for a bit?" she asks, glancing around at the now-empty store.

"Fine, fine. Go have lunch—and lunchtime nookie—with your hot husband," I tell her, shooing her with my hand.

"I thought you were all for helping me give the vag a dick-break. Now you're encouraging me to go attack it like a Christmas ham."

I pull a face. "Who attacks a Christmas ham?"

"Have you ever had Kitty's ham? She puts a brown sugar rub and pineapple rings on it to sweeten it up. It's amazing," she sings.

"If I ate pig, I'd totally eat that."

"Right? Anyway, I think he brought leftovers. If there's any left, I'll bring some to you."

I have her off. "Don't worry about it. I know how much your husband eats. I can run across the street and grab a salad from the deli."

"If you're sure," she says, giving me a look.

"Definitely. Go eat. I'll be fine. See you in a bit," I tell her, turning back to the counter and ringing up my new purchase.

"See you soon."

And then I'm left alone with a room full of lingerie.

I spend the next ten minutes refolding the panties in the bins, displaying them just the way Harper likes. Just when I'm about to move on to another task, the bell over the door chimes. I'm actually super stoked to have a customer, hopefully to help pass the time. However, when I turn around, it isn't the face of a happy customer. Oh, no. This one looks awkward as fuck, and he's trying his damnedest not to look at any of the sexy displays.

Samuel.

I'm so shocked to see him at the front door of the one place everyone knows makes him horribly uncomfortable; all I can do is stand there and stare back.

"Hey," he says, reaching up with one hand and adjusting his necktie. "I, uh, thought you might need lunch."

"Oh," I stammer, still completely shocked he's here.

He glances down at the bag in his hand. "If you've already eaten, I can just head back to work," he starts, but I quickly cut him off.

"No, I haven't eaten anything. I'd love to have lunch."

Samuel takes a tentative step forward, his eyes darting to a nice satin negligée on a mannequin. "If you're sure," he says, very slowly, clearing his throat.

"Definitely," I say, finally recovering. "Come on back here. Your sister is next door with Latham, so I should stay up here and man the counter."

"Okay," he replies, quickly glancing around at the pretties hanging and displayed near him. I can't help but smile at the blush he's trying to conceal by dropping his head.

I move everything off the back counter as he sets down a bag and pulls a few containers from within. Chinese. He opens steaming tubs of vegetables and rice, teriyaki noodles, and sautéed mushrooms. My stomach growls instantly. "This looks yummy," I tell him, grabbing the two stools and moving them to the table.

"I wasn't sure what to get, but I remembered you talking about the vegetables and rice."

"It's my favorite," I reassure him.

I could run back to the small kitchen area in back but decide against it. Instead, we use the chopsticks provided, and eat together out of the containers. I thought Samuel would say something about germs and sharing, but surprisingly, he hasn't. When I dive into the veggies and rice, he helps himself to the teriyaki noodles, and after a few bites, we switch it up.

Who knew sharing Chinese food could be so easy and satisfying.

When my stomach is full of goodness, I pat myself on the belly and push away the food. "Thank you so much. I didn't realize I was starved until I started eating and couldn't stop."

"You're very welcome," he says, patting his mouth with a napkin and picking up the empty containers. "You've brought food plenty of times to work at the funeral home. It's the least I could do," he tells me.

"And doing it without asking first? Look at you and your sudden bout of spontaneity."

"It's new to me," he confesses with a sheepish grin. When he does it, laugh lines appear around his eyes and he suddenly looks younger. Carefree. It's an appearance I'm not used to seeing on Samuel.

"You're doing just fine," I reassure him, patting his hand.

Suddenly, an idea sparks to life, and even though I definitely *shouldn't*, I'm definitely *gonna.*

Glancing around the empty store, the moment he throws all the trash in the bin, I reach for his hand. He seems a little hesitant at first, but follows behind me as I guide him toward the dressing rooms. Even though he's most certainly a little uncomfortable as I lead him through the masses of panties, he doesn't say a word.

Not until I open the dressing room curtain and motion for him to step inside.

"Uh, Freedom?" he asks, giving me a look of both concern and horror.

I offer him my sweetest grin with devil horns and pull him completely inside. "Come on, Sammy. Live a little." Then, I push against his shoulders until he plops down on the small bench.

The surprised look on his face makes me smile even wider. "Wh-what are you doing?"

Before he can process what I'm doing, I drop to my knees between his legs and run my hands up his thighs. "I'm saying thank you for lunch."

"Thank you?" he asks, and then like the flip of a switch, he must realize what I mean. "What? Freedom! You can't do *that* here," he scolds, his voice low and harsh, yet there's no denying the hint of excitement in his eyes.

"I can, and I will," I tell him, reaching up to unfasten his belt. He doesn't argue, but he doesn't really assist either. He seems torn between what's right (not receiving a blowie in his sister's shop's dressing room) and what's wrong (enjoying the hell out of a blowie in his sister's shop's dressing room).

When I get his pants undone, and I need his assistance to get them down past his hips, he finally speaks again. "I'm not sure about this, Freedom." His voice is still low, like a whisper, but there's a definite current of desire with it.

"All you have to do sit still there for a few minutes. I realized I've never really done this to you, and I really, *really* want to wrap my mouth around your cock right now and suck you off."

His eyes widen and darken, his cock jumps in his pants. "See? He wants to come out and play too," I add, running my palm over the entire hard length of his erection.

"Shit," he mumbles. "But, what about…what about Harper? Or a customer?"

I blow out a breath. "I'll be able to hear the bell over the door. Plus, we'll be done before she gets back, if you'd actually take off your pants and let me get started."

As I stroke him through his trousers a few more times, I can see the moment I win the battle. He sags against the wall and he closes his eyes with a deep exhale. Then, he reaches down, lifts his hips, and helps remove his pants and tighty-whities.

Leaning forward, I waste no time. I take his long, hard cock in my hands and bend down. I lick the tip, tasting the salty wetness seeping from his erection, before taking him down my throat. A gasp fills the small space as his hips flex. "Shit," he mumbles.

With a sassy grin, I tell him, "Hang on, Sammy. This is going to be a wild and fast ride."

Chapter Nineteen

Samuel

Fast and wild.

No shit.

I can barely breathe as she wraps her mouth around my dick and practically swallows it whole. "Jesus." I gasp, trying to pay attention for the bell, listen for my sister's arrival, and watch as Freedom tries to devour my cock as if it were the main course in Nathan's Hotdog Eating Contest.

Then she reaches down and strokes my balls. My hips thrust upward, all on their own, as I try for a little more of that sweet friction her mouth creates. It's amazing, like her, especially when she palms my balls and squeezes. Not hard, but enough that I feel electricity spread through my blood.

Freedom continues to work me over, stroking long and firmly with her hand and taking as much of me into her mouth and throat as she can. And my eyes? They're transfixed on her. Her movements, her mouth, the way her throat bobs as she swallows and gasps for air. And her eyes? They're locked on my face the entire time. Something passes between us as our gaze locks.

Her tongue swirls around the head of my cock. It tickles, but the good tickle, and I feel it in my balls. They draw up and my orgasm is just within grasp. I'm not sure I've ever gotten off so quickly before by blowjob. But with Freedom? I'm ready to blow in less than two minutes.

That's when she goes for broke. She takes me as far as she possibly can and with a single finger, strokes and presses into this spot just behind my balls. I erupt. Her throat constricts around me as she strokes my cock with one hand and rubs behind my balls with the other. I don't even have time to warn her, but she doesn't seem to mind. Her eyes lock on mine once more as I rock my hips and empty myself down her throat. Even after I'm left with nothing but trembles, she watches me, and I her.

She gently slides my cock from her mouth, licking and sucking off any remaining wetness as she goes. I sag against the wall, thankful it's there to help keep me from falling to the ground. I'm suddenly boneless and spent, my body completely sated and happy. "Shit," I grumble, closing my eyes.

After a few seconds, Freedom giggles. "I knew that would work."

I open my eyes and glance her way. "Knew what would work?" I ask, finally recalling I'm sitting in my sister's dressing room with my softening cock hanging out.

As I stand up and start to pull up my pants, she laughs again, righting her long skirt and straightening her top. "Pressing the magic button. It makes a great blowie a fucking phenomenal one."

"Magic button?" I ask, almost absently. "Blowie?"

"You know, the spot behind your balls? Makes the cock erupt like Mount St. Helens in a matter of moments," she tells me bluntly.

"Jesus, Freedom," I whisper, shoving my shirt back into my pants, and spending several long seconds making sure my shirt buttons and the fly of my trousers line up perfectly.

"What? Did it not work?"

I open my mouth to argue but can't seem to find the words. Did it work? Does the sun rise in the east and set in the west?

You know it.

"We should get back out there," I tell her, adjusting my tie in the mirror. It has a slight wrinkle where she grabbed it, which is funny, but I don't recall her pulling on my tie at all. But I know she has this *thing* for it, and always has her hands on it, straightening or smoothing the soft material.

"We should," she says, a broad smile on her face. She looks beautiful. Happy. Carefree. I'm not sure what comes over me, but I wrap my arms around her and press my lips against hers. The kiss is tender, almost sweet, but causes a stir in my pants just the same. I never would have thought I could get hard so quickly, but here I am, starting to feel the tightness in my groin once more.

"Freedom," I start, trailing open-mouthed kisses across her jaw. "We shouldn't…"

She grabs me by the crotch and squeezes, making me jump. "We definitely should," she sasses, biting my jaw. "Tonight. I'll let you return the favor."

My cock jumps at the thought.

"Come on, Sammy. Let's get back out there." Freedom takes me by the hand, throws the curtain back, and steps out. I'm right behind her and slam into her back when she stops. Glancing up, I see the reason for the sudden halt.

"Samuel?"

I stare back at my sister and brother-in-law. They're both wearing a surprised look that's quickly replaced with humor. "Dude," Latham mumbles, nodding down to my pants.

When I glance that way, I find my zipper down. "Shit," I murmur, rapidly zipping my fly.

"Do I even want to know what you two were doing in my dressing room that would result in your zipper being down?" my sister asks, unable to meet my eyes.

She glances at her best friend, who just shrugs. "A blowie."

Harper's jaw drops to the floor as Latham bursts into laughter.

"Freedom!" I chastise.

"What?" she asks, glancing my way. "We were talking the other day about the magic button behind the balls, and I'm happy to report, it works just as well as you said it would." Freedom looks at Harper and nods happily.

"Oh, yeah, the magic button," Latham coos, smiling from ear to ear.

"Totally works!" Freedom replies to him, excitedly.

"Don't I know it." To my sister, he says, "Maybe we should slip into the dressing room and you can press the magic button."

I clear my throat and straighten my necktie. "I really don't need to hear that."

"And I don't really need to see you coming out of my dressing room with your fly down and that just got a blowie look on your face," Harper retorts with a smirk.

Quickly turning to Freedom, I tell her, "I should get back to work. I'll, uh, see you tonight?"

"Definitely," she sings, smiling widely as she walks my way. "I'll make dinner tonight, and then you can have me for dessert." With a wink, she heads off to get back to work, leaving me standing in the middle of the boutique with a smile and a hard-on.

"Gross," Harper says before kissing her husband and heading off to work.

Latham smiles, watching her go. Before he makes his way back to his own business, he leans in and whispers, "So, the magic button. No shame in barely lasting when that's pushed. Happens to the best of us." He slaps me on the back and heads back to the hardware store.

I can feel the burn of mortification on my cheeks, but after one last glance at Freedom before I slip out the door, I'm surprised that's not what accompanies me back to work.

It's the thought of dessert.

***

It's been a long day. Two families arrived almost simultaneously to plan funerals, and each one took time. Elma was there and helped, but all I kept thinking about was how great Freedom and I work together. Elma's well past retirement age, and I can't help but wonder what it would be like if Freedom were there all the time. Well, it'd be chaotic, I'm sure, in true Freedom fashion. But it would also be enjoyable and soothing having her close day in, and day out.

I pull into my driveway and park my car beside her beat-up old POS. She really needs a new car. Something more reliable. However, if I know her as well as I think I do, she won't accept one as a gift, nor will she openly talk about it, unless it's her idea first.

When I reach the door, I go to slide my key into the lock when I find it slightly ajar. Worry steals my breath as I gently push the door open. "Freedom?"

"Hey!" she bounces down the hallway, a load of laundry in her arms.

"Why was the door open?" I ask, stepping inside and closing it securely behind me. Then, I throw the lock.

"It was?"

"Yes," I tell her, a hint of annoyance in my tone. "You can't leave the front door standing wide open, Freedom. Did you know more than 325,000 houses are still broken into a year? Even with security systems and those fancy doorbells that take video. That's every thirteen seconds, Free."

She's staring at me across the room, her eyes wide. She doesn't say anything for several seconds, not an argument or even a roll of her beautiful eyes. She just stands there, and I'm starting to wonder if she's okay. "Free?"

Suddenly, she drops the dirty clothes she was carrying on the floor and practically launches herself into my arms. I stumble back a few steps, but am able to quickly right myself, considering she's so small and weighs practically nothing. Then, her mouth slams into mine so hard, I wonder if we didn't just crack a few teeth. But I don't pay the jarring any further attention when her tongue presses into my mouth and dances with my own.

She groans as she tightens her arms around my neck, pressing her chest into mine. My hands grip her ass as she rocks into my erection. I move, walking her to the wall, and pressing her back against it. Freedom wiggles and I can feel her nipples pressed through each of our shirts. It makes my hands itch to touch them.

When I'm mere seconds away from taking her to the bedroom, she rips her lips from my own, her eyes hooded with lust. "Shit, Freedom," I gasp, the ache in my pants prominent. "What was that?"

She smiles widely. "You called me Free. You've never called me that."

"And you felt the need to attack me?" I ask, trying to wrap my head around it.

"No, that was the hum between my legs talking, Sammy," she says as she pats my shoulder. Carefully, she slides down my body, her hands smoothing out the wrinkles that now appear on my shirt. "Come on, let's go cook dinner. I'm starved."

She turns and heads to the kitchen, leaving me and my erection with the pile of dirty clothes to go into the washer. "Me too," I mumble as I scoop up the clothes and follow her, the entire time, picturing what she would look like splayed out on top of my bed, naked.

I walk past her in the kitchen and make my way to the laundry room. I set the clothes on the floor, noticing instantly the weird mix of clothing. There's a little of hers and a bit of mine, and the combination has a somewhat calming effect on me. It's been almost two decades since my clothes were washed with someone else's, and I find myself smiling as I look down at the dirty items.

After adding the clothes, closing the lid, and turning on the machine, Freedom hollers from the other room. "Will you restart the dryer for me?"

Curious, I open the dryer and find it full of brightly colored, wrinkled garments. They're cool to the touch, but dry, which tells me they've been in here for a while after dried. "What is this?" I ask, closing the door and finding the right heat setting for the material.

"Yesterday's load," she bellows in reply.

"Yesterday? These have been here since then?" I ask, as I enter the kitchen and close the laundry room door.

Freedom shrugs. "Yeah."

I sigh, rubbing my forehead. "Freedom, you can't just leave clean clothes in the dryer."

"Why not?" she asks, and I can't tell if she's genuinely curious or on the brink of laughing at me.

"Well, because…they…if you don't…" I stop. And can't really think of a reason besides 'it wastes electricity by running the dryer a second time,' and for some reason, that sounds really dumb. Trivial, in the grand scheme of things.

Freedom doesn't roll her eyes, as I expect. Instead, she smiles, heads my way, and wraps her arms around my waist. She leans her cheek against my chest and sighs. My arms automatically go to her shoulders, holding her close. I could definitely get used to this.

"What do you say we make dinner?" she asks without moving.

"Sounds good." I don't move either.

After a few minutes, she whispers my name.

"Yeah?"

Brilliant blue eyes gaze up at me. I don't know what I'm expecting her to say, but I'm pretty sure this isn't it. "Do you want to skip dinner and go make out naked in bed?"

My cock jumps in my pants as all of the blood I possess starts to rush its way. I open my mouth to explain why we should eat now, when I answer, "Yes."

She smiles that wide grin I can't seem to get enough of and reaches around and slaps my butt. "Good answer, Sammy. Give me five minutes," she tells me before turning and practically sprinting from the room.

I sigh and run my hand down my face. What am I doing? Well, besides about to make love to my wife. *My wife.* I spy my bag over by the entryway, and with leaded legs, head over to retrieve it. The envelope is still inside, the one I've been ignoring for weeks now. I head back to the kitchen and pull the contents out.

Divorce papers.

My heart starts to ache in my chest as I scan the documents. There's not a lot of information there, but considering we've only been married for a month I imagine that's sufficient. I scan them over, hating them and needing them all at the same time. I'm still battling with myself. I need to right this wrong before it's too late. Divorce is the best way to go about that. Then, we can start over, with a clean slate.

When I get to the last page, to the lines with our names below them, I have to look away. I hate seeing her name beside mine, knowing we're both going to sign them, effectively ending our short-lived marriage.

But then we can start new. I can ask her out, the right way. We can date and enjoy each other's company.

Kind of like we do now.

I hear my bedroom door creak open, and I quickly shove the documents back into the envelope. I turn and stuff it in the top kitchen drawer that I use for mail and bills. The moment the drawer is shut, I catch movement out of the corner of my eye. When I turn, I find Freedom there, standing against the doorway, wearing a light green bra and panty set with little white eyelets.

My jaw practically hits the ground.

Her hair is down, hanging loosely around her shoulders, and all I can think about is running my fingers through it. I take a step forward, my eyes riveted to the beauty before me. "You look absolutely stunning," I whisper as I reach her.

"Yeah?" she asks, reaching up and grabbing my necktie. "And you look like you're wearing entirely too many clothes."

She tugs my tie and walks backward, leading me down the hall and to my bedroom. *Our* bedroom. No, it's not anything official, but she's slept here every night since we returned to Rockland Falls. It's where she belongs.

As she drags me to bed and throws her arms around my neck, pressing her lips to my own, I forget everything.

Including those papers in the drawer.

Everything but Freedom.

Chapter Twenty

Freedom

I think I'm coming down with something. Even though the sun is shining high in the late morning sky, I've felt…off. Tired. Like I've been staying up way too late at night participating in a variety of games in the Bedroom Olympics.

It's true.

I have.

My sleep pattern hasn't been what it usually is while I've been in Samuel's bed. Not only do we fall asleep a little later, but several times, we're woken up in the night with a need that only the other can quench. For someone who's had decent sex in the past, I've never experienced anything like it. This all-consuming desire that takes over, day or night.

I think he feels the same. I find him touching me more, even when we're at the office. Two weeks ago, that wouldn't have happened at all. I did my job and he did his. But now, when I'm there, he pops by the office often just to see how I'm doing or if I need anything. And his hands always seem to graze against my skin, especially my neck. It's soothing and exciting, all at the same time.

We've even stayed up way past Samuel's self-imposed unofficial bedtime, and he has barely grumbled.

I'm smiling as I collect my things. I have a massage appointment and Reiki healing treatment over the lunch hour, and then I'm helping Harper at the boutique again. Her part-timer had to have a tooth extracted this morning, so I agreed to help a few hours a day for the next handful of days. I don't mind, though. Spending a little extra time with my bestie is a bonus on this Friday.

As I head out the front door, our mail lady is approaching. "Hey," she says pleasantly, pulling our mail out of her bag. Well, Samuel's mail. I never did a change of address for my apartment, mostly because the plan has always been to go back once it's finished. However, now, I'm not so sure I want to go back. I kinda *like* living here, with Samuel.

I like it a lot.

"Good morning," I greet as I take the stack of envelopes. There are a few regular-sized envelopes, mostly bills, and a larger one. The mail lady waves as she heads back down the sidewalk and toward the neighbors to deliver their mail.

Since the door is still open—don't tell Samuel—I head back inside to throw the mail in his mail drawer. The return address on the large envelope catches my eye. Las Vegas. When I look at the addressee, my heart stutters in my chest. *Mr. and Mrs. Samuel Grayson.*

Ripping that envelope open like it's Christmas morning, I smile down at the papers. It's our marriage certificate. It seems so official, seeing our names printed on the fancy document. My fingers slide over the paper, the simple double rings on my left ring finger shining beneath the sunlight.

I realize I'm smiling so wide it hurts my face, and even though we've been living this life for the last month, seeing our names on the certificate, makes it real, and a bubble of hope erupts in my chest. Hope for our future. Hope for our relationship.

Maybe before I come home tonight, I'll stop by the store and grab a frame. I could have the certificate framed and on the counter when he comes home tonight. I pull open the drawer to add today's mail, and find a large envelope already shoved inside. It was roughly thrown in there, the papers crumpled a bit and sticking out of the top.

I remove it from the drawer to properly store the documents inside, shocked that Samuel would have put it away like that.

The heading catches my attention immediately.

Petition for Divorce.

I scan through the documents, which basically says we both keep our pre-marital assets and neither contests the divorce.

Irreconcilable differences.

My stomach drops to my sandals, a wave of nausea sweeps in. The papers blur as tears fill my eyes. Samuel still wants the divorce. Even though he hasn't mentioned it in weeks, he still plans to go through with the legal separation. I thought we'd been connecting, getting along. The way he holds me and kisses me doesn't scream divorce, but apparently, I've been blind. Blinded by my own happiness and the love I feel for him.

He doesn't feel the same way.

And he never will.

My hands shake, but I read the entire document. When I get to the last page, I see the line where I'm supposed to sign. Sign my name to grant Samuel the divorce he's seeking. You can't make someone love you. I know that now. That's why I grab one of the many ink pens from the mail drawer and sign my name. I scribble it across the paper, the tears slightly blurring the line. But it's there.

Done.

My heart aches. It hurts more than ever before. More than being left in the hospital to fight an illness alone until my grandmother came to get me. More than learning how to thrive in an actual home, surrounded by things and people, when I've never known it. More than when my grandma passed a few years ago, and my own parents didn't even attend.

I move to my bedroom. Not the one I've been sleeping in for weeks, but the guest room. The one I was supposed to sleep in. My things are still there, and with shaking hands, I gather it all up. I toss it all into my old suitcase. There's a box sitting in the closet with a few other things I brought from my apartment. I toss the rest of my personal effects in there and secure the lid.

I glance around at the place I've called home for the past four weeks. At the memories I've made. The good times, and the bad. The painted walls and vibrant décor in the kitchen. The familiar bodywash that sits in the shower right next to where my razor once sat. With tears in my eyes, I head for the front door. Before I close it completely, I spy the papers left on the counter. The marriage certificate we just received and the divorce papers, signed and ready to go. My heart breaks all over again for what could have been.

Stupid girl.

I knew he was struggling with our quickie marriage, but I was stupid enough to think he maybe wanted me like I wanted him.

Stupid girl.

I head to my car and throw my bag and box in the trunk. My stomach growls angrily, but I ignore it. I pull out of the driveway and take one last look at the door. The vibrant blue door that made him so mad, yet he hasn't changed it back.

A single tear slides down my cheek as I look away and face the road. Swiping angrily at those pesky tears, I sit up straight and put the car in drive. I still have a job to do, and now isn't the time to break down. Now is the time to pull myself together and do what needs to be done. First, the massage appointment, followed by the Reiki treatment. Then, I'll grab a sandwich or something from the café before I meet Harper at Kiss Me Goodnight.

Just the thought of her business name makes those stupid tears well up in my eyes.

So, like the goddess I am, I force them back down and get to work.

There's time for drowning my hurt in Rocky Road later. Now, I have a job to do.

***

My phone rings as I'm getting out of my car. My heart starts to beat at the idea of it being Samuel, but then reality sets in. When I glance at the screen, it's not Samuel's name I see. It's Mr. Monet. "Hello?"

"Hey, Free. Just wanted to tell ya your place is ready. We got the appliances back in earlier so you're set. You can get your stuff back in anytime."

"Oh. Uhh, thanks."

"No, problem," he says before we sign off.

I stare down at the phone. I guess it's all happening just the way it's supposed to, right? At least I have a place to sleep now. Of course, I don't have my bed and stuff, but I'm sure I could ask Latham, Jensen, and Rhenn to help move me out of Mary Ann's garage this weekend. Until then, I've got enough in my car to get me by. All I need is a blanket and a pillow, and I'll be fine.

Looking up, I head for the back door. "Hello!" I sing as I enter my bestie's boutique.

She turns around after finishing up with a customer, and the smile on her face instantly drops. "What's wrong?" she presses after I set my bag down in her office.

"Nothing," I insist, painting on my brightest smile and tough girl attitude.

"Bullshit. Your eyes…they're swollen." She squints her own eyes and glares at me, as if reading me like the pages in a book.

I blow out a big exaggerated puff of air. "You're crazy. My allergies are acting up," I insist.

Harper continues to stare at me, and eventually, turns back around to face the register. I'm grateful she doesn't call me on the lie. She knows I don't have allergies. There are two more customers in the boutique, so I make myself useful and offer to assist the one wandering in the far corner.

I'm able to successful avoid my best friend for nearly an hour. Even though we work almost side by side at her store, we're busy with customers and filling internet orders, something new she's trying after being encouraged to do so by her cousins in Virginia. She spends a modest advertising budget on ads and promotions online, and the result has been an increase in sales through her website. I gather up a few sample packets from under the counter—a variety of lotions, creams, and body products—and stick two in each online package. That technique is proven to successfully help bring in additional revenue. Several customers have placed an additional order, just by the wonderful smelling lotion sample or eye cream sample they received.

"I'm going to walk these down to the post office," she says when both boxes are sealed and ready to go. "Do you need anything?"

My stomach is still not right, and I'm sure a big part of it is there's nothing in it. I still haven't eaten today, my appetite completely gone since I left Samuel's house. "Yeah, let me grab my wallet," I tell her, turning to head for the office.

"Oh, stop it. I'll buy. Just tell me what you want," my bestie insists, like the amazing, selfless, big-hearted person she is.

I can't help it, but tears prickle my eyes. I blink rapidly and avert my gaze, thankful that she doesn't seem to notice. "I'd like some soothing tea. Maybe a chamomile or peppermint. My stomach's a little squeamish today. Also, maybe a little soup? Whatever they have is fine," I insist.

Harper just stares at me, but I refuse to give her anything but a quick smile to reassure her I'm okay. With the boxes in hand, she gives me one last look before she slips out the front door. I feel a sense of relief when she's finally gone and not watching me, waiting for me to crack and tell her what's going on. I'm not ready yet.

I get to work straightening up a display when I hear someone enter from the side, whistling a Patsy Cline tune. Latham gives me a wide grin and doesn't even miss a beat of the song.

"Hey, Latham," I say as he glances around, no doubt, looking for his wife. "Harper ran to the post office and café."

He smiles the moment I say his wife's name, and by some stroke of really bad luck, wetness seems to gather in my eyes once more. He's so excited just by hearing her name and doesn't even care he's wearing the biggest, dopiest grin ever. "Damn, I was hoping to steal my afternoon kiss."

"Well, you're going to have to wait for her return. I don't kiss married men," I reply with a smile.

"And I don't kiss a married woman besides my wife," he adds, laughing.

My smile falters, and he notices instantly, standing up straight and tall. The casual man before me is replaced with something else, something edgier and more serious.

I try to brush off the concern I know is coming. "Anyway, I'll send her over as soon as she gets back for that kiss." I busy my hands again by straightening the stack of bras I've already tidied.

"Hey, Free? Is everything okay?" he asks, taking a step closer.

"Yeah, sure, fine. Why?" I ask, wishing I hadn't asked that question.

He studies me for a few seconds before answering. "You just don't look yourself, sweetie. You look…"

"Tired?" I ask with a snort. "I haven't been sleeping well," I add with a dismissive wave of my hand.

He takes another step closer, almost into my personal space. "Is everything okay with…you know?"

I blink several times. Is he referring to me and Samuel? I mean, I'm certain Harper told him about finding us in my hotel room, married, back in Vegas, but no one has ever really said anything about it.

When I don't reply, he goes on. "Did you guys have a fight or something?"

I can't stop my snort. "You could say that," I mumble.

He shrugs and relaxes a little against one of the cabinets. "I'm sure you guys will figure it out."

I glance down at my hand—at the rings on my finger. "I'm not so sure about that," I whisper, grabbing the wedding band and spinning it around. "I'm sure Harper told you? About Vegas?"

He laughs. "No she didn't."

That gives me pause. When I look up I can tell he's serious.

"Actually, Samuel told me."

I gasp. "He did? When?"

"That night we had dinner at his mom's place. I don't think he really meant to tell us guys, but he just sort of blurted it out."

"Wow," I mumble, taking in this new revelation.

"Yeah, and when we got home that night, I might have mentioned it to Harper after swearing her to secrecy. Turns out, she already knew. At first, I was pissed she didn't tell me, but when she explained it was because it was you and Samuel and you had a lot of stuff to figure out, I guess I understood. I mean, she wasn't lying to me or intentionally keeping it from me. She was just protecting you."

My eyes burn again. God, what the hell is up with all these tears?

"Anyway, he mentioned it when we were cleaning up, but didn't give too many details."

My mind wanders back to that evening, to dinner. When we left, he seemed to have a lot on his mind, but he usually does when his family is involved. "So you all know?"

"Well, I can't speak for everyone, but I would assume Rhenn told Marissa and Jensen told Kathryn."

"And Mary Ann?" I ask, my heart suddenly up in my throat.

Latham opens his mouth to respond and then shuts it quickly. "That doesn't mean anything," he insists when my face falls.

It means more than he thinks. He hasn't told his mother because he knew it wouldn't last. He knew about the divorce papers. Why would you tell your mom about getting married if you'd planned to have it taken care of as quick as possible? You wouldn't.

My sandals are suddenly the most interesting thing ever, and my eyes are glued to them.

"Hey, don't get upset about that, Free. He's a different guy," Latham insists, as if telling me something I don't already know.

Not really knowing what to say, I reply with, "I know." And I do. He's different. He's anal as hell, but while not everyone understands him, I do.

Or at least, I thought I did.

I smile when I see Harper coming out of the café across the street and heading our way. "Thanks for the talk," I tell him, even though we really didn't discuss anything we didn't already know.

"Anytime, Free, and I mean that. We're here for you," he says before he goes to the front door and holds it open for his wife. Harper presses her lips to his the moment she steps over the threshold. "What did you bring me?" he asks, looking down, longingly, at the bag in her hand.

Grinning, she heads to where I'm now standing at the counter, and I can't help but laugh when I see his eyes following her ass the entire way. She knows it, of course, and adds a little extra swing in her steps. "Here's a peppermint tea and some vegetable soup," she says, taking one of the two coffee cups from the holder and setting it down beside me. She reaches into the bag and pulls out a small bowl of soup and two small packages of crackers.

Latham looks over her shoulder, presses a kiss to her cheek and asks, "What'd ya get me?"

She takes a large cookie out of the bag and hands it to him. "S'more crunch," she tells him, as he shovels half the treat into his mouth.

Before he's even swallowed it, he presses a kiss to her cheek and waves goodbye. "See you at four thirty," he mumbles with food in his mouth as he disappears into the hardware store.

"I forgot you're leaving early," I tell her as I open the container of soup. The moment I smell the vegetables, my stomach clenches. Without drawing attention to the fact I'm about to get sick, I reach for the tea and take a tentative sip. The peppermint seems to have an instant calming sensation to my unhappy belly.

"You're still okay to close, right? Snuggles' appointment is at five," Harper says. "I can't believe the little hussy went and got herself knocked up. I mean, when she got out, she was gone for like ten minutes."

"Most men only need about three," I remind her, taking another drink of my tea.

"This is true. When we hunt down the dog that did this, he's going to pay child support," Harper insists, which makes me snort. I can count on Harper to always provide a few laughs.

The rest of the afternoon passes quickly and before I know it, Harper and Latham are heading out take Snuggles to the vet. I promise to throw them a baby shower soon and find myself actually smiling as they leave to take care of their dog. Of course, now that I'm alone and left with only my thoughts, they're returning back to the man I've fallen in love with.

No doubt about it, I love Samuel Grayson. I have for a while, even if it was merely a carefully guarded secret. I knew, but I made sure no one else did. Especially Harper. Her family is so close, and the last thing I needed was to cause a rift.

Like now.

When this all comes out, and we know it will, I'd hate to think of the repercussions. Will my best friend have to choose sides between hanging out with me or doing something with her brother? Will I ever be invited to Grayson family dinners again? No, probably not. The thought of not seeing Mary Ann again, except in casual passing, makes my heart hurt almost as much as leaving Samuel. Realization sets in. I'm losing so much more than just my husband. I'm losing his family too.

I'm just a ball of fun and excitement as the clock finally approaches six. I'm grateful tonight isn't the later night to be open. All I want to do is head back to my apartment, curl up with a blanket (on the floor, mind you), and have a good cry. Maybe when I stop and buy a new blanket and pillow, I'll grab a tub of Rocky Road ice cream and some tequila.

My stomach rolls, letting me know that's not the best idea.

I go through the closing process, including closing out the cash register, processing all the credit card payments, and turning off the light. There's a small gate that extends between the main doorway to the lingerie shop. It keeps gawkers from wandering around when the shop is closed. There are a few things in the expansion between the two businesses, but those are things like lotions and other body products that the hardware store can sell if needed. The rest of the goodies are separate and only sold when Kiss Me Goodnight is open.

I head up to the front door to flip the lock and turn off the two light switches on the front wall. After securing the lock, my head starts to feel…funny. I'm definitely coming down with something. I haven't been able to eat right all day, and the thought of eating that soup I stuck in the fridge makes me want to vomit.

My next stop is the vestibule between the two stores. Whoever is closing down the hardware store already has their lights out, so I pull the small gate closed, make sure it's secure, and return to the desk. As I'm walking by the counter, heading for the back room, another wave of nausea hits me as the room starts to spin. I reach for the closest solid structure, but it's no use. I go down. Hard.

The last thing I remember before the blackness consumes me is worrying for Samuel when he finds out I'm gone.

Chapter Twenty-One

Samuel

I'm all smiles as I make my way home. Robert let me go early. Well, early considering I'm usually the one to stay late for visitations. He offered to stay for the last few hours and told Aaron he was staying too, which didn't make the son very happy. Usually, I'd insist on staying and overseeing the entire visitation, start to finish, but for some reason, I decided to take him up on his offer. I left work.

Before the work was complete.

After a quick stop at the florist to grab a bunch of daisies and meatless tacos from the restaurant at the edge of town, I'm finally heading home. To Freedom. And it's only six o'clock.

I pull into my driveway, surprised she's not home yet. Another quick glance at the clock lets me know she should be here soon. The shop closes at six on Fridays, so I can expect her within the next fifteen to twenty minutes. Just enough time to run through the shower.

Inside, I set the flowers and food on the coffee table and head straight to my bedroom. *Our* bedroom. I strip off my suit, making sure it goes in the dry-clean bin, and make my way to the bathroom. I can still smell her soap as I start the water, and the smile is instantaneous. Her scent is embedded in my soul, just like her. She has quickly become the very reason for my existence. A few weeks ago, I wouldn't have thought that was possible, to want or need anyone, but here I am, needing her like crops need rain. She's the air I breathe.

I reach for the bodywash, but something seems off. I can't really pinpoint it, but the shelf just seems...different. Freedom probably rearranged everything on me again, which I'm pretty sure she only does to annoy the crap out of me. It works too.

After a fast shower, I return to my bedroom to get dressed. I opt for a loose pair of shorts and a T-shirt. I rarely wear them, especially this early in the evening, but there are times when I just don't feel like putting on a suit and tie. Not often, but it does happen.

I run a comb through my hair and finally return to the living room. Six fifteen. She should be home any minute. I grab the flowers and dinner and take them into the kitchen. I find a vase beneath the kitchen sink and fill it with water. I realize I'm humming a happy tune as I place the daisy stems in the water, carefully arranging the white and yellow blooms as if I knew what I were doing.

Turning the oven warmer on low, I place our food one two plates and stick them inside to stay warm. Then, I grab a bottle of beer from the fridge and pop the top open, my hip resting against the counter as I wait.

A few minutes turns into another fifteen, then twenty, and I start to worry. Freedom's rarely not home by six thirty, unless she's working at the massage parlor. I know she's not, though. She was filling in this afternoon with Harper, whose employee had dental work done, and since she's been a little tired lately, she didn't schedule anyone this evening.

I've noticed her exhaustion. She may not realize I've picked up on it, but I have. That's why my plan for tonight was dinner, a relaxing bath, and bed. I can keep my raging libido caged for the night just so she can get a little rest. I'm not that much of an animal.

Deciding to head back to the living room and check the driveway, a stack of papers catches my eye. They're lying on top of the countertop, directly above my mail drawer. It's sticking out slightly, so I use my hip to close it. Freedom must have put today's mail in there. She's notorious for leaving a drawer or a door open. Drives me crazy.

Grabbing the papers, I smile when I see what it is. Our marriage certificate arrived. My heart starts to sing as I stare down at our names. Something about seeing this document makes our marriage, I don't know, official. Sure, I've found the receipts and the rings, but with no true memory of the wedding taking place, I guess it never really felt…well, real.

Smiling, I decide to pick up a frame tomorrow after I leave work. I can frame this and possibly display it on the wall or our dresser. I know she's been itching to decorate my bedroom, so maybe this is a great first step at making the space ours.

I set the license down and realize what else I'm holding. The divorce papers. The ones I had shoved in the drawer the night before. I can barely breathe as I gaze down at the document in my hand. It's the last page, and it's signed. Her name is there in her bubbly, slightly angled signature, and I'm pretty sure my heart actually breaks in my chest. I've broken up with past girlfriends, and while it hurt, this is something different. Deeper.

Excruciating.

With the papers still in my hand, I take off down the hallway, stopping in front of the guest room. It's empty. Sure, the furniture is still there, but all of her personal effects, the *life*, is gone. I step across the hall and realize right away what's wrong with my bodywash. It's alone on the shelf. The pink razor and fancy shower gel are gone. Only my belongings remain.

I already know what I'll find—or, specifically, what I won't—but I make my way to my bedroom next. There's nothing there but empty white walls and clutterless furniture tops. No knickknacks. No sage burning too close to the curtains. No water rings on the nightstand from her glass of ice water.

Nothing.

The entire house feels…lifeless.

My head is spinning. I have to find her. But where would she go? I know her apartment isn't ready, and even if it were, her belongings aren't there yet. She'd have no bed, no couch, no real belongings. But then again, that's such a Freedom move. It's the only place that's *hers*, so why not go there anyway.

Determined to find her, I head for my dresser to grab my phone, wallet, and keys, not even caring I'm wearing old shorts and a T-shirt. My attire is the least of my worries. Right now, I need to find Freedom and explain those papers. Maybe, just maybe, she'll see why I had them drawn up.

And how seeing her name on that line makes me realize I don't want it.

Not at all.

My cell phone rings as I'm slipping my bare feet into the pair of old Nikes I wear for yardwork. I almost let it go to voicemail but realize quickly it could be Freedom. "Hello?" I answer, without looking at the screen.

"Hey, Samuel, it's Latham."

"Hi, Latham. Listen, now's not a good time," I start, but he cuts me off.

"I need to tell you something. It's about Free."

My heart drops to my toes and a lump the size of a golf ball lodges in my throat. There's something in his tone, in the way he says her name. My lungs flat out refuse to work, though that may be okay, because if something's happened to her, if I've lost her for good, I won't need air.

I'll be as good as gone myself.

Chapter Twenty-Two

Freedom

The steady beep of the monitor keeps me company as I watch my bestie pace the emergency room floor.

When I woke up, I was lying on the floor at Kiss Me Goodnight. I didn't remember how it happened, but I found Harper and Latham hovering over me, freaking the fuck out. Harper called 911, even though I insisted I was fine. Latham refused to let me get up, maintaining no one passes out just because. And I knew he was right, I just didn't want to admit it. Thank goodness she forgot some orders she wanted to review and went back to her shop.

The ambulance arrived a few minutes later and took my vitals. Even though I was feeling much better by that point, we all agreed—and by that, I mean Harper guilted me into it—going to the hospital to get checked out was for the best.

The ride to the hospital was fun. Harper rode with, asking a billion questions to the poor female EMT who was just doing her job to make sure I was stabilized for transport, while Latham brought his truck and met us here. Before I was whisked away to be stuck with five needles, I made them both promise to just keep this to ourselves. There was no reason to get everyone all worked up—specifically, Samuel—when we didn't know anything. I could tell by the looks on their faces they didn't approve, but neither argued with me.

So here I am, waiting for the results of my lab work to come back, while my best friend works on wearing down a pacing path on the old tile flooring. I'm in one of those standard hospital gowns, my clothes balled up on the chair by the door, and wishing I had my phone. It's probably still at the boutique, since I don't recall Harper grabbing it after she snatched my purse out of her office.

"What's taking so long?" Harper asks, pacing back and forth.

I shrug. "Dunno. Maybe they all went on a coffee break," I mutter, picking at the tape holding down my IV.

"That's not funny," she says, her hands on her hips. "I wish you'd let me call—"

"Stop right there. I've already told you we're not calling anyone. I'm sure there's nothing wrong here, and the moment they let me go, I'll head back to my place and everything will be fine."

She stops her pacing and gazes at me. "Your place? You mean Samuel's house? Aren't you living there permanently now?"

"Oh, uh," I stutter, trying to think of something to say. When nothing comes to me and her stare becomes more intense, I finally say, "I'm moving back to my apartment. It's ready to go." I throw on a wide smile, so she can tell how happy I am about the news.

Harper comes over and stands next to my bed. "But…what about living with Samuel?"

Again, I start picking at the horrible tape stuck to my skin. "It was only temporary. I live at my apartment." My heart starts to ache just thinking about moving back into the place I've lived for the last few years.

Alone.

My bestie drops onto the plastic chair sitting beside the bed. "But…why? I mean, you two are married," she whispers so no one else can hear. After all, our marriage is one big ugly secret, right?

I shrug and feel my eyes well up. I open my mouth to reply, to tell her it doesn't always work out the way you plan, but we're interrupted by the attending physician. "Good news, Freedom," he says as he comes into the room. "Most of your lab work looks good."

"Great," I reply, ready to get up out of this bed.

"Wait, what do you mean most of her lab work?" Harper says, stepping up and taking my hand.

The doctor smiles. "Well, you're a little dehydrated, and your blood sugar was very low. I'm certain that's why you passed out. We see that a lot in the early stages of pregnancy."

Well, I didn't eat much today because—

Wait.

What?

I glance at Harper, whose eyes are locked on me, her mouth hanging to her chest. Okay, so my hearing is going bad already. Swell. I could have sworn he said—

"Pregnant?" Harper asks.

The doctor smiles. "Yes. I'm assuming by the shocked look on your faces, this wasn't something you already knew."

Slowly, I shake my head.

"Can you tell me again what you ate today?" he asks, pulling out the chart with the test results.

"Uhh…well, I didn't really eat anything," I say softly, wishing the bed would swallow me whole.

"Are you throwing up? Nauseated?"

"I've been nauseous a few times in the last week or so," I recall, my eyes dropping down to my still-flat stomach.

"Well, I'm going to prescribe prenatal vitamins for you. If you can get that filled tonight still, that would be beneficial. Start taking them tomorrow morning. I'm also going to suggest you make an appointment with an obstetrician. Let them know of your ER visit today. I'm sure they'll want to schedule you just to check everything over. If you don't feel like eating much, make sure you're still drinking plenty of fluids. But at the least, try to eat small meals and snacks. Crackers, breads, things like that. Do you have any questions?"

I shake my head, my eyes still glued to my midsection.

"Well, thank you, Doctor," Harper says, reaching her hand out for him to shake.

"I'll get your discharge papers in order and have the nurse bring them in."

"Thank you," I whisper before he leaves the room.

The silence in the room is deafening. I can no longer hear the beeping of the machine, no longer hear the busy commotion in the emergency room vestibule. All I can hear is the rapid beat of my heart. The swoosh of blood through my ears. Pregnant? How is that possible? I mean, I know exactly how it's possible, but...pregnant?

"Freedom?" Harper whispers beside me. She takes me hand, careful not to jar the IV sticking out of my hand. When I look at her face, I see a mixture of shock and excitement, and I'm certain it rivals my own. "Are you okay?"

Am I okay? That's the million-dollar question. I just found out I passed out because my blood sugar was crazy low, I was dehydrated, and apparently, pregnant to boot. Am I okay?

I realize quickly the answer is yes. Yes, I'm more than okay. I'm ecstatic and scared and worried. Worried I'll be an absent parent, like my own. Worried I'll make too many mistakes and mess up an innocent life for the rest of theirs. Worried I'll have to do this alone.

But as quickly as that thought creeps in, I dismiss it. Samuel won't let me do this alone. I know it in my bones. He may not have signed up for this, but he's loyal and committed to a fault. So even though he may not be mine anymore, I know he'll be there for his child.

Our child.

The tears are falling before I can stop them, and this time, I don't. I let them slide, unchecked, down my face, as the weight of the day finally sets in. Strong arms wrap around me as Harper practically climbs onto my bed and holds me tight. She doesn't say a word, just lets me cry and is there for me. Like she always is. The one person I can always count on.

No, that's not true.

I know Mary Ann, Marissa, Jensen, and the rest of their gang is there for me. They have been since I was a teenager with knobby knees and mismatched clothes.

And Samuel.

He's always been there too, even if I didn't really notice it at the time. But now, looking back, I see him, waiting in the corner, always willing to lend a helping hand, even if he grumbled about it first.

"I'm okay," I whisper, wiping the wetness from my eyes.

Harper grabs a Kleenex from a nearby counter and brings it to me. "I take it this was an unplanned surprise?" she asks softly.

"Yeah," I tell her, blowing my nose in the tissue and then reaching out my hand for another.

She brings the entire box to me and sets them on the bed beside me. "Apparently Snuggles isn't the only hussy in town."

The laughter that bubbles from my chest is freeing, and the next thing I know, we're both practically rolling on the floor—err, the bed, since I can't get up at the moment. "Oh my God, I so needed that," I tell her through my giggle fits.

"Sorry, you know I love you," she says.

I reach for her hand and place mine around it. "Yeah, I do. Thank you for being here with me."

Harper grins. "Nowhere else I'd rather be," she says as she takes her seat beside me again. "And I assume since you didn't know, Samuel doesn't know yet."

"Obviously."

"Well, he's going to be so excited," she says, gazing off at the wall. "He'll make a great dad."

"Yeah," I reply softly.

She picks up on the tone of my word, though. It's sad and resolved. "Free, what's going on? You've been a little gloomy today, and even though you've tried to hide it, I'm certain you've been crying. What's up?"

Sighing, I glance down at my flat stomach. "It's over."

"What's over?" she asks, concerned and a little alarmed.

"Samuel and me. I signed divorce papers." Just saying the words brings back that moment again, when I found them in the drawer. The unexpected popping of the happiness bubble I thought we lived in.

"What?" she gasps harshly. "Why?"

I shrug. "You know as well as I do things aren't always what they seem. And you also know your brother. He's very…set in his ways."

"Anally-retentive?" she asks with a smile.

"That, yes. And I think this entire thing has been difficult for him," I tell her. "I mean, who falls in love *after* they accidentally get married in Vegas, right?" I ask with a laugh, but even though I try for humor, it hurts the same, because I know the truth.

I fall in love after accidentally getting married in Vegas.

Me.

Hell, I loved him before Vegas.

But he's not built that way. I knew it before, and I definitely know it now. Even if the quickie wedding was his idea, it was the booze talking, not him. Samuel would never willingly do anything so rash, so rushed, and so impulsive. That's not how he's wired, and that's okay. It's part of what makes him *him.*

Latham appears in the doorway, rubbing his neck. "Uhh, hey."

Harper instantly smiles. "She's being discharged. We're waiting on the papers, and then we'll take her home. I can run and fill the prescription," Harper is saying, but Latham seems…nervous.

"Listen, so remember how we agreed to not call anyone?" he asks, his eyes on me. The hairs on the back of my neck stand up as I slowly nod. "Well, here's the thing," he starts, but is cut off by the commotion coming from behind him. Samuel bursts through the doorway, almost knocking Latham down. He doesn't say a word to his brother-in-law, his eyes are wild and locked on me.

As he approaches my bed, I catch Harper moving away out of the corner of my eye. She heads over to the doorway, where she and Latham slip out of the room to give us privacy. "What are you doing here?" I ask, trying to sit up a little straighter in bed. I'm sure I look a fright, with my hair all askew and my fancy hospital gown hanging awkwardly off my shoulder.

"What am I doing here?" he asks, a little winded and definitely a bit frazzled. "I came to see you." His eyes scan my body from head to toe, as if searching for injuries. "Are you okay?" his voice is hoarse and thick, his eyes landing on the IV sticking out of my hand, and the I swear he blinks a few times rapidly.

"I'm fine," I reassure him, hating how my body aches to lean into him, to find comfort in his arms.

I don't know if he's been home yet, if he knows about the signed papers, but the more I look at his frazzled appearance, at his older T-shirt and the shorts he usually wears to bed, I can tell he's been home. While I might be used to seeing him like this, the world is definitely not accustomed to seeing him in anything but a suit and tie.

He takes the empty seat beside me and carefully reaches for my hand. I almost pull it away. Not because I don't want him to touch me—oh God, do I want him to touch me—but because it'll make it that much harder for me to walk away.

"What happened?" he asks as he strokes my knuckles, careful to avoid the tape around the IV.

"I passed out at Kiss Me Goodnight. Harper and Latham returned after taking Snuggles to the vet and found me on the floor."

He drops his head to his arm. I can hear him trying to take deep breaths. When his eyes return to mine, there's so much pain there, it almost makes it hard to breathe. He clears his throat. "Thank God they showed up."

"I'll be fine, Samuel." It's meant to reassure him, as well as myself. Because I will. Be fine.

His hurt eyes practically pierce my soul. "You called me Samuel."

Chapter Twenty-Three

Samuel

She said my name. My full name.

And I hate it.

Sure, she's said it while we were intimate, but this is different. This feels heavy settling in my chest, like a thousand pound weight.

Her brown eyes shine with confusion. "That's your name still, right?" she says with the hint of a smile. Usually, I'd argue with her sass, just for the sake of arguing. But now? Now, I just want to hold her in my arms and never let her go. For her to call me Sammy, just to get under my skin.

But the truth of the matter is I love it. I love that stupid nickname I've always despised, but only when it comes from her lips. I love it because I love her.

So fucking much.

"Don't leave," I blurt out as the emotions of the evening get the best of me.

"Well, I can't yet. Not until they release me and take the needle out of my hand."

I ignore her sass and shake my head. "No, Freedom. Don't. Leave. Stay with me."

Her eyes widen as she gazes back at me. "What?" she gasps.

"I know I'm different. I'm organized and anal as hell. I can't stand clutter or understand the need for colored towels, but I feel…better when I'm with you. Understood. Loved. Despite all of my quirks, I feel whole when I'm with you."

Now it's her turn to blink rapidly as she tries to keep the tears at bay. She goes to open her mouth, but nothing comes out. For the first time in her life, I think she's speechless.

"So, I guess what I'm saying is I'm done."

I can see the moment my words register. There's a flash of shock, followed by a world of hurt on her gorgeous face. Even lying in a hospital bed, she's still the most beautiful woman I've ever known. "You're done?" she whispers, unable to mask the pain.

I reach over and place my palm against her cheek. "Done living this life without you." It takes a moment for my clarification to sink in, but the moment it does, the most stunning grin spreads across her dry lips. Bending forward, I place my lips against hers. The moment we touch, it's a homecoming. Life is finally righted again.

"I have something to tell you," she interrupts, pulling back to look me in the eyes.

"I have something to tell you too. Those papers? I'm tearing them up. I don't want a divorce," I start, letting all of the words just flow like a river. "I just had it in my head that we did this wrong, you know? That we couldn't be married before we dated." I take a breath, but rush on. "And that was my full intention, Freedom. I wanted to date you. When I spoke with that lawyer, I had every intent to right the wrong I thought we committed in Las Vegas." I take her hand once more and carefully bring it up to my lips. "But do you know what? The only wrong would be a divorce. I love you."

My heart is both dancing in my chest and trying to beat out of it. I just told her I loved her. I just blurted it out in the middle of an ER examination room, and I'm not panicking. I feel cool and calm, two things rarely ever associated with me. But I just feel so…happy. So excited. So carefree. Like confessing my love for her is just another part of the day.

She finally opens her mouth to speak. I'm expecting a declaration of love in return, but am nowhere prepared for what she actually says. "I'm pregnant." It comes out in a big rush of breath, like she just completed a half marathon.

My smile falters, but only a second, as I absorb the news.

Not giving me a chance to say anything, Freedom continues. "I was just as surprised as you are. When I passed out, it was because my blood sugar was low, and I was dehydrated. Apparently, when they did the blood test, it came back positive for pregnancy. I'm pregnant. We're having a baby," she rushes out, her eyes wide with a mixture of shock and joy.

Her words hit me hard. Right in the chest. I wasn't expecting to hear we'd created a child together, but I feel an odd sense of calmness sweep over me. I smile so bright, my face starts to hurt, and all I can do is reach for her. My throat feels tight and my eyes burn, so I grab Freedom, mindful of the IV still in her hand, hold her as close and as tenderly as possible. Our chests are pressed together, and all I can hear, all I can feel, is the beat of a single heart.

Our heart.

Together.

When I pull away, our eyes meet. "Marry me."

She looks surprised, and all I want to do is kiss those lips. "But…what?"

"I know we're already married, Freedom, but I want to do it again. In front of my family and our friends," I tell her, bringing my hand to rest on her belly. Her wide eyes look down as tears gather in them. "We can do it whenever, wherever, but I'd like to marry you before our baby arrives." I search her eyes, waiting for a response. Fortunately, I don't have to wait long.

"I'll marry you again, as long as it can be at the bed and breakfast. Maybe by the beach out back?"

Smiling, I respond, "That's perfect."

She reaches up and rests her hand on the collar of my T-shirt, much like the way she does when I wear a tie. "And I'd like to get married right away. Maybe in a few weeks?"

I can only grin. "Yep. I want that too." And then I lean forward and press a kiss to her forehead. "I can't believe you're pregnant."

"Me neither, Sammy. Talk about a shock to the ol' ticker!"

I snort a laugh, but before I can reply, the nurse enters. "We have your discharge papers ready. I'm going to remove the IV now, and you'll be able to head home and rest."

As she pulls the tape and tube from Freedom's hand, I keep her attention on me. Running my hand over her head, I tell her, "Home. We're going home to my place, okay? I know you were probably about to head to Harper's house—"

She winces when the tube is removed and pressure placed on her vein. "Actually, my apartment is ready. I was going to grab a blanket and pillow and head there."

I give her a disapproving look. "No way, Free. You're coming home with me. Where you belong. You and the baby."

Her lips brush against mine once more. "Okay. Let's go home."

***

This is what I've been missing. This bone-deep contentment, as I hold my wife in my arms.

The moment we got home, we ripped up those divorce papers. I'll make a call to the attorney first thing in the morning to let him know we're not proceeding. At least, not with the end of our marriage.

My second call will be to my regular attorney who drafted my will. In the event of my death, everything will currently go to my mom and siblings. I learned the importance of a last will and testament back in college, when I was interning at Hanson Funeral Home and discovered how many don't have proper planning for end of life. It bothered me instantly, so I met with an attorney to draft my own. Now, I'll be making a change. Freedom is the one I'll be protecting in the event of my passing.

Freedom and our unborn child.

After we shredded the papers, I propped the marriage certificate up on the counter. It was the only way I could think to display it until I can purchase a proper frame. Harper and Latham ran to get her prescription and brought home dinner, and over sub sandwiches, shared the details of Snuggles' vet appointment.

Now, our house is empty and the night sky full of stars, but most importantly, the woman I love is home and sleeping in my arms. I can't seem to stop touching her, though I'm making sure to keep it PG. She needs her rest; she's growing a tiny human.

I'm not going to lie and say I wasn't terrified when Latham called me earlier. I tore out of here like my ass was on fire and broke more laws than I care to admit to get to the hospital as quick as possible. I make it my personal mission in life to make sure she's never dehydrated or having issues with low blood sugar again. I don't care if I have to force-feed her food and water.

Freedom softly snores on my shoulder, and I can't help but smile. As I gaze up at the white ceiling in the bedroom, inspiration hits. I reach for my phone and fire off a text to my sister.

Me: *I have an idea.*

Harper: *How can I help?*

I spell out my plan, one-handed, which is difficult, but I manage. I smile as she replies with a dozen emojis.

Harper: *Yes! Perfect! I'm in! See you Sunday at eleven.*

Me: *Thank you.*

Harper: *insert kissy face emoji* *Anytime! You and Free deserve this.*

We sign off, but I don't set my phone down. Even though it's nearing ten, there's one more call I need to make. I slowly extract myself from Freedom and head for the door. Before I leave the room, I stop and turn around, watching as she sleeps. Her breathing remains even as she turns on her side and curls into a ball. The sooner I make this call, the quicker I'm back in bed, with her in my arms.

I enter the kitchen and flip on the light. As I bring my phone to my ear, I grab a glass of water and fill it up.

"Hello?"

"Hey, Mom."

"Samuel, is everything okay?" she asks, her voice laced with worry.

"Everything is fine."

"You never call this late," she reminds me.

"I know, I apologize."

"Well, don't apologize if nothing's wrong. It's just unlike you."

I can't help but grin. "Yeah, I know. I've done a lot that's unlike me lately," I reply, almost absently.

She's quiet for a few seconds before asking, "Well, are you going to tell me what's going on?"

"How about dinner tomorrow evening?"

Again, she's silent on the other end. "Okay," she finally agrees, but I can hear the hesitancy in that word.

"Can you come here? I'll cook."

"Well, sure. What can I bring?"

"Nothing. Freedom will be here, if that's okay."

Now, she chuckles and I can practically hear her relax. "Of course it's okay. I mean, she's staying there with you while her apartment is worked on, right?"

I clear my throat. I hate I'm lying to her, but this isn't something you tell your mother over the phone. That's why I say, "Right."

"What time?"

"How about five? We can enjoy a few appetizers before dinner at six," I offer, spelling out my timeline for the evening.

Some things never change.

"I can't wait," she says, and I can hear the smile in her voice.

"Great. See you tomorrow," I tell her.

"Yes. Oh, and, Samuel?"

"Yeah?"

"Are you sure everything's okay?"

I lean my hip against the counter, spying the marriage certificate still propped against the wall. "Everything's exactly as it's supposed to be," I tell her honestly.

We sign off, and I take a few minutes to make a grocery list for dinner tomorrow night. I'll grill steaks and portabella mushrooms. Freedom loves the mushrooms with loads of grilled vegetables and cheese. She also prefers chopped potatoes in a foil packet over a big baked potato, so I add a few additional ingredients to my list before setting the paper on the counter for tomorrow.

Making sure the doors are locked for a second time tonight, I grab the glass of water and head back to my bedroom. *Our* bedroom. I set the glass on the nightstand and slip into bed. "Hey," I whisper, pulling her into my chest.

"What time is it?" she whispers in a sleepy voice.

I run my hand over her head, loving the way the long locks feel sliding between my fingers. "Almost ten thirty. I brought you some more water."

She yawns. "If I drink that, I'm going to pee for the tenth time since we got home, and I'm tired of peeing."

I chuckle as she burrows into my side. "You're tired of peeing?"

"Yes. They pumped me full of a bag of fluids at the hospital, and you've made me drink two glasses of water since we've been home."

Home. I love the way she says it.

"How about just part of the glass?" I coax, moving and reaching for the glass. Freedom grumbles but takes the glass from my hand. She ends up gulping more than half the glass. "Jesus, remind me to never challenge you to a chugging contest."

She exhales loudly as she sets the glass back on the table. "Don't do that, Sammy. I could chug cheap beer like no other when I was younger."

We turn on our sides, her back pressed to my front. Freedom yawns again and rests her cheek against my arm. "This is comfy."

"It's perfect," I tell her as I kiss her head. "Go to sleep. We have a big day tomorrow."

"What's tomorrow?" she asks.

"Mom is coming over for dinner. We have some big news to share," I reply, running my hand over her arm.

"Yeah?"

"Yes. Well, you're okay to tell her, right?" I ask, worrying she isn't ready to tell people about the baby. I, on the other hand, am ready to scream it from the rooftop.

"Definitely," she replies through another yawn. "I mean, Harper and Latham know, so it wouldn't be fair to keep it from everyone else."

I hug her to my chest. "Good. And I'm going to tell her we're married, Freedom. I want her to hear it from me, but also that we're planning a re-do."

"Well, considering we want to do it on the beach, we should probably let her know," she teases, but all I heard was *do it on the beach.*

"Go to sleep, Free. We'll figure it out tomorrow."

She sighs. "Okay." After a few minutes, she asks, "Samuel?"

"Yeah, love?"

"I'm not wearing any panties."

I groan. "Jesus, Freedom."

She giggles the sweetest sound. "I'm just saying. It wouldn't take much to free the willy and slide 'er home."

My cock responds immediately, hard and ready to go. "Good night, Freedom."

"Fine, but I expect to be woken up with your dick between my legs," she says just as another yawn erupts.

Sighing, I settle in to sleep. "I love you."

"I love you too, Sammy."

With a smile on my face, I let myself drift off to sleep, my wife in my arms and our child nestled protectively in her body. This may not be the life I expected, but there's no other life I'd choose to live.

Chapter Twenty-Four

Freedom

"I'm so glad you called," Mary Ann says, as Samuel places a kiss on her cheek. "It's been forever since I've enjoyed a meal with you and talked about what's going on in your world."

My heart tries to gallop right out of my chest as I think about the bombs he's about to lay on her.

"And Freedom," she says when she sees me. Her arms are extended and she immediately pulls me into a hug. "I'm so glad you're here still." She glances at her son before adding, "Someone has to keep my oldest in line."

I chuckle, but it feels awkward. "Well, I appreciate Samuel letting me stay here." He gives me a look, letting me know he doesn't really like my answer. Shrugging, I lead the way to the kitchen. "Come on, Mary Ann. Sammy made some delicious dip and crackers." My stomach growls at the thought of enjoying more dip. He had me taste it this afternoon when he was making it, and I've been itching to get more since.

"It smells delicious," Mary Ann says as she heads to the table.

I dive in right away, but feel bad when I see her looking at me, the slightest hint of a smile on her lips. "Oh, sorry. Guests first," I mumble over the chip I'm trying to chew.

She waves me off. "Girl, please eat. You've always had a hearty appetite when you'd come over as a child."

If she only knew…

Samuel clears his throat and joins us at the table. He's wearing a collared polo shirt, a look that's much more casual than his usual suit and tie, but looks amazing just the same. He's in a pair of nice

Dockers, which make his ass look amazing. He gives me a look, as if he knows I'm objectifying him in my head. I grin as he takes a seat and filling up my small plate with yummy snacks.

"So, there was something I wanted to tell you. A couple of things, actually," he says to him mom.

"Oh, yes," she replies, sitting up straight in her chair.

"You know the night before Harper and Latham's wedding, we all went to the magic show? Well, when you and the Douglases went back to the hotel, we all went to a club and celebrated." Mary Ann nods her head. "Anyway, Freedom and I, well, we went out. Alone."

She glances my way and smiles, looking as cool as a cucumber. While I feel like my heart is going to explode out of my chest.

"We ended up…doing something," he adds.

"Doing something?" she asks, glancing back to her son.

"Yeah. We, uh…"

I can tell he's struggling with how to put this, so I decide to help him out a bit. "We went and got completely schnockered, and then found this all-night wedding chapel place and got hitched."

She looks surprised. Samuel looks shocked. I shovel a little more dip in my face.

"Freedom," he sighs. "That's not exactly how I was going to tell her."

"Well, you seemed to be struggling finding the right words."

"Wait, you're married?" Mary Ann asks, bringing us back to the other issue at hand. The fact we just told his mom that we got married. A month ago. And didn't tell her.

"We did," Samuel answers, as he reaches over and grabs my hand.

She glances back and forth between the two of us, and I start to feel a little moisture in the pit area. Is she mad? Happy? Shocked speechless? Finally, her eyes water as a smile crosses her face. "You're married," she says again, as if trying it on for size.

"We are," I confirm.

The scrape of her chair pushing back startles me. Mary Ann gets up, and panic starts to set in. She's leaving?

But she doesn't leave. Instead, she stops in front of me, throws her arms around my shoulders, and…cries. "I'm so happy for you two! I can't believe you're actually married," she says, running a motherly hand across my cheek. "You have always been a part of my family, Freedom, and I'm so excited to make it official."

My vision blurs with my own tears. "Really?"

"Oh, sweet girl, really. You have no idea how happy this makes me. I mean, I'm a little shocked, to be honest. If any of my kids were going to elope in Vegas, Samuel is the last one I'd suspect," she says with a giggle.

Then, she goes over to her oldest son and hugs him tightly. She places her palm on his cheek as well, and grins up at him. "I'm so thrilled."

"Well, if you think that's exciting, just wait for the rest," he says with a chuckle.

"There's more?" she asks, her eyes wide with surprise. "Don't make me wait."

"Well, Freedom and I would like to renew our vows next month behind the house on the beach. We'd like to invite close family and friends only."

"And we'd have the entire meal catered, so you don't have to do a thing," I add quickly. Even though Mary Ann and Marissa love to cook and bake, I could never expect them to prepare a meal for our wedding.

She holds up her hands. "What if I insist? Marissa and I would love to prepare the meal. I'm not the best baker when it comes to elaborate cakes, but we could whip up so many specialty desserts. I mean, if that's what you want. You pick what you two want, but just know the offer stands," Mary Ann says.

"Thanks, Mom. We'll discuss it later and let you know?"

"Sounds good," she says with a wide smile. "Wow, I can't believe it. Married and getting remarried. What a great surprise," she says, as she takes her seat again and places a little food on her small plate.

"Actually," Samuel says, struggling to hide his excitement.

Mary Ann's hand stops halfway to her mouth. "There's more?"

Samuel glances my way, his eyes so full of love and joy. "You're going to be a grandma again."

Well, if I thought Mary Ann was excited with the wedding and renewal of vows part, the scream that fly lets me know *this* surprise is her favorite of all. She jumps up and throws her arms around her son. "Really?" she asks, glancing my way with more of those pesky tears in her eyes.

"Really," I confirm with a nod, my hand automatically going to my abdomen.

She hugs me next, rocking us back and forth as she holds me in her arms. When she pulls back, her tears lay, unchecked, on her cheeks. "You, my dear, are glowing. I've never seen you look lovelier than you do right now. Thank you for making my son the happiest I've ever seen him."

My throat is too thick to speak, so I just hug her in return. I want to tell her she has it wrong. That it's the other way around. In fact, it's her son who makes me the happiest I've ever been. But then

I glance his way and see the look in his eyes, and I realize the happiness is a two-way street. We're in this together, Samuel and me.

Mary Ann squeezes me one last time, but before she releases me whispers, "Thank you for loving my Samuel."

Her blue eyes shine brightly as she smiles at me, her hand cupping my cheek in that tender way she does. I can't speak, so I just nod.

Mary Ann nods before finally stepping back. We return to the table and start to snack on the appetizers Samuel made this afternoon. With a plate full of food and a smile on her face, she turns to me and says, "Now, let's talk about this wedding."

***

"Where are we going?" I ask as I slip into Harper's car.

"It's a surprise." She gives me an ornery grin as she pulls out of the driveway.

To be honest, I'm a little surprised Samuel allowed my bestie to whisk me away for a few hours. He's been completely overprotective, hovering almost, since we got home from the emergency room Friday night. Now, here we are on Sunday, and he practically pushed me out the door.

"I'm just happy to be free for a few hours," I tell her with a smile. "What's first on our list of debauchery?"

"Lunch!" Harper declares, as if she knew I'd be hungry.

My stomach growls, making us both giggle. "Perfect."

She drives to our favorite Mexican restaurant. It's not yet quite as busy as it will be, but there aren't too many tables open. Sundays after church are a very popular day for dining in Rockland Falls, and it always seems like every place you go is packed.

I order an ice water and dive into the chips and salsa the moment the server sets them down on the table. "How have you been feeling?" she asks, toying with her napkin.

"Fine," I tell her over the large smothered chip I just shoved into my mouth.

"Good. No nausea?"

I shrug. "Maybe a little every now and then, but not too bad. I haven't actually thrown up, which is a plus, because I really, *really* hate throwing up."

"Ugh, yeah, so gross." Harper reaches over and dips a chip in the tomato goodness and munches away. "I hear you had company for dinner last night."

The smile is already crossing my lips. "Yeah, we did. Samuel told her about the wedding, the rewedding, and the baby."

"I bet Mom was about to burst with excitement."

"You know it. She was really surprised it was Samuel who ended up eloping in Vegas," I tell her.

"No shit! We all are. I mean, I'd pick Marissa or Jensen hand-over-fist to run off and get married before Samuel."

I laugh. "That's pretty much exactly what she said."

"Well, I'm super happy for your two. And just so you know, Latham and I were totally out in the hallway at the hospital, listening."

I glance up, my eyes wide with shock and humor. "Shut up!"

She's already nodding. "Totally. He didn't want to, but the moment Samuel started talking, he was glued in place like a teenager girl."

I can't help but laugh. "Well, I was a bit surprised by his confession. I mean, I was prepared to go to my apartment Friday night. Finding those papers, well, I thought there was no way we could move forward."

"I probably would have thought the same. Actually, in a way, I did think the same. When Latham won the bid on that building, I was so pissed off. I had no idea he wanted to share it with me. Not until he put in all that work and made it a joint space."

"Then you shagged like rabbits," I tease, recalling exactly how everything played out that night he told her he loved her and showed her the building. I was a part of it, making sure she was still there that night.

Harper snorts. "He's definitely a male rabbit. He could go anytime, anywhere."

"He's a man, so…"

She snorts and smiles at me. "You know, I love oversharing with you, right?" When I nod, she continues, "But I really don't ever want to know about my brother's rabbit tendencies. Deal?"

"So, you don't want to know that he really likes to take me from behind?"

Her mouth falls open and a look of disgust mars her beautiful face. "Shut up!" she gasps.

"He's really good with his—"

Harper's hands go to her ears as she makes noises to block out my words, drawing attention from a few tables around us.

I reach over and move her hands. "Sorry, I'll be more considerate."

"Thank you," she says, dropping her hands completely and grabbing another chip.

"I won't tell you how much I love riding your oldest brother's massive cock."

I hear a gasp, but it's not from Harper. It's from the sweet old lady at the table across from us. She looks horrified by my statement, which makes me blush a little.

"See? That's what you get for being disgusting and talking about my brother," Harper whisper-yells.

I just shrug my shoulders, relaxing and enjoying the rest of my lunch with my bestie.

After we eat and she pays the bill—actually, I was told it was Samuel who paid the bill—we head out to stop number two. Relaxation Spa is across town and is the best place for mani/pedis. The place is busy, but when Harper approaches the counter and gives our names, they quickly usher us back to the two open pedicure chairs.

We spend the next hour having our feet and hands pampered. Just when I think we're done, we make our third stop of the day. The massage parlor. When I glance her way, she just smiles. "You're here for your own relaxation massage, not to give one. Samuel wanted to treat you," she tells me as we exit her vehicle.

Inside, I find two coworkers and smile warmly. Patti takes me back to her room, and for the next hour, proceeds to massage me from head to toe. At one point, I think I fall asleep, which is crazy considering the amount of sleep I've been getting lately. Man, growing a baby sure is tiring work.

Harper's just coming out of her room as I exit, a sleepy smile on her face. "That was heaven," she says, handing a stack of bills to both massage therapists.

"Here, let me," I start, digging in my bag for some money.

"No, Samuel got it. Tip too."

Finally, we make our way to our fourth and final stop of the day. The ice cream parlor. I feel like a kid as I order a double scoop of Rocky Road and Cherry Jubilee ice cream in a dish, with whipped cream and a cherry. Harper goes with a scoop of chocolate chunk and banana split, and at the table in front of the window, we eat our sweet treats.

By the time we're done, I feel truly pampered and loved.

"Ready to head home?" Harper asks, as she throws our bowls in the trash.

"Ready," I confirm, anxious to get home and thank Samuel for such a wonderful day.

When we pull up to the house, Samuel and Latham are standing on the porch. Latham waves goodbye to Samuel, gives me a kiss on the cheek as he passes, and climbs in the passenger seat I just vacated. I turn around just in time to wave goodbye, curious as to what the hurry is.

"Where's the fire?" I ask as I walk up the steps.

"They just wanted to give us a little privacy," Samuel says, taking me in his arms and kissing me hello.

"Well, good afternoon to you too," I tell him.

He takes my hand and leads me into the house. "Come on, I have something to show you."

We head inside, bypassing the kitchen and heading straight for the master bedroom. The door is shut, but I can smell the fresh paint. The anticipation is getting the best of me as I try to picture what he's done. When he opens the door, my imagination didn't do any justice of the actual finished product.

"Wow," I whisper as we step inside.

Samuel clears his throat and moves us to the center of the bedroom. "One of my favorite things to do with you is watch the stars, so I brought them inside."

The former white walls are now a gorgeous shade of blue that continues to the ceiling, but it's what's stuck there that has tears burning behind my eyelids.

"I know it might be a little cheesy," he starts, his paint-covered hand messing with the collar of his T-shirt. "I remembered Marissa had these on her ceiling when she was younger, and I got to thinking, they would be perfect for here. For us."

I'm smiling as I look up at the dozens of stars on the ceiling. It's not dark enough in here yet for them to shine, but I can picture it perfectly, the beautiful glow of the stars later tonight. "It's amazing. I love it," I tell him, noticing for the first time that the furniture isn't pushed back against the walls.

"Tomorrow we'll move it all back to the walls, but I didn't want to take the chance of the paint not being completely dry. I've never painted an entire room so fast in my life," he confesses.

Turning, I throw my arms around his neck. "You did this for me," I whisper, nuzzling my nose against his neck, inhaling the familiar scent of his soap.

"Yeah, well, for both of us. That white was so…boring."

I can't help but laugh. "It was," I confirm. "But you've made great strides and stepped out of your comfort zone on a lot."

He nods in agreement. "I have, because the woman I love has made me see there's nothing wrong with a little splash of color." He runs his lips over my forehead and just breathes me in.

We stand there for several minutes, soaking in the warmth of each other and the changes around us. So many changes, but when I'm next to Samuel, those changes don't look so daunting. "Thank you for today."

He wraps his arms around my shoulders and pulls me into his chest, his front to my back. "Anytime, Freedom. You deserved a little pampering."

"And for this surprise. It's my favorite room in the house," I confess.

He beams at me. "Oh, Marissa brought over some dinner. It's in the oven."

"Well, I had a double scoop of ice cream not that long ago, so I'm not quite ready for dinner yet."

His eyebrows shoot up and a wicked grin spreads across his face. "No?"

"Not yet."

"Whatever shall we do?" he asks, his hands sliding down my arms and drawing goosebumps in their wake.

"Well, we could talk about our next color change," I suggest.

Samuel pauses. "What else could we possibly change? Every room in this place has color in it?"

With my own wicked smile, I reach down and tug on his shorts. The elastic gives easily as they drop below his narrow hips and fall to the floor. His cock starts to harden right before my eyes, and I lick my lips as I gaze down at it.

When my eyes meet his, I just smile. "Let's talk about these tighty-whities."

Epilogue

Samuel

I've never seen the beach look so amazing. Freedom, Mom, and my sisters did an amazing job of setting it up for today's festivities. There's an arch along the shore that Latham built and a few rows of white chairs we borrowed from the funeral home. There are small handfuls of daisies tied to the end chairs, creating a sea of flowers on your way to the altar.

That's where I stand, with my brother by my side.

My entire family is here. The Summer clan from Virginia drove in for the occasion, including my aunt and uncle. When we extended the invitation to them, we didn't think they'd all show up. But they did. All six cousins, their spouses, and kids in tow. It's a tight fit getting everyone a place to stay, but we've made it work. Thankfully, it's the low season for bed and breakfasts in the area, so we were able to secure a few rooms elsewhere too.

Whimsical music drifts from the speakers in back, and I can't help but smile. It's the same relaxing melodies she plays when giving a massage, which seems a little fitting to me because it's just *her*. I'll admit, I'm starting to sweat in my suit under the late afternoon sun, but I refuse to complain. We have perfect weather for a beach wedding in Rockland Falls.

My family all files in, taking any available seat. The Hansons are here too, along with Bud and Kitty Douglas, and a few other friends. It's a small affair, which is exactly what we both wanted.

Mom is the last one to take her seat in the front row. Beside her is Kathryn and Max, as well as Latham, Marissa, and Rhenn. Everyone I love is front and center on the biggest day of my life. Well, the second biggest. Even though I don't remember most of it, our Vegas wedding will still be the best day. That was the day I made her mine.

The one person absent is my father. I still haven't reached out to him. I don't know when I'll be ready, if I ever will be. There's so much hurt and betrayal there, I'm not sure if I'll be able to let it go. No, I take that back. I will be able to, just not today. Today is for celebrating. Today is for Freedom and me.

Everyone turns and looks toward the clearing in the trees as Harper makes her way to the beach. She's wearing a flowy taupe dress and is holding a bouquet of white daisies. She even has one in her hair, which makes me smile. Harper walks to the front and takes her position beside the minister. My sister gives me an excited smile and a wink before turning to face the trees once more.

When I turn, my heart stops beating. There, standing amongst the oak trees, is a vision in red. Yes, red. My wife is wearing a long flowy dress in a color as bold and vibrant as she is. It's seductive, sexy, and dips low in the front. Her long dark hair is pulled up on her head with a halo of flowers surrounding her.

She's beautiful.

Breathtaking.

Mine.

As she makes her way toward me, I notice her feet are bare, and I can't help but grin. My eyes return to her face, and all I see now is her smile. It's wide and full of happiness, and to see that look on her face, knowing I put it there, brings tears to my eyes. I don't even care that I could cry in front of my family, in front of my brother who'd no doubt tease me mercilessly. I don't care because I feel that same happiness too.

Freedom stops in front of me. "Fancy meeting you here," she says, making those around us laugh.

I shrug. "I had nowhere else to be," I tell her with a wink as I reach for her hand.

"Damn right, you didn't." She shifts the flowers to her left and takes my hand with her right, and together, we turn to face the minister.

The ceremony is quick, but it feels amazing to repeat our vows, especially in light of the fact, I don't exactly remember them the first time. Even though I listen to what he says, my eyes are only for her. She truly looks stunning today, on our wedding day.

Rewedding day, as Freedom likes to call it.

The moment the minister pronounces us man and wife, I pull her into my arms and kiss her. It's probably not a church-appropriate kiss, but I don't care. She's my wife, and there's nothing I want more than to seal this moment with a kiss. As I pull away, my left hand, the one with my wedding ring, drops to her belly. It's still flat, but we could see in the ultrasound we had three days ago that our peanut is getting bigger every day.

Freedom hasn't had any more episodes of passing out or getting dizzy. We make sure she's well hydrated, and thanks to only minor nausea, she's eating like a champ. She still works too many jobs, I'm just happy to report she has scaled back on them. She still massages a few of her regular clients, as well as continues to be a Reiki practitioner (still don't really know what that means), but she's stepped back from Kiss Me Goodnight, only working as a backup for the backups. She's also still working part time at the funeral home, which I love because then I can keep an eye on her. And besides the times she completely disorganizes my filing system (which she does regularly), I love working beside her.

We make a great team.

After the ceremony, we take a few pictures on the beach, but we're both anxious to go up to the backyard of the bed and breakfast.

There, we have tables and chairs set up and enough food to feed half the town. When Mom and Marissa begged to make the meal, we had no idea they'd go all out. They even whipped up a big selection of desserts in place of the traditional wedding cake. Freedom's eyes glazed over as she saw the spread, so I'm happy.

Happy wife, happy life.

It was laid-back and casual, but most importantly, everyone who means anything to us is here, celebrating right alongside us. "Ready to eat some food, Mrs. Grayson?"

"Hell to the yeah," Freedom bellows as she eyes the varieties of food laid out for us.

I lead my wife to the tables of food, grab two plates, and watch with delight as she starts piling on the food. I'm surprised as she takes a small scoop of beef tips, mainly because she doesn't eat meat. She must see the shocked look on my face because she holds the spoon up and says, "Baby wants beef."

I hold up the hand not holding the plate in surrender. "Sweetheart, you eat whatever you want, though I do have to say, I'm worried your system might not like it since you haven't had it in forever." I actually read an article online recently where a woman took several years off from eating red meat and then the moment she did, her body rejected it. Violently.

She waves her hand dismissively. "I don't care. I've been smelling these bad boys for the last fifteen minutes. Besides, if I get sick later, you'll be there to hold my hair again, just like last time."

I stop and look her way. "You got sick last time?" Since I barely remember anything about our first wedding, I had no idea she was ill.

"We both did, Sammy. Why do you think we ended up in the shower?"

I pull a face, but she doesn't seem to care, just continues to place food on her plate. I follow behind, taking a little bit of everything, since my mom and sister are the best cooks I know. "To answer your question, yes, I'll hold your hair later."

She stops at the front of the line, not even caring that she's holding everyone up. "What if I don't actually get sick? Will you still hold my hair?" Freedom wiggles her eyebrows suggestively, which makes my cock jump in my pants.

"Nothing beats a good hairpulling from behind, right?"

I gasp and turn, noticing for the first time Aunt Emma standing right behind me.

"Oh, wedding nights are special. Everyone thinks you need sweet lovemaking with missionary positions."

"Stop talking," I beg, but Freedom leans forward, all ears at whatever Emma is about to say.

"But that's not true, right, Orvie? On our wedding night, he took me hard from behind with his hands pulling my hair like he paid for it."

I gasp as Freedom chuckles.

"She kept that long hair for decades for a reason," Uncle Orval says loud enough to draw the attention of half our guests.

"Anyway, my point is, we all know it's not your first time having *the sex*, because you're already knocked up, but just because it's your second wedding night doesn't mean you can't get dirty and have some fun," Emma says, nodding along as if giving the world's best advice known to man.

"Please, stop," I beg, but my wife steps in front of me, her plate overflowing with food.

"No, I totally want that. Sammy, you're pulling my hair later!" she hollers, making Emma smile widely.

"Good," Emma replies, grabbing her food and heading toward their table. "Oh, and, Samuel?" I'm almost afraid to look her way, but I do. "You can thank me later for the wedding night gift." With a wink, she turns and walks away, leaving us standing at the food table and wondering, what the hell they bought us.

"Come on, Sammy. Baby and I are starved," Freedom says, pulling my thoughts away from what is sure to be a completely inappropriate gift from my aunt and uncle.

After dinner, Jensen stands up and toasts us as husband and wife, even though we've already held those titles for two months. My family has done everything to make this the wedding we missed out on and the celebration we deserve, including stringing white lights from the big oak trees and playing music. All and all, it's the perfect day.

I'm standing off to the side, chatting with Levi, Linkin, and Ryan when Freedom comes up and wraps her arms around my waist. My own arm instantly goes to her shoulder, pulling her to me and breathing her in. "Hey, holding up okay?" I ask, always worried about her overdoing it.

"I'm great," she says, holding up a cannoli. "I was able to snatch the last one of these bad boys before Max got to it."

I laugh, picturing her grabbing the treat before our nephew. "I'm glad you were able to steal it from the clutches of a five-year-old."

She snorts. "Right?" she says, as she drops it on the ground. "Shitballs." Freedom drops to her knees in the grass and scoops up the dessert. Before she stands back up, her eyes lock in on my shoes.

"What? Did I step in something?" The thought makes me cringe.

Freedom reaches over with her cream-cheese filling covered hands and grabs my pant leg, ripping them up and exposing my socks.

"Oh my God! You're wearing the socks!" she bellows with a huge smile on her face.

I glance down, trying to shake my leg, much like I did all those months ago in the funeral home. "Get up, Freedom. People will get the wrong idea," I tell her, noticing how everyone is smiling over at us. Freedom is on her knees in front of me, and I can only envision the image it creates.

"You love me," she coos, smiling at the sex position socks she got me for my birthday last summer.

When she stands up, I take her in my arms, careful to avoid the cream cheese mess she has made, and place my lips to hers. It takes all the control I possess to not deepen the kiss the way I want to. The way I intend to later this evening when we're alone.

I look down at my wife, and feel the waves of contentment and joy wash over me. "And you love me."

If you were to tell me I'd someday find myself married to the one woman who has the ability to drive me mad, I'd have argued you were a liar. But here I am, against all odds, married to the woman who completes me, who drives me crazy, who sees my flaws and loves me despite them. The woman who carries my child, and will, hopefully, one day give me more. My polar opposite.

Freedom.

My love.

Another Epilogue

Mary Ann

"Good evening, Mary Ann."

I turn in my seat to find Stan Phillips, the minister who married my son just a few short hours ago, standing behind me. "Stan, so good to see you again," I tell him, taking his offered hand.

I'll be honest, I've only seen the man a handful of times in the last few years. Word on the street was if he wasn't at the church with his congregation, he was home, taking care of his ailing wife. Grace Phillips passed away last year after a lengthy battle with ovarian cancer. Her story actually reminds me of my niece's story. Even though I didn't know Trish, Orval and Emma have shared enough to create a lasting, loving impression of their daughter in my eyes.

He points to the chair beside me. "Do you mind?"

"Not at all," I tell him before taking a nervous sip of the red wine in my glass.

"You look well," he says with a small smile, and I'm suddenly grateful for the darkened backyard to help hide my blush.

"Oh, uh, thank you."

"You have a beautiful home here," he adds, looking around and smiling as we watch my children visit and carry on with their cousins.

"Thank you. I apologize for not coming to church lately. I don't get away from the house often."

Stan chuckles. "Mary Ann, you haven't been to church in about fourteen years," he says, his eyes dancing with delight.

His eyes. I don't know why I've never really noticed them before. They're this beautiful shade of hazel. A mix of green and gold that makes my heart skip a beat. And his dark hair has definitely grayed since the last time I saw him. He has that whole salt-and-pepper thing down, and all I can think about is how handsome he looks in his pressed shirt and black dress slacks. I glance down, feeling that blush spread up my cheeks. "Oh, uh, yeah. It has been quite a while."

Stan waves his hand dismissively. "I didn't come over here to badger you about coming to church, Mary Ann."

The way he says my name, it does weird things in my chest. Things I haven't felt in...well, forever. Clearing my throat, I ask, "Oh? Why did you come over here?" Then I feel like a real heel. "I'm sorry! I didn't mean that the way it came out," I insist.

Stan just smiles at me. "Would you like to have coffee with me sometime?"

Okay, I wasn't expecting that.

I sit up a little straighter in my chair as I gaze back at him in surprise. "Yes," I tell him before I even have time to really consider his offer. The truth of the matter is I do want to have coffee with him. I'd love to catch up and have adult conversation with an individual of the opposite sex, who isn't someone I'm related to or a guest in my home. Stan's smile is warm and friendly, and when flashed my way, makes me feel like a young schoolgirl again with a crush.

He leans forward in his chair. "Is tomorrow too soon? I have a luncheon after church, but then I'll be free around two. We could meet at the café on Main Street?"

"Sounds perfect. I'd like that." And I realize I would very much enjoy a coffee date with Stan Phillips.

Wait. Is this a date?

"Perfect. I can't wait," he says as he reaches out and places his palm on my hand, giving it a gentle squeeze. All sorts of heat rushes through my body. It's foreign, yet familiar, and makes me feel so very alive.

"Me either," I confess with a smile.

He clears his throat again and glances around. "So, did I hear you made all of those treats on the table?"

Smiling proudly, I reply, "I did, with the assistance of my youngest daughter. She's more of the baker than I am, but together, we make a great team."

"Care to escort me up there? You can show me which ones are your favorites." Stan stands up and extends his hand. There's no hesitation as I place my palm against his and rise.

As we make our way toward the patio, I seek out my children. Samuel and Freedom are dancing on the grass, swaying back and forth under the bright stars and white lights we strung in the trees. Harper and Latham are sneaking off behind the cottage, and I can't help but smile as they disappear from sight. Jensen and Kathryn and playing with Max and Nolan, one of my brother's great grandkids. And Marissa and Rhenn are sitting at a picnic table with Meghan and Nick.

My family is content and healthy, and that's all I've ever wanted, all I've ever strived for. It was hard to run a business, even out of your home, and keep up with four children, but I managed. I managed alone for so many years. Now, my family is grown and creating families of their own.

And I couldn't be happier.

Stan's hand feels warm against my own as we approach the dessert table, and I realize something as he turns and smiles those soft, friendly hazel eyes. It's my turn. I've done my part, raised my children to the best of my ability. Now, I get to live my life.

Find my happiness.

I'm ready.

The End

Thank you for reading!

If you'd like more of Emma and Orval, you'll find them in the

Summer Sisters series!

Don't miss a new release, reveal, or sale! Sign up for my newsletter at www.laceyblackbooks.com/newsletter

Acknowledgments

There are so many that help in the production of a book, and I'm going to try to not forget anyone!

Regina Wamba – Thank you for this amazing cover photo. It was a pleasure working with you!
Nikki and Frankie – You have brought my characters to life on this cover – thank you!
Melissa Gill – Thank you for another gorgeous cover.
Give Me Books – Thank you for your tireless work organizing the cover reveal and release.
Kara Hildebrand – Thank you for your editing expertise.
Sandra Shipman, Jo Thompson, and Karen Hrdlicka – Thank you for beta and alpha reading, and for your help in making the storyline consistent.
Kaylee Ryan – Thank you for always being just a text or phone call away.
Holly Collins – Thank you for always believing in me.
Brenda Wright, Formatting Done Wright – Thank you for another amazing format.
My ARC team – Thank you for the early reviews and for sharing the book with the world.
Lacey's Ladies – Thank you for your continual support and for making me laugh every day.
My family, husband, and kids – Thank you for always standing by my side.
Bloggers and Readers – Thank you, thank you, thank you!

About the Author

Lacey Black is a Midwestern girl with a passion for reading, writing, and shopping. She carries her e-reader with her everywhere she goes so she never misses an opportunity to read a few pages. Always looking for a happily ever after, Lacey is passionate about contemporary romance novels and enjoys it further when you mix in a little suspense. She resides in a small town in Illinois with her husband, two children, and a chocolate lab. Lacey loves watching NASCAR races, shooting guns, and should only consume one mixed drink because she's a lightweight.

Email: laceyblackwrites@gmail.com
Facebook: https://www.facebook.com/authorlaceyblack
Twitter: https://twitter.com/AuthLaceyBlack
Website: www.laceyblackbooks.com

www.ingramcontent.com/pod-product-compliance
Lightning Source LLC
Chambersburg PA
CBHW060528260626
47161CB00003B/804